Celia looked up at him.

Her eyes were as grey as clear water before a storm, Kit thought. Her face as calm as that of one of the many statues of the goddess Diana he had seen in Italy. It was not a holy, but a classic calm. If he touched her damask cheek, would he feel flesh, or marble?

Kit's hand rose. He checked himself. To win his bet would be far more difficult than he had thought. To go too fast would be to lose her.

Dear Reader

We have some superb stories for you! Elizabeth Bailey is back with a bang with FRIDAY DREAMING, a Regency you will adore, while Paula Marshall gives us THE ASTROLOGER'S DAUGHTER, where Celia turns the tables on Kit and the Great Fire of London finally brings them together. Our American offerings are CHRISTMAS MIRACLE by Ruth Langan, a touching story, and ANGEL OF THE LAKE by Ana Seymour, based on a true incident. Have a very happy Christmas!

The Editor

Paula Marshall, married with three children, has had a varied life. She began her career in a large library and ended it as a senior academic in charge of history in a polytechnic. She has travelled widely, has been a swimming coach, and has appeared on *University Challenge* and *Mastermind*. She has always wanted to write, and likes her novels to be full of adventure and humour.

Recent titles by the same author:

REASONS OF THE HEART
Trilogy: THE MOON SHINES BRIGHT
       TOUCH THE FIRE
       THE CAPTAIN'S LADY

THE ASTROLOGER'S DAUGHTER

Paula Marshall

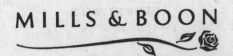

MILLS & BOON

MILLS & BOON LIMITED
ETON HOUSE, 18–24 PARADISE ROAD
RICHMOND, SURREY, TW9 1SR

MILLS & BOON, the Rose Device and LEGACY OF LOVE are trademarks of the publisher.

*First published in Great Britain 1994
by Mills & Boon Limited*

© Paula Marshall 1994

*Australian copyright 1994   Philippine copyright 1994
This edition 1994*

ISBN 0 263 78861 X

*Set in 10½ on 12 pt Linotron Times
04-9412-83529*

*Typeset in Great Britain by Centracet, Cambridge
Printed in Great Britain by
BPC Paperbacks Ltd*

AUTHOR'S NOTE ON THE LANGUAGE IN
THE ASTROLOGER'S DAUGHTER

IN THE seventeenth century, when the action of the novel takes place, the English language was undergoing a period of great change. Until then all women, whether married or single, were called mistress. But early in the century it often became shortened to miss when used to address a very young unmarried woman—but not always! This confusion persisted until late in the following century. Thus Celia is always named as mistress, although she was unmarried, because she was over twenty and the mistress of her father's house. The Queen's maids of honour were, however, always called miss, and so I have named them in THE ASTROLOGER'S DAUGHTER.

Similarly, you, your, thee, thou and thy were interchangeable and often mixed up in the same sentence. Again it was the eighteenth century before the present usage of you and your at all times became customary. I have followed the fashion of 1665/6 to make the dialogue more authentic-sounding.

Kit's song on pages 10 and 11 was written by the author and is copyright to her.

5

CHAPTER ONE

KIT CARLYON was pleasuring a woman against a wall in an ante-room in the Court of Whitehall. She was one of the maids of honour of Queen Catherine of Braganza, wife of King Charles II, and the enjoyment of both parties was heightened because they might be found by anyone at any moment.

Kit Carlyon's pleasure was even greater than his partner's because he was winning a bet with George Buckingham that he would swive this particular maid before anyone else would be able to do so, and that the act would be performed in the precincts of the court itself.

Consummation achieved, there was no further time for enjoyment. Voices and footsteps could be heard and, laughing and cursing, Kit tied up his black velvet petticoat breeches. The maid, who had certainly lost the right to that title long before she reached King Charles's court, was pulling her skirts down and frantically doing up the bodice which Kit had undone in the early stages of their encounter.

By the time the door had opened and George Villiers, second Duke of Buckingham, the handsome son of an even more handsome father, had entered with a group of his cronies, Kit was sitting down again. He had picked up his discarded guitar and was playing 'Greensleeves' while Dorothy Lowther, the maid, was looking out of the window

7

so that sharp eyes should not see her swollen, scarlet face.

Kit's eyes met Buckingham's as he began to sing and a silent message passed between them. At a pause in the song Buckingham said, a trifle ruefully, 'You have been entertaining the lady, Kit?'

Kit said, head bent over his guitar, 'Oh, I hope so, George, I do hope so.'

Dorothy Lowther's head swung round at the sardonic note in Kit's voice. She was a plump girl with an emptily pretty face and had been fortunate to achieve a place at Court. Kit Carlyon was not the first man whom she had favoured, as he had rapidly discovered, nor was he, he thought, the first man she had favoured at Court, but so far she had always been discreet. She looked from him to Buckingham who was pulling a silk purse from the heavy skirts of his splendid scarlet coat, and was proffering several guineas to the singer.

Kit raised his head to stare at his friend and said briefly, 'Twice that, George. I was right on both counts.'

Buckingham began to laugh. Dorothy Lowther went first pale and then scarlet as she watched Buckingham toss the guineas into Kit's lap, remarking through his laughter, 'I have to accept that you are not cheating me, Kit—on either count.'

Before Kit could answer, Dorothy Lowther was between him and Buckingham. 'You whore-son rogue, Kit Carlyon, you bet upon me with him!' And she swung her right hand with such force as to leave a bright red mark on Kit's left cheek.

He put down his guitar, caught at her hand and

kissed it as she swung it to strike him again, announcing in a voice of such calm reason that he left her aghast at his coldness, 'Since, my sweeting, you have chosen to broadcast to all the world what we have so recently been doing, you may as well tell George, here, that I was not the first man to plough your particular field—he might not believe my unsupported word. I bet upon your lack of virginity as well as your complaisance.'

Dorothy Lowther had gone bright red but his last words left her ashen. She stood away from Kit, looked from his mocking saturnine face, framed in chestnut curls—he wore his own hair—to Buckingham and his laughing friends, and said slowly, 'They warned me what you were, Kit Carlyon, and I chose not to believe them. I thought that you were different from the rest, that you liked me a little, but I see that I was wrong. I hope that one day you will know what it means to love—and to be betrayed.'

'Love,' sang Kit to the music he was playing. 'And what the devil's that? You enjoyed yourself and so did I. Isn't that enough? Must you have more? Seize the day, as the Ancients said, and, by God, we have just seized it together. As for the money, it's yours; you've earned it.' And he rose and stuffed the guineas into her hand.

As rapidly as he had bestowed them on her, she raised her hand and threw the guineas at him. They rolled and clattered beyond him upon the polished floor. She turned on her heel and prepared to run from the room.

Kit was not a whit abashed. He raised his guitar

to salute her and said over the top of it, 'My pretty dear, I have a song for you. Only stay, and you shall hear it.'

'A song!' cried Buckingham, no mean performer on the guitar himself and, like most of King Charles's court, given to writing poetry—and even, on occasion, a play. 'A new one, Kit? Say it is a new song. I am weary of the old. We lack invention these days.'

'New, quite new. But the theme is old—all the best themes are old.' And he began to sing in his pleasant baritone. Even Dorothy Lowther stayed to hear, caught by the melancholy beauty of both the music and the words. Kit was so intent on his performance that room, courtiers and maids of honour alike vanished. He was alone with his creation; the harsh realities of life had disappeared. For a brief moment he was a boy again, joying in his newly found power to create, the world lying all before him. . .

In the middle of his song the King himself, drawn by the sound of music, came into the room followed by yet more courtiers. He placed his finger on his lips, mutely asking Kit's audience not to acknowledge him so that the music should not be disturbed.

Yes, it was a new song and yes, the theme was old, but, for a moment, it held King and courtiers in its spell.

Love is joy, love is fleeting,
And parting is as sure as meeting.
'Tis the burden of my song,
That love, alas, is never long.

So enjoy it while we may;
Tomorrow is another day—
If love should last until the dawn,
By dusk its farewell we shall mourn.

Seize then the hour before it passes,
For sure there will be other lasses.
Time and chance may change my song,
But love, alas will ne'er be long.

The last haunting notes hung in the air. There was
something so plaintive, so sad, about both the song
and the singer that for a moment no one spoke, and
then the King, striking his hands together, came
forward to greet Kit, his courtiers parting before him.

Charles was not a particularly regal figure, but
then he never had been. Informality reigned at
Whitehall in 1665 as it had done ever since Charles
had come home from his travels in 1660. He was
wearing a crimson velvet coat, laced with gold, and
a vast lace cravat; his petticoat breeches—wide
culottes falling to his knees—were black, his shirt
loose over the top of them. His stockings were of
scarlet silk with gold clocks and his black leather
shoes had red heels. His wig was long, curling and
black, and added another couple of inches to his
height of over six feet. He towered over every man
in the room.

'Well sung, Kit. No, do not stand, man. The song
is your own?'

'Yes, sire.' Kit obeyed his monarch and remained
where he was.

'Passing fine, Kit, passing fine. I missed the first
verse. You will sing it again?'

It was formed as a question, but was really a command. Kit nodded and once again the strains of the song filled the air. One or two, including George Buckingham, began to hum along with it by the end.

'I am not sure, Kit——' Charles was judicious '—whether I prefer the music or the words. Both are rare. You will let me have a copy of both, will you not? I would like to hear Castlemaine sing it.'

Few dared to laugh at this somewhat double-edged statement. Charles II was free and easy with his court, but whether he would have appreciated any comment on his mistress, Barbara Palmer, Lady Castlemaine, singing a song about fleeting love—her own hold on the King being the opposite of that—was quite another matter.

Kit looked up at his master, his friend since they had fought side by side at Worcester field in 1651 and had fled that doomed battlefield together—Kit barely seventeen years old and Charles already a man of twenty-one, cynical beyond his years.

He rose and bowed. He was not much shorter than the King in height and, like the King, was well-built and athletic—Charles sometimes teased him with his nickname 'Shoulders', and frequently demanded that he play opposite to him at tennis.

'Certainly, sire. As always, your wish is my command.' And he gave yet another bow—as perfunctory as the first had been. The King's eyebrows climbed. Kit's words might sound obedient, almost servile, but there was nothing of either in his manner. He was neither as rebellious nor as insolent as the young Lord Rochester already was, occasionally being condemned by the King to short periods in the Tower for his *lèse majesté*, but he was always his own man—as Dorothy Lowther had found.

'You were not formed to be a courtier, Kit. Natheless, lend me your shoulder for a moment.' He flung his arm around Kit, leaning on him, and began to walk him to the tall glass doors which led on to one of Whitehall's many lawns.

The palace by the river was a rabbit warren. It had been built over the reigns of many different monarchs and it was Kit's joke that, like Theseus pursuing the Minotaur in the labyrinth, one needed a thread unwinding behind one to find a safe way in and out of it.

Behind them both streamed not only the courtiers but also Charles's small spaniels, yapping their pleasure as they ran into the open. The King made for one of the many seats scattered about the grounds. He released his human prop, saying, 'Another song, Kit, and then you may retire—to please yourself, perhaps,' and his black eyes shone, leaving Kit in no doubt that his monarch knew perfectly well of Kit's dalliance and neither approved nor disapproved of it.

Kit had carried his guitar in his left hand as he walked along and, standing, he lifted a foot on to the bench before beginning to sing Herrick's poem 'Delight in Disorder'. He had set it to his own music the other evening and his eyes rested on Dorothy Lowther as he sang it. She had followed him and the King into the gardens almost unwillingly, and blushed a little at the opening words of the song:

A sweet disorder in the dress
Kindles in clothes a wantonness. . .

which he sang to her in defiance of her displeasure.

Once more King and Court applauded him. The King raised his hands and said, 'Go, Kit. Let your time be your own. I shall call on you again soon.'

Kit, now released, bowed gracefully this time—he was supple and elegant in all his movements despite his size—and walked slowly away from the King, his guitar by his side. He had hardly reached the paved walk which ran alongside the lawn, some of the little dogs following him, before George Buckingham caught up with him.

'Stay but a while, Kit. Old Rowley may have released you, but I have not done with you yet.'

Kit turned to face him. Buckingham was both an old friend and a rival. Despite his delicate beauty, rapidly running to seed, there was an aura of brutality about him which many of Charles's old friends and courtiers possessed. It was a relic of the days when they had followed him around the courts of Europe, penniless, begging for a living, hardly knowing where the next crust was coming from. It had made them all hard, and they had seized with both hands the pleasure of ruling England again after Charles's restoration in 1660.

Their boyhood had been harsh and penurious; their manhood was making up for it. Buckingham and Rochester were among the leaders of the self-styled Merry Gang who surrounded and amused the King, their antics often bordering on cruelty.

'Come, Kit,' Buckingham said, his smile a rictus, not a smile at all—he never liked being bested. 'Easy enough to pleasure the little Lowther, eh? Nothing to that, you must own. Her nay is always her yea. Now, I have a proposition for you of another coin. A trial of a different kind. A wench who not only flaunts her virtue, but clasps it tight to her. Now, if you could but breach her. . .that would be a triumph indeed, for she hath resisted so many. Could she resist you, think you? What would you wager with me on that?'

Kit looked at his friend, who was his enemy—for Buckingham was all contradictions—and mocked back at him. 'Nothing to that, indeed. Who is this paragon? Not to be found at Court, I'll be bound.'

'No, never at Court—until you bring her here, perhaps to joy us all. After you, my friend, always after you. *That* is the wager. She is the astrologer's daughter, no less.'

'What, William Lilly's get?' Kit was incredulous. 'I had not known that he had any.'

'No, not Lilly. His friend, his colleague, his rival. They live near to one another, hate each other's guts, cast horoscopes at one another instead of stones.' Words were pouring in a torrent from Buckingham; he could never resist them. 'Who but Adam Antiquis, who hath a fair daughter, Celia, a most chaste maid, who meets your eyes so steadily and says with hers, Stand off, do not touch me, I am cold Diana, I was born beneath the sign of the moon. Be Apollo, Kit, the Sun himself, and conquer, and I shall give thee—the manor of Latter, no less.'

'And if I lose? What then, George, can I give you, having so little?'

'The ruby on thy finger, Kit. I have long coveted it. The setting is magnificent—Cellini might have made it. Come, man, be not a laggard. You lose but a ring and you stand to gain Latter, which, my boy, would give thee a better hearth and home than that scrub you own in Cheshire, crowned with a burned-out ruin where your father, old Sir Kit, once held court. I'll never love thee again if you do not humour me. A good friend, but a bad enemy—you know my way. Besides, the wench hath flouted me most cruelly. I would see her endure love's pangs and love's shame—and who better than you to ensure them?'

At the mention of the ruby Kit looked down at the ring which blazed on his finger. He knew that Buckingham coveted it, knew also that he had vowed never to part with it. It was all that was left to Kit Carlyon of another life, another time, when he had been young and innocent, a man who would never have treated Dorothy Lowther as he had just done.

'I'll wager anything you like, George. But not the ring.' There was a hesitancy in his voice, he knew, for Latter was a temptation. At a stroke he would gain a competency, a home. Why, he might retire the Court, cease to be one of Charles's gentlemen, not need his small bounty; late though the King often was in paying those who served him, at least it was pay.

'But not the ring,' he repeated slowly.

Buckingham saw his hesitancy, threw back his head and laughed. 'Oh, Kit, Kit, why not the ring? Sure, you'll not fail, you never do. The girl once yours, you keep the ring and gain Latter too. As for the girl, whether you keep her or not, why, that's another matter.' And he began to sing Kit's song back at him.

Madness seized Kit. What was there left for him,

after all? Thirty-one years old, a bachelor, nigh penniless, no kith nor kin—why hang on to the dream of a lost past? Why not cut loose? To risk the ring would be to say that Kit Carlyon was still alive, not mourning that dead past. As for the girl, this Celia Antiquis, she must take her chance. If she were truly virtuous then she had nothing to fear; if not, then she deserved Kit Carlyon, did she not?

'The ring against Latter, let it be. Do you wish a term for this, George?'

'Nay, not I—or yet, perhaps this twelvemonth, Kit, there shall be a reckoning. Say a year from now. And now let's to the river to feed the ducks, to watch our master.' And he flung his arm around Kit's shoulders, as Charles had done, and walked him down the steps towards the riverbank, calling to the ducks as he did so, so that they scattered across the water, the King swearing at him genially as they fled, and the courtiers laughing.

And Kit Carlyon?

Why, Sir Christopher Carlyon, Bart, thought himself Judas that he wagered what was precious to him on such a thing, with such a creature as George Buckingham had become. Save that I am no better he thought, and, yes, the girl must take her chance.

'Now, my Celia, my wench, if thou hast cast the horoscope for which Sir William asked, then let me have it. You have saved mine eyes the pain.'

Adam Antiquis, outwardly hale at sixty, although inwardly failing, stood in his luxurious parlour at the back of his fine house in the Strand. Once he had been able to enjoy the view of the gardens outside, see the small wooden summer-house where he was wont to sit on a fair evening, listening to Celia as she played the viol for him, but latterly his sight had begun to dim.

Celia, her hand on the parchment on which she had inscribed Sir William Harmer's horoscope, lifted her blonde head and smiled at him. 'And what reward for *my* pains, sir?' she asked demurely, teasing him a little, for he well knew that she never asked for reward, being content to serve him.

Adam was about to answer when Mistress Hart, their housekeeper, came in carrying a flagon of good sack and two metal goblets on a silver tray. 'Master, mistress, as you commanded,' she said, and placed the tray on the oak table before Celia, neatly avoiding the parchment, inkhorn and Celia's quill.

'Pour out the drink,' commanded Adam in his most noble vein. He had been born a poor yeoman's son in Leicestershire, by the name of Archer. But nobler far was Antiquis, he had thought, for one who had set up as an astrologer, counting Elias Ashmole as his master and William Lilly, another Leicestershire man, as his friend and rival.

Nothing of his origins remained. He was as finely dressed as any courtier—if more soberly—in black velvet with silver trimmings, to match his luxuriant silver hair. Celia was the child of his middle years and his wife had died at her birth. She was like her father, not her dead mother. Her face was noble, classic—a Greek nose, great grey eyes beneath fine black eyebrows, her mouth long and firm, but generous. Her blonde hair, deeply waved, was caught simply back in a great knot.

Her clothes were simple too. A grey gown with a while linen collar edged with fine lace, all spotless.

Both of the Antiquises were spotless in clothes and body—for Adam had long noted that the clean lived longer than the dirty and were less inclined to agues and bad humours. He and Celia bathed frequently in water drawn from a well far from cesspits.

'I would thou gave me a reward,' he said, putting down the goblet. 'A reward which would please me, seeing that I am old and failing. I would not die leaving you alone and unprotected. Robert Renwick, the goldsmith, came yester eve to ask if he might offer for you. He would want a dowry, he said, to which my answer was, "No heed of that, Master Renwick, for Celia is all I have and will inherit all that is mine." He is a good man, Celia, and would treat you well, I have no doubt. His first wife was well cared for, 'till the sweating sickness took her.'

Celia rose, holding the goblet before her, and stood quite still to say at last, 'I have a mind to die a virgin, as you have long known, Father. I also have a mind to carry on your work. You have trained me well, but I think Robert Renwick would not want his wife to be other than his housekeeper and his bed-mate.'

Adam sighed, walked to the window, peered out of it, inwardly cursing his blurred sight and his failing body.

'I should not have trained you as I would have done a son,' he answered her. 'It pleased me to do so, and well you have rewarded me. You are better than most sons and, for a woman, your grasp of matters both plain and arcane is remarkable. But I have done you no favours. Times are changing, daughter. Sarah Ginner might be an astrologer under the Commonwealth, but the lives of women become ever more straitened. You would be safer as Renwick's wife. I would not die thinking you in danger, or penniless, or to be despoiled by the ruthless. Say you will obey me in this. You have never refused to obey me before.'

He had never asked such a thing of her before. Robert Renwick was well enough. He was older than she was—thirty-five to her twenty-two—but that was not it, either. He was heavy, dull: he would not wish his wife to know more than he did. He would cabin her—confine her to his kitchen, his bed, to be the mother of his sons. He was not asking for her out of love, she thought, but out of expedience—and Adam was passing rich. That must weigh with him, for all would come to him if he married her, and she—why she would be his chattel, nothing more.

Adam had made her his equal—and now he wished her to be another man's slave. She drank long and deep, but hardly tasted the sack.

'Allow me but a time to think,' she answered him.

'Aye, you may have that. But not too long—the stars say that my time on earth is nearly run and my body answers yes to them. And catastrophe awaits London—whether the plague or the fire, as Lilly thinks, I do not know, but I would have thee settled first.'

Celia knew that he was disturbed when he used thee and thou so freely. She put the goblet down on the table. 'And meantime, Father?'

'Meantime, my Lord of Buckingham comes this afternoon, my girl. He wishes me to make an election. Of what, his messenger did not say. But he will pay well, I think, and he is not a man to deny. You will be my eyes, will you not?' Writing was beginning to be a burden to him and Celia was his hand as well as his sight.

He added, abruptly for him, 'And he is a man you would be safe from if you married Renwick. He would have no occasion to meet you then. I would not have you with us when he calls, save that my sight needs thee. You understand me, daughter?'

Oh, Celia understood him. She had not known that her father had read Buckingham, and read him aright. He frequently visited Adam, to commission him to draw up an election, which was a decision on some important matter, to be made by consulting the disposition of the stars. But he also came to pursue Celia, to place a careless hand on her when she passed him and then, when her father was not by, to suggest with obscene directness that she become his bawd, his plaything.

Celia did not like him. Handsome he might be, and the housekeeper cast sheep's eyes on him, but there was something about him which made her shudder. Besides, the stars said that he was a danger to her. Adam had cast Buckingham's horoscope for him and she had written it out, and there, lo, when she placed it beside her own, was the message that she was in an unknown way tied to him.

Fear rode on her shoulders, for Buckingham was great, and she and Adam, for all their arcane knowledge and the respect in which the commonalty held them, were small.

There was a bustle outside—a noise. It was the Duke, come with all the train which his state demanded, rowed downriver from Whitehall in his barge, doubtless, surrounded by his minions, to come to leer at Celia Antiquis while using old Adam's knowledge which increasingly, as he aged, was her knowledge.

The door was rapped upon, was opened. Mistress Hart was there, curtsying to the visitors, her head held low. A steward stood before her, a white staff in his hand. Today my lord of Buckingham had come as Duke, not as he sometimes did, informally, to lean on Adam's shoulder and call him friend.

Buckingham entered. He was all gravity, in black and gold. There was a pearl in his right ear; the wig above his handsome dissipated face was like his silver-blond hair—except that it had not faded with age. He had his right arm draped round the broad shoulders of a man whom Celia had not seen before and was whispering in his ear. None other was with them.

Celia, curtsying, avoided the eyes of both of them. Like a wild creature, she would not give the Duke a direct glance of her eyes, keeping her head submissively low, focusing her attention on the white bows of her polished black shoes.

His Grace would not allow her that. He pulled his arm away from his companion's shoulders, nodded briefly to Adam, put a hand under Celia's chin to tip her face towards him.

'I would have a proper greeting from you, mistress. And one for my friend, Sir Christopher Carlyon, too. He hath a mind for you to cast his 'scope, or provide him with an horary—is not that so, Kit? What question shall thy horary answer? Nay, that you must tell the maiden, not myself. She is your eyes, is she not, Master Antiquis?'

If Adam disliked His Grace's easy handling of his daughter there was no show of it in his manner. He murmured his agreement, offered the Duke a chair as Celia bowed to the two men. Sir Christopher stood beside it, leaning on the chair-back, curious green and hazel eyes roving the elegant parlour.

Celia had been compelled by the Duke to look Sir Christopher Carlyon straight in the eye. She saw a tall man, taller than the Duke, more carelessly dressed in green and silver, whose face was deceptive, for while he was not handsome there was something compelling in it. As she looked at him, the room moved around her. For a moment Celia was lost. She had had such a fit before, where her body remained but her spirit roved, but never such a profound one. Adam knew of her rare trances and they frightened him, for nothing he had read, or been taught, could explain them.

She was in the open. There was a smell of burning and the sky was not blue, but black and orange. The air was not fresh, but hot and humid. People were shouting and the face of Sir Christopher Carlyon was before her, strangely distorted. She thought that he was shouting but she could hear nothing.

And then she was back in the parlour again, the sweet smell of spring was coming through the window, the smell of fire had gone. No time at all had passed, and yet an infinite time had held her imprisoned.

The green and hazel eyes were hard on her. She knew that her face changed on these occasions, that her eyes became wide and blank. He had seen the change, the shift of her consciousness, and he said, leaning forward, 'You are ill, mistress? Master Antiquis, your daughter needs attention, I think.'

His voice was beautiful, a caress, the voice of a singer or an actor. For sure he was neither. Her spirit, that sometimes remained with her after her trance had passed, told her that he was, or had been, a soldier. The spirit vanished. She was ordinary Celia Antiquis again, saying in a submissive voice, as colourless as she could make it, 'It is nothing, sir. A passing malaise only.'

She was surprised that he had registered that something strange had happened to her. It supposed a sensitivity in him which she would not have thought he possessed. The green eyes were suddenly veiled and Sir Christopher waved a dismissive hand. 'Enough, then, Mistress. George, I must not stop you from your business here.' He looked through the open window at the pretty garden and turned his green eyes away from Celia as though, restored again, she bored him.

Celia's surprise was now at herself. She sat down at the table, listened to her father taking the Duke's instructions, heard her father's answers and wrote in her clear plain script at his instruction, and was, astonishingly, piqued at Sir Christopher's lack of interest in her.

Kit, his friend called him. Or was the Duke his master? She thought not. No one was his master. Green-eyes was owned by none. How did she know that? She did two things at once, a trick Adam had taught her. She was achingly aware of Sir Christopher's every movement while appearing to be absorbed in her work. He was listening to the

grass, already yellowing. It had not rained for weeks.

Kit's man brought his guitar, Mistress Hart the wine and goblets. Adam was proud that his possessions were so fine. The yeoman's cottage where he had begun his days seemed far away. The steward came and a man following him in the Duke's colours handed the wine about. Kit tuned his guitar, bent his head over it, looked up and this time collected Celia's eyes.

'A song for you, mistress, seeing that you have been a good and obedient clerk. It is one of the late Will Shakespeare's and is a favourite of George's. The cherubim will envy this.' It was the longest speech he had yet made. His musician's hands plucked the strings. He sang, and his voice was so soft and tender that the tears started in Celia's eyes.

O mistress mine! where are you roaming?
O! stay and hear; your true love's coming,
   That can sing both high and low.
Trip no further, pretty sweeting;
   Journeys end in lovers' meeting,
   Every wise man's son doth know. . .

What is love? 'tis not hereafter;
Present mirth hath present laughter;
   What's to come is still unsure:
In delay there lies no plenty;
Then come kiss me, sweet and twenty,
   Youth's a stuff will not endure.

Kit had kept his eyes on Celia while he sang and, when all was silent at the end, repeated, 'Youth's a stuff will not endure,' not in his singing mode but low, breathily, as if he were giving her a message and they were alone in the garden, Adam and Eve together. But the serpent—where was he?

Buckingham spoke. It was to quote from *Twelfth Night*, the play from which the song was taken. '"A mellifluous voice, as I am true knight." Well sung, Kit. Thy singing matches the wine. Matchless, Master Antiquis, like your talent—and your daughter. A toast to thee, Mistress Celia. A fairer face never adorned the court.'

There was mockery in his tone, but Adam was deaf to it. He took all as his due. This was his zenith, his apogee, to have a Duke in his garden, one of the King's favourites singing to his daughter—for he knew of Kit Carlyon if Celia did not—wine before them and a meal waiting in his parlour, for the steward was at the garden door summoning them to eat.

Celia heard the Duke's mockery, saw his knowing eye on her, and thought how much she preferred his friend, who had behaved so quietly, who had noted her earlier distemper, but had not refined on it to distress her. So, when Buckingham said to the steward, 'In with you, man; Master Antiquis will accompany me and Sir Kit will take a turn around the garden with Mistress Celia before he brings her in to dine with us, for he hath a great interest in posies as well as poesies,' she felt no fear of Kit.

She allowed him to take her arm after he had handed his guitar to his waiting servant, whose grin after Celia had walked away from him, her hand on Kit's arm, was as knowingly insolent as only a servant's could be.

Kit had not known what to expect when

Buckingham had collected him at Whitehall. He had watched the Duke order the hampers of food to be loaded into the barge. He had laughingly told Kit to take his guitar with him to old Antiquis's home, 'For music undoes more ribbons and buttons than fingers do—as well you know.'

He had passed the house on the Strand many times. It was a decent place with its own curtilage. Many of the dwellings had gardens at the back. He had not accompanied the Duke to the astrologer's before. Kit had grave doubts about astrology—he thought it a fraud and those who practised it mere tricksters.

Adam and his home had impressed him. There was a decency about it, a plainness, nothing tawdry. He had expected toads, perhaps, dried and pinned to the walls, mystic cabala—all the trappings of the charlatan—but nothing to that. Master Antiquis's home was as grave as an Oxford scholar's, like the rooms he remembered being tutored in that last year before the world fell in and he became a penniless rover around the principalities of Europe and the Turkish dominions.

Celia was a surprise, too. She was quite unlike Buckingham's usual fancies. He had supposed her to be a knowing lass, sure of herself—George had told him that she was her father's clerk. He had also called her a chaste Diana—but anyone who held him off was a chaste Diana, until she became the Whore of Babylon in his arms. Once the girl was conquered, George moved on. One day, however, Fate would play one of her tricks on him and cause him to fall desperately in love with someone quite unworthy, and leave him unable to move on—but that day lay in the future. For the present, he enjoyed life and defied it to rule him.

Yes, that grave face, the cleanly dress, the modest deportment—for there was nothing tawdry about the astrologer's daughter; she matched his home—came as a surprise. But she was a woman and therefore to be won. What lay behind that demure mask? Could Kit Carlyon transform her to desire itself, writhing in his arms? To win her would be to win a trophy worth having, but only a cur would despoil her innocence.

Almost he cancelled the bet, handed George the ring he coveted. And then, why then, she showed the cloven hoof! Belial had laid his mark on her. The coy trance into which she had fallen was there to fetch him—or the Duke—was it not? Why, if Buckingham had but continued to pursue her, he could have had the sweet cheat for himself. Her tricks, like her father's, were not obvious ones, but tricks they were.

What was it that Shakespeare had said? 'Springes to catch woodcocks.' He, Kit Carlyon, would not be a woodcock. She had given him her blind grey look and he had refused to answer it. Oh, she had known that he was there and had refused to look further. Another sweet trick.

He had sung to her and for a moment their eyes had met again. When she rose to accompany him on the Duke's order, all in one fluid movement, her body was momentarily outlined beneath the concealing gown and he caught his breath at the sight of it. It was as purely lovely as her face with its classic profile.

But oh, he must go carefully with her. He had

spoken little. To win her would need all his arts for, were he to be clumsy, as Buckingham had been, sure in his power to woo and win, he would lose her. Never underestimate a clever woman—and the astrologer's daughter was clever.

He put out his arm for her to hold and, when she took it, there was the sweet smell of her—lavender, a country perfume for a town girl—and he led her along her garden path—to perdition and surrender, he hoped.

CHAPTER TWO

'A FINE garden, Mistress Celia. Are you the
gardener?'

Celia shook her head and said a little timidly,
which was most unlike her, for she was usually
controlled where the opposite sex was concerned. 'I
tend the herbs only, Sir Christopher. Our handy-
man, Willem, cares for the rest.'

'The herbs?' Kit looked about him but saw no
herbs. Celia gestured towards a wicker arch, with
climbing plants wreathed about it, through which a
further garden could be seen.

'If you are interested in herbs, Sir Christopher,
then mine lie through there.'

'Then I would visit them, Mistress Celia.' And he
led her through the arch to find himself in a knot
garden where, instead of flowers, herbs were
arranged. Along the brick wall which divided them
from the next property stood terracotta urns, filled
with more plants whose scents perfumed the air.

Kit bent down to pluck a sprig of thyme and sniff
it before handing it to Celia. 'You use herbs in your
mysteries, Mistress Celia?'

Celia crushed the thyme in her hands before
smelling it and answered him. 'I have no mysteries,
Sir Christopher, but yes, I use the herbs. Like
Mistress Ginner, of whom you may have heard, I
serve those women among us who need help in their
sicknesses. Culpepper hath shown us the virtues

herbs possess, and both my father and I believe that they possess others, yet unknown. Since the willow gives us surcease from pain and mould from many plants aids in healing wounds, may it not be that other plants have their virtues, too? It is for us to discover them and to use them as the stars direct.' And she slipped the thyme into the small pouch which swung at her wàist and walked composedly on.

Kit, from his great height, looked down on her. She was not small, he noted, but neither was she over-tall. A woman to reach above a man's heart, he thought. And what a strange woman. She had spoken to him as soberly as though she were a scholar and he another, nothing of a woman's traditional coquetry about her.

He answered her as he might have done a scholar. He thought that George might have failed to win her because he spoke to her lightly, as he did to all women.

'And the plague, mistress? Do you think there might be a specific against that? A fine thing if there were.'

Celia knew, as Kit did, that the plague was abroad in London and the numbers dying from it were growing each day. From being a thing distant from the haunts of the powerful and the comfortable, like Adam and herself, it was coming disturbingly near and to catch it meant almost certain death.

'No herbal specific of which I or my father know, but. . .' Celia paused; she was fearful that he might mock her if she spoke of what her father thought that he knew.

'A "but", Mistress Celia? What does thy "but" conceal or reveal? Pray tell me.'

Celia looked up at him. Her eyes were as grey as clear water before a storm, Kit thought. Her face as calm as that of one of the many statues of the goddess Diana he had seen in Italy. It was not a holy, but a classic calm. If he touched her damask cheek would he feel flesh, or marble?

Kit's hand rose. He checked himself. To win his bet would be far more difficult than he had thought. To go too fast would be to lose her. She would close herself against him as she had closed herself against Buckingham. She would live in a bubble, would be seen, spoken to, but not reached—forever sealed away from him.

Would she be so for any man? Or was there some Hodge, some decent, dull merchant to whom she would surrender her treasure? Or had she vowed herself a vestal virgin to the pale moon?

His hesitation, the thoughts hastening pell-mell through his head, took but an instant of his time. Celia barely noticed his movement, or his hesitation, and said again without artifice, 'But Father thinks that perhaps we misunderstand the cause of the thing. He says that if it is mere bad air then why does the plague so often confine itself to the poor? The air is as bad in many great houses and yet the plague most often leaves them free. He thinks that perhaps it is because the houses of the rich are spacious, and not huddled together, hugger-mugger; that instead of shutting those infected away, as the law has recently ordered in St Giles in the Fields, we ought to put them outside and let them live in the open. What is there, he also asks, that the rich do and the poor do not, which makes the difference between them? Or mayhap it is the other way around; it is what the poor do.'

She fell silent. She had spoken too long and too vigorously, but she and her father had thought much about the plague and how to contain it.

'And the stars?' asked Kit slyly, for he thought astrology a cheat, but would not tell the astrologer's daughter so. 'Why do they not tell your father where, how and why the plague works on us as it does? If they are so powerful over our destinies, *that* is a question which they can surely answer.'

'That I know not,' said Celia frankly, her brow a little troubled. 'The stars do tell us when the plague is coming. All the charts which my father and I prepared for our almanack this year foretold its arrival, and it has come. Master Lilly, too, agreed with us. Perhaps there are things which we may not know. . .'

'You dispute as well as any scholar,' remarked Kit, fascinated by her, admiring first her full face turned towards him and then her profile, pure against the dark of the house.

'So I have been taught,' she answered. She had never spoken so long with any man other than her father and had not thought to spend an afternoon discoursing with one from Charles's court. Nor had she thought that he would speak to her so gravely. Buckingham had always teased her, tried to make her talk nonsense, and had talked nonsense to her. She had no answer to that, so rarely answered him.

This man, now, was different. She stole a glance at Kit and admired his powerful face, his haughty pride, barely held in check. She knew he was proud because he bore the marks of it as the old text she had recently read had told her: 'head high, eyes steady, mouth firm—he looks to the distant, not the near—carriage erect, voice sure'. To win his respect would be a fine thing, and already he spoke to her not as a woman to be lightly handled and then thrown away but as a fellow soul to dispute with, as he would have disputed with her father.

'You do not believe in astrology, then, sir?' she asked him as she would not have done had he merely played the light game of love with her.

'I do not believe in anything that I cannot see, touch, or experiment with. I am with Prince Rupert in that,' was his reply. 'But, mistress, we must to the house again. The Duke and your father will wonder what has kept us and will not be like to believe us if we say that we were having a most scholarly discourse. Such is not the usual converse of man and maid left alone together!'

Celia did not blush, or raise a hand to flap at him, but nodded her head in agreement. 'I had forgot how long we had been alone,' she said, 'in the pleasure of our discourse. You are perhaps a member of the King's great society which seeks to discover the secrets of the world in which we live.'

'Most surely,' agreed Kit, leading her back to the house. He was a little surprised that she knew of the Royal Society, but then if her father spoke freely to her of his work, and she had read widely, as it was plain that she had, then she was like to know of it.

'Oh, I wish,' said Celia wistfully, looking up at him so that Kit felt that he was about to drown in the grey waters of her eyes—and what a splendid death that would be—'I wish that I were a man that

I might be present and listen to the sages and the learned men speak. Sometimes when Father hath company I am allowed to be present, but I am not allowed to speak. I may merely listen.'

'And what a waste——' Kit was suddenly a gallant, a true member of the King's dissolute court '—that would be. That you were a man, I mean, mistress. You are too fair to be a man.'

'And that,' she said gently, as they reached the door to the house where they could hear Adam and the Duke speaking together, both having drunk too well, and their voices rising and falling almost as though they were singing, 'is what I most complain of. That it is my looks which men think of and never of me—the Celia who has thoughts and dreams that a man might have, but may rarely express them.'

She had thought him different but she had been wrong. He was a man and a courtier and he might dally for a moment with her and speak as he might have done to one of his fellows, but that was no matter, she was, forever and ever, merely a woman, and that she must endure.

Kit knew that he had sounded a false note, and that with it he had lost all that he had gained with her. But no matter. He could not believe that she was so different from all the other women he had known. Her wooing and winning would take longer, and would follow a different path, but the end would be the same—if only he guarded his tongue and showed to her that face of him which she would most like to see.

Buckingham lifted his glass mockingly to them as they entered the room. 'Hast been a devil of a long time admiring the flowers, Kit, my boy. Or is that all you admired? Nay, do not answer me; I would not have the fair Celia put out of countenance. That would never do, my sweeting, would it?' And he rose and bowed to her.

Kit felt a flash of anger at such boorishness. He saw that Adam had drunk too well to mind the Duke's grossness, but he need not have feared for the lady at his side.

Celia curtsied and put out a hand to the dish on the table to take a sweetmeat from it, refusing the wine which the Duke's servant offered her. 'Why, Your Grace,' she murmured, before she bit into the sweetmeat, 'we did but speak of the plague and specifics against it. Sir Christopher was of a mind that an herb might be found, and so we spoke on. And of the King's society, too. The flowers were not outfaced, I think. Was not that so, Sir Christopher?'

Kit made her a great leg, in respect for her wit, and the Duke gave a great shout.

'Oh, the astrologer's daughter is a pearl of great price!' He turned to Adam, who was beaming at the compliment. 'Why, man, when you bring my election to Court when thou hast finished it, bring thy daughter, too. Pearls are to be admired by all, not only by such lucky dogs as Kit and myself.' And he threw back his head and laughed, the drink strong in him.

'If you so command,' replied Adam, too dazzled by such condescension to think of the dangers to his daughter of being seen by the denizens of Whitehall's labyrinthine corridors.

Kit Carlyon's reaction to the Duke's carelessness was extraordinary. For a moment he felt a cold rage on the girl's behalf, that she should be exposed as

prey to those who might feed on her. After that
came the thought, like cold water thrown over him,
and what are thy intentions, Kit, friend of this
whoremaster? What of the bet? What makes that of
you?

He looked at her, smiling a small smile, a goblet
in her hand from which she was drinking lemonade.
He repressed his feelings. She's but a woman after
all, no better nor no worse than the rest, and he said
again what he had said to himself on the day of his
bet—she must take her chance, as we all must. If
she be chaste, why, she's in no danger, for I'll never
force her. I've never forced a woman yet.

Now why did Sir Christopher Carlyon walk through
her head? He had nothing to do with her—she must
forget him, which was difficult. He was with her
when she rose the morning following the Duke's
visit and he walked with her on her chores about the
house. He was a haughty ghost who bent his head
and spoke kindly to her as few men had ever done.

Adam had a bad head, rose late and broke his fast
lightly—food nauseated him, he said. He decided to
work after noon, when his head might have cleared.
He had had second thoughts about the Duke's visit
and, sober now, regretted that he had promised to
take Celia to Whitehall. So far she had kept herself
clear from that world, and he regretted even more
that he had not persuaded her to marry and forget
that she was the astrologer's daughter.

'You will receive Master Renwick when he comes,
will you not, daughter?' he asked her as she prepared to go shopping. 'And you will be a good

daughter, I know, and give him the answer he—and I—wish to hear.'

What could she say to that? He had been a kind father and she did not want to distress him but, talking to Kit Carlyon, brief though their speech had been, had made her even less inclined towards a marriage with Master Renwick. He was not an unkind man, she knew that without needing an astrological chart to tell her so, but he was not the man for her. Perhaps there was no man for her and, if so, then Amen to that. Except that her father did not want to hear that particular Amen!

'I like Master Renwick as a friend,' she said gently, her head bent a little, 'but I do not wish to marry, Father. You know that. Not him or any man.'

She thought that she spoke the truth but, for a moment, was there not such as man as *he* had seemed to be yester afternoon whom she might wish to marry? She straightened up and looked her father full in the eye, for she would have refused to marry Robert Renwick even if the Duke had never visited them and brought his haughty friend with him.

'Say not so, daughter, before you speak with him.' Adam uttered no threats, no words such as, You will do my bidding daughter, or be thrashed and remain in your room until you agree to the marriage. It was not his way. Besides, he had done an election, soon after rising, and the election had told him that his daughter would marry, and that her marriage would be long and blessed. It did not tell him whom she would marry, but reason said that Renwick was the man—for who else could there be? No need, then, to act as most men did towards their daughters when they flouted their authority. Time and chance were on his side.

'Very well, Father. I will listen to Master Renwick, speak him fair, but I warn you, I do not think that I shall change my mind.'

Adam was pleased to take this as a half-submission and said, 'Go to, then; go to. Do this day's duty. And should he chance to come today, why, then do that duty too.'

All the way down the Strand Celia walked, not with Robert Renwick, that decent man whom her father wished her to marry, but with Sir Kit. Oh, it was not just the fashion in which he had spoken to her which entranced her, but it was the whole man. So tall, so proud, the green eyes flashing at her and his voice, that seducing voice when he sang.

What a fool I am; how many women has that beautiful voice seduced? Why should that voice not wish to seduce me? Why should he see me as any different from the other women he has known? Celia suddenly walked with a pride as great as his. I am no court light of love, I am Celia Antiquis—and if I do not wish to be Robert Renwick's wife, neither do I wish to be Kit Carlyon's whore, for that is all I should be. Great men do not look at such as I am for other than a passing entertainment. But a girl may dream of other things, so long as she understands that dreams and daily life may never meet!

Willem thought his mistress a little more distant than usual that morning as she bargained with the mercer over stuff for a new gown. A pretty wench, Mistress Celia, but cold. Robert Renwick would be taking an icicle to his bed.

Robert Renwick came that afternoon. Celia and

Adam were working on the Duke's elections, for he had made several. Neither father nor daughter was to know that the true reason for Buckingham's visit had not been the elections, useful though they might be to him, but to introduce Kit to Celia, to start the consequences of the bet on their way.

Buckingham was mischievous. It would be as good as a play to watch Kit lure Celia Antiquis into his toils. It might even make a play for him. Who knew what the future held for any of them?

Robert Renwick thought that he knew. He was a goldsmith and saw men and women as an extension of his craft, particularly women. They were malleable, could be bought and then bent to the whim of the craftsman or the master. He knew his worth and thought that both Antiquises did. He had spoken often with Celia, and she pleased him. Modesty always pleased a man and Celia was truly modest, save only that her father had unfortunately chosen to treat her as his acolyte. No matter. Her nature, woman's nature would mean that she would become Robert Renwick's acolyte and, in so doing, would relinquish what her father had taught her.

He stood in the parlour where Buckingham and Kit had stood the day before. He admired it, particularly the presses. He thought that one day, perhaps not long distant by Adam's looks, they would grace his home and grace it well.

He ignored the view of the garden through the window. Gardens were for women and his sole thought of it was that Celia might make such a one for him. She entered and was before him.

Celia had thought and thought what to say to him. She neither liked nor disliked him. He was someone with whom her father had supped and spoken. She had known Nan Barton, his first wife, and liked her. She had grieved at her death in childbirth, had watched with pity Robert's grief at his loss. He was a good man, she thought, but not a good man for Celia Antiquis to marry.

He was finely dressed and, although the day was warm, he had put on his best murrey-coloured doublet with the fur collar. He wore one of his own gold chains and carried a pair of fine gloves in his strong craftsman's hands. He was not as tall as Kit Carlyon, but broader. His eyes were not flashing green, but brown pools. Why did she think of Kit Carlyon at this juncture?

'Mistress, you will be seated, I hope.' He handed Celia into one of her father's high-backed chairs. Few stools for the prosperous Antiquises, Robert had noted.

'Indeed, Master Renwick.' Celia arranged the skirts of her pale blue dress about her. She was neat and careful in all her ways, a good sign for a prospective husband. The house was neat, too, most carefully tended. Her studies had not kept her from her proper work, Robert noted with pleasure.

'I understand that your father has spoken to you of my visit and its purpose, Mistress Celia.' He was standing, his back to the light, so that she could not properly see his face. She supposed it was set in lines of pleasant determination. She was right.

He was sure of himself—as who would not be? He had her father's favour, and the daughter was obedient. Almost, Celia gave him his yes, and then, as she began to frame the words, something inside her rebelled. To wed him would be to go from freedom to servitude. She had secretly vowed never to marry any man for, as a single woman, she might own her own property, run her father's business while he lived, own it after his death. She would be in all things the equal of a man.

But if she married Robert Renwick she would lose all. Her property would pass to him for him to use without consulting her. As a separate person she would cease to exist. She would be Robert Renwick's wife and that would be all. Now, if she loved him, she could perhaps bear that servitude, become his chattel—for that was what a wife was, a chattel, nothing more. But, since she loved him not, she would on marriage give up all to receive—nothing.

The words of acceptance stuck in her throat. She would speak him fair, be kind to him, but she would not marry him. As to what her father might say, well, she would have to live with that.

'He has so,' she replied. 'He has told me that you wish to marry me and that if I wish to accept you, he will give us his blessing.'

For a moment Robert thought that she *had* accepted him; his face lightened, then darkened again.

'And you, mistress, do you wish to be my wife? I vow to you that I will treat you most lovingly. You were my Nan's good friend. You know how well we dealt together. I believe that you and I could be as happy. A man would be proud to call you wife, mistress.'

He would treat her lovingly, he said, but he had spoken no word of love. Nor had he asked for hers.

Well, that was common enough, but the word might have reconciled her.

She curtsied to him, and something he saw in her face darkened his. 'Master Renwick, you are a good man, I know, and your offer is a kind one, made in good faith, and as such I have considered it most carefully since my father told me that you wished to speak to me. It grieves me greatly to refuse you, but refuse you I must. I have no mind to marry any man, but were I to marry one, then, Master Renwick, that man would be you. The world is wide, London is large, and there are many maidens who would be happy to be your wife. I wish you happy with one of them.'

He advanced on her, his face grim. Celia suddenly saw that he could be cruel, and her refusal, which had sounded capricious to her as she made it, no longer seemed so. She had thought him tame but she had misjudged him—and the power which her own sex held over the other.

'Good Mistress Celia, I want no other maid, I want only you. I have dreamed of you as my wife, lo, these many years, and now it has become possible. I shall speak to thy father and persuade him to command thee to accept my offer.'

'I think not,' said Celia spiritedly. 'He has never yet forced me to do that which displeases me. He may lament my refusal of you, but he will not force me.' Something he had said struck her. He had wanted her 'lo, these many years', but Nan had died only six months ago. . .

'No!' she exclaimed, the colour deserting her face. 'I hope I have misunderstood you. You wanted me when Nan. . .' And she paused, as Robert threw himself on his knees before her.

'I have wanted thee since I first saw thee as a maiden of sixteen on the day I married Nan. God forgive me, when she died I could only think that it freed me for you. It has been torture for me to see thee about my house. I had not meant thee to know, but when you refused me, my tongue betrayed me.'

He seized her hand and the words of love were pouring out at last, and now Celia knew more than ever that he—and his tainted love—was not for her. Nan's shadow would lie forever between them.

'Oh, accept me, I beseech thee. Do not let me burn longer. I will buy thee a silken gown, make thee a fine chain, jewels for thy fingers. Robert Renwick's wife will be as fine as any lady of the court. You cannot turn away such love.'

Celia pulled her hand away. 'Please stop, I beg of you, Master Renwick. To learn of this makes my mind more fixed than ever. I can never marry you. Nan was my dear friend. Her ghost would lie in our bed reproaching me.'

It was hopeless and, knowing that it was hopeless, he lost all self-control. 'What, have you a lover, then, mistress, a secret one, that you should treat a good man so? No wench who looks as you do could truthfully prate of staying single. Was the court gallant who came here yesterday with my lord of Buckingham a man to please you more? Or is it the Duke himself you have an eye to? He hath haunted thy father's house. Was it for thee he came?'

'For shame.' Celia was at the door. She had heard a hundred songs which told of the bitterness of unrequited love, but to see that bitterness exposed, to feel it lashing about her as though he had taken a whip to her was more than she could endure. 'My nay is my nay, Master Renwick. My father did not breed me to be a weak fool. There is no other man in my life, save in thy sick imagination. I will leave you, Master Renwick. You have had your answer.'

Her small hand on the door latch was covered by his large one. 'Why, mistress,' he said, panting slightly, 'never think that this is the end of the story. Robert Renwick hath always got what Robert Renwick wants, and this is no time for him to begin to lose that reputation. If I find you have lied to me, why, mistress, I make a good friend, would have made thee a good husband, but I am a bad enemy. Think on that.'

Celia wrenched her hand from under his and was through the door, sobbing slightly between fright and disgust. The calm which had ruled her life until this day was shattered quite. She had seen the face of naked lust in one whom she had thought was free of such a vulgar passion, had learned how little she knew of the true face of the world, and it had frightened her.

She fled to the sanctuary of her room.

Celia Antiquis walked with Kit Carlyon that day. She was with him when he woke with a thick head. He rarely drank heavily, and seldom gambled, having little with which to gamble. But at Whitehall on the night of the first day that he had met her he sat down to Basset and lost. The old saying went, lucky at cards, unlucky in love. He staggered to his bed, hoping that the reverse held good.

He had supposed that to win his bet he would also

need to win something which he did not want—a woman's love. He had thought that the astrologer's daughter would be such that he could woo and win her and toss her away without a thought, as he had tossed away Dorothy Lowther.

Aye, and that was the worst of it. He saw Dorothy Lowther that morning and felt only shame at the sight of her. What! Had one walk on a pleasant afternoon among the herbs and shrubs and flowers with a sweet-faced virgin at his side unmanned him quite? He was run tearing mad. He would forget her—but he could not.

The day was fair, the sun shone, the King was not capricious. The Privy Council met in the morning. In the afternoon the court walked in the open, down an alley whose fruit trees were flowering early. The talk was of the coming war with the Dutch.

The Duke of York had left to join the fleet, Charles Berkeley with him. Berkeley was a friend of Kit's. It might be more truthful to say that he was a friend of everyone, universally loved by all, from the King downwards. He had written a song before he had gone and early in the afternoon the King called on Kit to sing it—his reward a game of tennis with his monarch in the cool of the day.

The role of courtier fretted Kit. But what else could a landless, penniless man do, who knew no trade save war? For that reason, Latter beckoned. A home of his own, an occupation to see his small lands well-run. Like many others, the late Civil War between King and Parliament had deprived him of his inheritance. At first, to serve the King, adorn his court, had seemed some recompense but, as the years drew on, he found himself needing security, his own home—a wife, children around him.

But to gain Latter, find that home, he must betray Celia Antiquis, and Buckingham, clever devil that he was, had thought of the one way to bribe Kit to do for him what he had failed to do for himself. Being Buckingham, he could not fail—he would succeed through Kit.

Kit finished Berkeley's merry ballad, 'To all you ladies now on land', and Celia Antiquis popped into his mind again. The King saw his melancholy and, being a melancholic man himself, had compassion for him. 'Why, Kit man, what ails thee? Hast taken a fever? Is there none here to please thee, haul thee from the dumps?' He waved a hand at the assorted beauties sitting or standing in the sun. His queen had accompanied him and held court from a bench beside an urn of unseasonally early flowers.

Kit shrugged and laid down his guitar. 'Nothing that a game of tennis will not cure, sire.' And that was true, he knew. Action always dissipated melancholy for, in the violent doing, the mind disappeared and the body took over.

'Buckingham tells me that you and he hied to the astrologer, Antiquis, yesterday and that he hath invited him here, and his daughter, too. He says that the daughter practises his trade, knows his mysteries. Is that the truth, or Buckingham's extravagance talking?'

Kit looked at the King, his master. He was wearing a royal-blue coat with a silver sash and trimmings; his petticoat breeches were of a deeper blue and a scarlet garter bound each stocking. He had a spaniel on his lap and toyed with its ears—as he was toying with Kit's in a different sense.

'The truth, sire? The maid is as knowledgeable as the father.'

'And is she fair?'

Kit's eyes were on Charles again. Was this mere idleness, or had the King the thought that a new sensation might be found in toying with the astrologer's daughter instead of a noble beauty? Actresses had graced his bed, Nell Gwyn and Moll Davis; why not a maiden from the city streets?

'Very fair,' he said at last.

The King began to laugh. 'Why, I verily believe I have found the cause of Kit Carlyon's melancholy. And is she chaste, as well as fair, and has she refused Buckingham and looked sideways at thy good self? Fie, for shame, you cannot have wooed her properly. Kit Carlyon to be bested by an unknown virgin?'

What to say? For he knew that Charles was truly toying with him, that Buckingham had told him of the bet and all the court were agog to see whether a cit's daughter could do what the maids of honour could not, and deny Kit Carlyon what he wished.

Kit picked up his guitar again, stared at the scarlet ribbons which decorated it and thought how often its music had helped him to a worthless victory over women whose virtue had long vanished. What true pleasure lay in that?

'The maid scarce knew that I was with her,' he said at last. 'Her eyes are fixed on a greater master than——' and he dared to say it '—than you or I.'

Charles took no offence—he rarely did. 'And what master is that, good Sir Kit, who is more attractive than any man, even one who wears a crown?'

'Why knowledge, sire. The lady would be a sage, know the secrets of the universe as well as those of the stars. She wishes that she were a man, able to sit at the meetings of our society and dispute the meaning of our findings with us. She does not see men as lovers, or husbands, I dare swear.'

'Oh, a rare wench, indeed. When she comes hither I must see her. Arrange it, Kit. I would talk with a maiden who is fair, chaste and does not wish to deal with men but with natural philosophy. Yes, a rare creature, indeed. Go now, but do not forget our game this evening. I would play with someone who does not fear to beat me. I grow weary of "A splendid stroke, Majesty" — "Oh, a fig for my play, you have bested me quite" — and that after I have been given the game!'

Kit watched him go. Charles held out his hand to the Queen as he passed her and Catherine of Braganza, dumpy, with a pleasant monkey face, was only too pathetically glad to take it. She loved her careless husband and was grateful for the crumbs of his attention. She possessed but one thing to hold him, and that was the promise of a legitimate child, but so far the child had not come, nor, some whispered, was like to. Recently she had been ill and in her delirium had thought herself delivered of the wanted children. Charles had been kind to her, but kindness was all she got. It was his love she wanted, and that she would never have.

Kit was thinking on this as he walked back to his lodgings to change to play tennis, and to rest a little. He met Buckingham coming from his quarters which faced the Privy Garden; Kit's were not far from the tennis court.

'Well met, Kit. Hath Old Rowley done with thee?' Old Rowley was the King's nickname after a notorious goat, given because of Charles's many loves. Charles knew of it and, in his sardonic way, was amused by it.

'Not yet. I am to play tennis with him later.'

'Sooner thou than I.' Buckingham became confidential, put his arm through Kit's. 'I had news today which should give us all pause. They say that the plague is far worse than the Bills of Mortality suggest. That it grows apace and leaves the warrens of St. Giles and Alsatia behind and advances towards the City. I should have had old Antiquis perform an election on it.'

'His daughter said that they forecast that the plague would come this year, and that it would be a great one. . .'

'So, that was the burden of thy talk. Small wonder that you progressed no further with her than you did if that was all you could find to speak of!'

Kit shrugged. 'I think,' he said slowly, 'that I may have progressed further than I thought. I am not sure, George, how far I wish to pursue this bet, even though by winning I might gain Latter.'

Buckingham laughed maliciously. 'Too late, man, too late. The die is cast. The bet is made that you will make the fair Celia no longer a maid.'

Once, Kit would have continued to play further with words, but not today. 'Did Antiquis say how much time might pass before he brought your answers to Whitehall?'

'Oho!' Buckingham laughed again. 'So hot to see

her, Kit, that you cannot wait? He said it might be a week, but should you wish to see her sooner, why, you know the way to the Strand. Her father would welcome thee, so pleased was he that the Court now patronises him. Would his pleasure agree to the surrender of his daughter's virginity, think you?'

Commonly Kit might have continued jousting with him after this fashion, but today he was uneasy, sick at heart, and did not know why.

'Oh, I can wait,' he answered. 'What was it that the old Roman, Fabius by name, said? That the best generalship draws the enemy on by slow degrees to destroy him utterly.'

'A soldier's answer,' responded Buckingham gaily. 'Well, I live to see that day, Kit, when she comes and you retreat and retreat so that alone, in enemy country, there is no retreat for her, but only surrender. I do not wish thee well, mind, for I covet thy ring.'

He was gone. Quicksilver in mind and body, a man whom few would trust, but old hardships shared bound him and Kit together. Had he told his friend the truth it would have been that he wished to see her again and soon, if only to find that his memory of her was false—that she was but another woman, after all.

CHAPTER THREE

'I WOULD have had thee wed Robert Renwick, but
since you will not, then you will not. I will only ask
you to consider such a marriage carefully, for he
tells me that he is of a mind to ask you again. You
trouble me greatly, daughter, for by the nature of
things you must shortly lose me and, in so doing,
lose thy protector. More, I am not sure that I ought
to take thee to Whitehall this day, but the Duke so
commanded and I dare not disobey. He would be a
powerful patron. They say that the King is power-
fully interested in astrology and, were we to see
him, who knows what might happen? The stars
foretold a change of fortune for me, but they did
not say what shape it will take. They are capricious,
as you know.'

Celia and her father were collecting their parchments and papers to take to Whitehall, the Duke's
commissions having been fulfilled. Willem would
accompany them to carry them and other necessi-
ties, for Adam was hopeful that their visit to
Whitehall might be productive of more than thanks
and a few guineas. This was his great opportunity to
woo and win the mighty. Why, he might even see
the King's Majesty himself.

He was unaware that Charles had already
arranged with an amused Buckingham to be present
at some point during the Antiquises' visit—in order
to see the astrologer's daughter, not the astrologer.

Celia saw the last parchment stowed away then said softly, 'I have little mind to go to Whitehall, Father. The courts of kings, I have read, are easily entered but not so easily left. The stars say that my fortune will change, too, but do not say whether for better or for worse. I want no change. I am happy as I am.'

Adam smiled, then frowned. 'Oh, child such a statement tempts the gods. When mortals say they are happy, they throw the dice to challenge that happiness. But, come, the wherry awaits us.'

They walked by Essex House, Willem following, down to the Temple Stairs where a wherry had been commissioned and was waiting to take them to Whitehall Palace. The river was the easiest mode of transport in London and was busier than any street. The Thames was both a port and a highway.

Celia had dressed herself carefully in a gown of middling blue. She wore a deep lace collar, but the neckline of her gown was modest and the pin at the throat of it was modest too. Her shoes were her best and she had dressed her hair a little more loosely than was her wont. She had not put in curl-papers to create the elaborate ringlets of the court ladies and was sure that she would look sadly out of fashion.

What she did not know was that the pure lines of her face, head and neck needed no ringlets. Classic simplicity had its own beauty which owed nothing to artifice.

'Speak when spoken to,' groused Adam gently. 'That was what Master Renwick said. They told him that before he went to Court when the King commissioned a loving cup from him, which, by the by, he hath not paid for. Will the Duke pay for his elections, I wonder, or will he follow his master's example? Yet, to have the King one's patron would be a fine thing, money or no. It hath brought Master Renwick many commissions, just to say that the King is pleased to employ him.'

Celia made no answer. She remained quiet as the wherry moved on its way to Whitehall. She was busy taking mental note of all that happened to her. She had seen the palace from the outside, marvelled at its size, at the coming and going of servants, courtiers and officials. Whitehall was the seat of Government as well as the King's home. Parliament might have tamed the monarch a little but, since his restoration in 1660, they worked in tandem—each side now up, now down.

She had never thought to find herself in it. A servant of the Duke's had been waiting for them at the top of the Privy Steps which led from the river. My lord expected them, he said. It was good that they had come betimes: he did not care to be kept waiting. A footman was there, who took Willem's burdens from him, and they set off in procession.

Willem was left at a small lodge, to be given ale by some functionary. There were so many servants and lackeys about that Celia wondered how she and Adam managed to live without them. They walked along a small paved road, through an archway into a large garden, a sundial in its middle. They had thought that they were to be taken to the Duke's apartments but, in reply to a question from Adam, it seemed not. They were to go to one of the state rooms, facing the garden, where the Duke had taken himself and his own small court—for there were courts within courts, Celia was to find.

Finally they went through double doors, held open by more lackeys, into a large long room with many windows—some from floor to ceiling, others with seats in them. There were glass doors opening on to yet another garden. The room was full of people, but contained little in the way of furnishings. The Duke was seated in a great chair facing the glass doors. Richly dressed women stood about, sat on cushions scattered about the polished floor or reclined on long settles. Some men and women were in the window seats; all their eyes turned on Celia and her father as they entered.

The Duke, on seeing them, rose, and conducted Adam to a high-backed armless chair placed a little to the right of his. Behind it Celia suddenly saw Sir Kit. He was seated on a long low stool of the type which stood before a fire. His guitar was on his knee. He was talking to a richly dressed woman who sat beside him. She was so superb, so proud and haughty, that Celia knew at once that she was a grand personage.

She caught sight of Celia following Adam, watched while the Duke demanded a stool be placed for her at her father's knee, then put a long finger on to Kit's chin and laughed into his eyes. There was something so secretive, so confidential about her action that it was plain that he and she shared a friendship or, perhaps even something more. Celia felt a strange pang at the sight of it. Which was foolish, for what was Kit Carlyon to her but the Duke's friend? He was not hers.

And all the time the Duke was speaking. His

voice, as beautiful in its own way as Kit's, went up and down. She must pay attention, for the elections and horaries had been as much her work as Adam's and at any moment he might call on her for her support.

The Duke held the parchments which they had prepared in his long-fingered hands, studded about with rings today. He was superbly dressed as though to emphasise to them that the man who had eaten in their parlour was also a man of great affairs.

'So, Mistress Celia,' he said, turning to her. 'Your father hath told me that you had a great hand in preparing these.' He handed the parchments to her. 'You might confirm his faith in you by expounding to me how I am to interpret them.'

'Why, Your Grace,' replied Celia, trying to hide how nervous she was to be so addressed before so many powerful people, 'it depends on whether thy question is an horary or an election, for the principles determining them are subtly different. Thy first question, as to when the time will be propitious for you to make a journey out of London, is an election and, therefore, looks to the best moment in the future to make thy journey—that is, the one when the moon and planets are most propitious. And here——' and she pointed to the horoscope '—is the day upon which my father advises you to leave, which you will see is in early July.

'But this——' and she lifted one of the parchments to display it to the Duke who now leaned forward, chin in hand, elbow on knee, to hear all that she had to say '—this one is an horary, because it asketh not of the future but is dependent on the present, and therefore the horoscope which determines the answer is drawn up showing the signs at the moment when the question was asked.'

The Duke put up his hand, laughing a little. 'Good mistress, I doubt me not as to your learning and, as to the use I shall make of it, why that I must ponder. You are a miracle of nature madam, a *lusus naturae*, as the Ancients had it. Sir——' And he turned to Adam who sat beaming at his daughter, lost in delight that his visit to the court was proving so propitious. And why, Adam thought, should that surprise me, for did not the stars tell me that great things would flow from it?

'Sir, you will continue where thy daughter hath finished. I would not have her overborne by her learning. Kit——' he turned towards his friend who was now tuning his guitar, head bent over it '—Kit, my friend, you will give the fair Mistress Antiquis a turn about the room while I speak further with her father.'

Kit, who had been supremely aware of Celia ever since she had walked into the room, rose, put down his guitar and walked over to where she sat, bowed and offered her his hand. She took it, felt its warmth and its strength. If he had been aware of her, then she had been as aware of him. More—as they touched, some message seemed to pass between them, for first her hand thrilled and then her arm, and finally her whole body. For a moment she was fearful that the trance was on her, but she could control it when warned of its coming, which she did, to hear him reply to Buckingham.

'Willingly, George, willingly. I would discourse again with the lady on matters philosophical.' And if there were a few who smirked behind their hands

at the notion of Kit Carlyon discussing philosophy
with a fair maid, neither Celia nor her father saw
them, both being too dazzled by the welcome which
they had received.

The welcome grew more remarkable yet. Hardly
had Kit taken Celia's hand in his to place it on his
sleeve, the tawny velvet of which matched the
curling locks which fell about his shoulders, than the
glass doors were opened and a party of courtiers
entered, led by a man whom Celia recognised at
once as the King.

She had seen him in the city streets—sometimes
walking with the Lord Mayor at his side, sometimes
on horseback and once in the Royal coach. She
could not be mistaken and, near to, she found that
his height and presence made him even more
remarkable. Only Kit Carlyon rivalled him as to
height; none rivalled his regality. Many bowed at his
entrance, and Celia curtsied. The King waved a
hand for them to rise.

'Nothing to that,' he declared imperiously. 'I
prefer my subjects on their feet, looking at me, not
on their knees, looking at the floor.' He examined
Celia closely, so that she blushed, and said, 'Kit, my
friend, thou hast a fair maid on thine arm. Pray
introduce her to us. I would not have a fair face pass
me by.'

Kit bowed, but not low, Celia saw, and replied,
'Sire, this is Mistress Antiquis, who is the daughter
and assistant of one Adam Antiquis, an astrologer
who hath come to Court today to bring George
Buckingham some horaries and elections which he
hath caused to be cast.'

'The astrologer's daughter and his assistant! That

is a rare thing. I must tell my Queen of this. Charles,' he commanded to a pleasant-faced young man who stood by him, 'run, tell my wife I have a rare thing for her to know of and I would have her by me when she is made aware of it.'

Sir Charles Sedley bowed in his turn and made for the glass doors to carry out his master's bidding. The King's attention was now on Adam and the Duke whom he commanded to present Celia's father to him. At last, after some fair words to the even more bedazzled Adam, he said, 'And you made thy daughter thy assistant, Master Antiquis. Pray why, if a mere monarch may enquire?'

'Why, Your Majesty, as to that——' Adam almost babbled, his usual stern composure almost melted by the rays of the imperial sun before him '—I had no son and an apprentice whom I took proving unwilling and slow, and she showing a turn for the mathematics and philosophy most unusual in a woman—and one so young as she then was—I thought to train her, almost in jest at first. Now the young pupil hath come close to equalling the master, as you may see by examining the work which she hath done for the Duke's grace.'

Bedazzled he might well be at such attention, thought Celia, watching him, for the King had kept light hold of Kit's arm as he spoke and her promised walk had been halted.

'A prodigy, then,' drawled the King, his dark eyes full on Celia, 'and a prodigy to be rewarded. No, no,' he said, waving away the parchments which Adam proffered him as proof of Celia's excellence. 'I take thy word, man. What, would thou deceive thy King? I think not; thy stars would tell thee otherwise!'

Everyone around them laughed at the King's small joke. Celia was fast recovering her wits and was already observing that the courtiers hung on their master's every word, rewarding him as frequently as they could for every imagined witticism or piece of wisdom offered. Only Sir Kit, at her side, refrained from doing so, even as he spoke to the Duke on terms of equality when she had already noticed that many splendid figures had been servile to him. Sir Kit was his own man, she concluded, and that pleased her. Why it did, she knew not.

Further talk was ended by the Queen's entrance, surrounded by her maids of honour, each one of whom outshone her in comeliness. The queen was not plain, but neither was she beautiful, and she appeared drab by comparison with them all—particularly the beauty who had been caressing Kit.

'My heart,' exclaimed the King, advancing on her to take her by the hand to lead her to where Celia and Adam were standing. 'Here is one Master Antiquis, an astrologer, and if you should ask why I command you to take particular note of him, it is because of his wondrous fair daughter, who stands by Kit, here. She is his assistant, he saith, and is as learned as he. Now, you were lamenting yester eve that you had none to advise you when you needed advice, and, seeing this fair maiden so learned and so young, it seemed to me that it might be fitting for you to have an adviser, here at Court. And what better than a female astrologer to cast thy horaries and elections?'

The Queen smiled kindly at Celia. 'My lord,' she

said in her lightly accented voice—her native country was Portugal, 'a kind thought. I welcome it. But what of her father? Does Master Antiquis wish to lose his assistant?'

To be the Queen's astrologer! To be at Court! So much was happening to her, so fast. The trembling hand on Kit's sleeve was the only outward evidence of Celia's inward agitation. Did she really want this thing? To be part of a court notorious for its lack of morals? How would she, a humble citizen's daughter, fare in such a place? Could she even learn to conduct herself properly? And what was proper here?

Yet a further thought struck her as the Queen spoke kindly to her father, and it made her hand tremble even more. If she came to Court, why then, why then, she would meet *him*, the man standing beside her, who, when he felt her hand quiver, had put his own large and strong one over it briefly, to reassure her. What a fine thing it would be to meet him every day to hear him singing in that voice which might draw the heart from one's breast, as it had drawn hers when he had visited them!

The hand which had briefly comforted hers—and how had he known that she might need comfort?—had had the same effect on her as it had had earlier. This time she could not stop the trance from consuming her. King and Court disappeared. She was in the dark, on her knees, staring at her hand in the dim light of a lantern. There was blood on it.

The vision was gone but Kit had felt her stiffen, had bent his head to look at her, and for a moment saw again the blind eyes she had turned on him in her own parlour. If it were a trick it was an odd one, for she drew no one's attention to it.

'Mistress Celia,' he said quietly, so that none but she might hear his words. 'Be not affrighted. The King means you no harm. Indeed, he seeks to do thee honour.'

'My father may not wish. . .' Celia began falteringly.

Kit's smile was humourless. 'Why, as to that, he will not decline such an honour for you, I am sure. He does but seek to discover on what terms the honour is made.'

'He should ask me first whether I wish to accept such an honour.'

Kit's lips twitched. Such an independent maiden for all her gentle quietude. Most would have curtsied and said modestly, As my father wills. But not the astrologer's daughter.

'You do not want the honour, mistress?'

'I am a little afeared of it, Sir Christopher.'

'Nay fear not. None will hurt thee. I will see to that.' And his hand covered hers again.

The King and Queen had finished their speech with Adam. 'Bring the lady to us,' Charles ordered and, when Kit had complied, the King said to Celia, 'Good Mistress Celia, thy father hath agreed that when the court is in London you should take lodgings here in Whitehall with us, to advise the Queen on matters astrological. When the court moves to the country thou shalt return to thy father's house, for he would not lose thee altogether, nor would I reft you from him. The Queen must manage as best she can, but country matters will not be so pressing as to demand thy services. Is not that so, madam?'

The Queen agreed with him, said in her gentle voice, 'Now, as to thy recompense, mistress, and thy lodgings, that shall be determined before you come to us, and thy father hath agreed a week's term for you to prepare yourself before you take up thy new position. This pleases you?'

She could not say nay to any of them, even if they had all determined matters without her. That did *not* please her, but she could not say so. She knew quite clearly, without the stars' help, that she would be happy to come to Court even if only to see Sir Kit again, to have his beautiful green eyes on her, perhaps to have his sensitive musician's hand cover hers again.

Celia made a great curtsy to them both and gave her assent. She had loosed her hand from Kit's arm so that he stood back.

The King would have none of that. 'Why, all's settled, then, and Kit, do not retire. I would have thee sing for us. Mistress Celia shall hear you, and learn that to work in the court of the King has its rewards as well as its pains.'

And so it was done. She was to go to Court, and her even life set in its pleasant quiet ways, would be no more. Time and chance had worked its will on her and Adam's horoscope, which had told of momentous things coming from this visit, had been a true one.

Listening to Kit sing, watching the King's face, sad amid the trappings of his office, she only knew one thing—that Celia Antiquis might be lodged in a strange place, but she would be plain Celia Antiquis still. None would cozen her, nor cheat her; she would hold true to the stars which governed her, even if the skies fell about her, as the old Latin saying had it.

Buckingham watched her as she listened to Kit sing his new song, for the King had demanded it again. Celia had not heard it and the words made her sad. A film of tears misted her eyes for the man who could both write and sing it. What unhappy experiences had brought him to this pass? Buckingham saw the tears and wondered. He leaned forward from his high chair to touch Celia's shoulder, for Kit had handed her to her stool again.

'The song saddens thee, Mistress Antiquis?'

'Oh, yes, the words so haunting and his voice so beautiful—his playing, too.'

'You are fond of music, mistress. Can it be that you play some instrument?'

Celia was forgetting her awe of him. He spoke so kindly, was so different from the man who had seemed to mock her father and herself when he had visited them. She did not yet know of the Duke's reputation for capriciousness, but in the coming weeks she would become aware of it. For now, he was pleasant and she was happy.

'I play the viol, but I am only an amateur, Your Grace.'

'George,' he said hastily, 'my name is George. I cannot believe that anything which you do will not be done well. You carry that look about you, mistress. Bring thy viol to Court when you come hither this sennight, and Kit and I shall play and sing with thee. You sing, mistress?'

'Again, a little. Then, daringly, because he had ordered her to call him George, which must mean friend, 'And you, sir——' for 'sir' seemed a fair compromise '—do you also play?'

'George, I said, mistress, and yes, I play the fiddle, and, like thyself——' he mocked at her with his voice again '—I sing a little. Kit shall write us a new song, or find us an old one—he hath a talent for discovering them—and we shall sing in concert and the great and simple shall be astonished by our talent, and Tom Killigrew will hire us to play in his theatre.' He pointed to a tall, fair man, of middle years, who sat listening to Kit, face rapt.

Kit finished his last song and refused, smiling, to sing any more. 'You will have a disgust of me if I sing too much. Let me leave and you will be happier to hear me again.'

Buckingham called him over as he finished speaking. 'I have discovered that thy astrological mistress hath a talent for music, Kit, and I have persuaded her to share it with us.' Which made Celia indignant for, sure, she had said no such thing and besides, she was not Sir Christopher's mistress. The Duke presumed too much, but then she supposed that he always did and, being great, none could say him nay.

She said so to Kit when he meekly obeyed Buckingham and walked her into the garden—and why should he do that? He was his own man, was he not? she thought, but that meant that he truly wished to walk with her, which made her happy.

Her father was happy, too, watching his daughter patronised by the great ones of the world and walking with one of the King's favourites—for it was plain by the King's manner that Kit was, and Buckingham favoured him as well. There were no clouds in his sky today, which was perhaps fortunate, since they might come later.

Kit led Celia down a gravel walk to a sundial which stood in the middle of the lawn like the one which she had seen in the Privy Garden. She read what was written about the rim: 'I tell only the sunny hours'.

'There are many sunny hours in this year,' she observed slowly, 'at least in such gardens as these. It is not perhaps so pleasant in St Giles in the Fields where the plague walks.'

'An ill thing to think on a fair day,' was Kit's only answer looking at her troubled, downcast face. 'I would have expected that such success as thou hast achieved today would have cast out gloomy thoughts.'

'I am a little like the old Romans,' replied Celia, her voice low, 'who, at the moment of their greatest triumphs, liked to be reminded of their mortality. Too much pride at today's work might gain me a reward I would not care for.'

Kit shivered at her answer and thought painfully of the true reason why the King had favoured her—that he was placing her in a position where Kit might—or might not—win his bet. In truth, her seemingly easy success owed little to her own merit, or to her father's, and he thought that she was clever enough to guess that—although the old man would not. He had too great an appreciation of his own worth and thought it was that for which he had been honoured, and not his daughter's chastity, which was to be held up for auction as it were.

Something told Kit that, while Celia might not guess at the truth, she knew that something lay behind the Antiquises' effortless success. For one mad moment he thought to tell her of the bet, and then hand George the ring as the price of his calling it off. He opened his mouth to speak, but was forestalled. Unknown to them both, as they stood admiring the sundial, the beauty who had spoken to Kit as Celia and her father arrived was on them. Behind her was a small train of pretty young women who seemed to be her acolytes.

'So, Kit, there you are, with today's new toy, no less.' Her beautiful, insolent eyes were hard on Celia, disparaging her plain dress, her neatly coiffed hair, her whole modest carriage. 'So, Mistress Celia, the astrologer's daughter, you have carried all before you this afternoon? The King and the Queen's grace, no less. And shall Kit write you a song to celebrate your success? What kind of song will he write, I wonder?' She said this after so meaningful a fashion that Celia, innocent though she was, was suddenly aware that the lady's words carried a double meaning.

'And doubtless, mistress, since you are new to Court, you will be asking yourself who addresses you so freely? Sir Christopher Carlyon, my erstwhile courtier—for I see that you have acquired a new mistress—pray introduce Mistress Celia to me and enlighten her as to who makes so free with her. And you.' Standing on tiptoes, she stretched herself languorously and placed her mouth on Kit's, to the accompaniment of screeches from the ladies who attended her.

Kit endured the kiss and made no attempt to respond to it, only saying coldly when, pouting, she took her mouth from his, 'My Lady Castlemaine, this is, as you already know, Mistress Celia Antiquis, now the Queen's own astrologer. I present her to you in the hope that if she needs protection you will protect her.' His eyes dared the lady to say otherwise.

Celia curtsied, her eyes enormous. This beauty, to whom Kit spoke so cavalierly, was Barbara Palmer, wife of Lord Castlemaine. She had been the beautiful Barbara Villiers and the King's first mistress when he came to England, and still held him, and many others, in her toils—for her amours outside her marriage to Castlemaine and her affair with the King were notorious. Had she been Kit's mistress, too, as Celia now realised that she had been hinting?

Well, what was that to her? Sir Kit was beyond her reach and she would never be his doxy—no, never. Neither his nor any other man's. Even here in Charles's dissolute court she would preserve herself, whatever the cost. She would be no man's light of love and, when she straightened up after her curtsy, that message was written plain on her face for both man and woman before her to see.

'Oho,' sighed Barbara Palmer plaintively. 'What have we here? The lady is consecrated to the moon, I think.' And she paused for Celia to say, astonished at her own daring,

'My sign *is* the moon, lady, which is clever of you to guess, and so I serve the moon. Diana is my mistress, and my mentor. She caused her hounds to gore Actaeon when he dared to dishonour her and I pray God that I, too, will so be able to treat any who might dare to dishonour her.'

For a moment she thought that she had gone too

far. Barbara Palmer looked thunder, but then her face cleared, and she began to laugh.

'By the sun, who is my master, I honour thee, Mistress Celia, and I hope that all the gallants of the court will avoid bringing thee into a dispute with them, for sure I could not tell who might win. Begin with friend Kit, here, for he will be the fiercest to rebuff, and if you can hold him off then you may dismiss anyone.'

'You honour me overmuch,' said Kit shortly. He was not happy that Barbara Palmer should so name him whoremaster.

Celia looked from him to the lady, not certain whether her description of Kit was correct. She had not thought him to be a pursuer of women; he had seemed so different from the Duke and others.

Her brow cleared. The lady was jealous. Not only because of Kit; common sense told her that Barbara would not look too kindly on any whom the King might favour. She would remember what the lady had said, but would not judge any man because of it.

After that, Barbara Palmer spoke of this and that to Kit and to Celia. Celia could not remember afterwards what she had said, only that it was light and jeering, that she was half warning Celia and half derisive in the warning. At length she dismissed them both, almost regally, to Celia's amusement. The King's whore thought that she was half a Queen, was her unkind and shrewd judgement on the lady, which would have surprised lady and Kit both by its worldly wisdom.

'So,' said Kit, taking her arm and leading her down to where the ducks swam and the Thames ran in the afternoon sunlight. 'What do you think of the lady? She seemed somewhat affrighted at you. Not unnatural, perhaps, for her hold on the King's majesty is not quite as sure as it was—although being something of a shrew she may often cow him, rather than woo him.'

'Cow the King?' questioned Celia, a little surprised.

'Aye. My master is an easygoing man, both kind and careless, easier to give way to Barbara than to fight her. After all, his day is not given wholly over to pleasure.'

'You have known the lady long?' asked Celia.

'Since I returned in 1660 with my master, the King.'

'And the King, have you known him long?' Celia knew that one should not question the great like this, but she wanted to know more about the man walking at her side.

'Much longer than I have known the Castlemaine. I fought beside him at Worcester field when I was still a boy and fled that field with him, parting from him only when it seemed that to stay with him would damage him more than me. Later I served him for a short space abroad, in exile.' He paused and added briefly, 'I did not like the life and made myself another.' He said no more, and Celia wondered what that life had been, but dared not ask him more.

She wanted this walk with him to continue, for it was pleasant to be with him. He made no demands upon her, whatever the lady had suggested, and when he said to her, 'Why should we not sit, Mistress Celia? Here is a low wall, with a hedge behind to cushion us, and we may watch the ducks paddle in the sun and wish we were there on the water with them,' she made no demur. She did not attempt to flirt with him, but allowed him to seat her where she might look both up and downriver, and watch the constant traffic of every different kind of craft pass them by.

The ducks came up to greet them. Kit made clucking noises and said, 'I wish I had brought my guitar with me. I might have played and sung to them and seen whether I might rival Orpheus and have the water-birds bow before me. Where stand such creatures in thy mysteries, lady?'

So, she had graduated to lady now! Yes, she was a lady of the court, she supposed. The astrologer's daughter was rising, like the sun—more, like the moon, except that her mysteries were performed in the day, not the night. The conceit pleased her, and Kit, seeing the small smile on her face, and already sensitive to her moods, leaned towards her and said softly, 'What amuses you, lady, that you smile so sweetly? Was it the thought of the birds honouring me, or something else? Grant me thy favour, and tell me.'

'Nothing of matter.' Celia's smile grew more mysterious, a thing of which she was unaware. 'Only that but two days agone, I had no thought that I would be sitting here, in the Palace of Whitehall, honoured by the King and insulted by Lady Castlemaine. I suppose that the last might be considered an honour, too,' she ended, a little slyly, offering Kit her most innocent smile.

'Oho, the astrologer's daughter has claws. I shall reward you for that.' And Kit leaned forward and kissed her gently on the cheek.

Celia was not prepared either for the kiss or for the sensation which shot through her when it was given. Nor was she prepared when Kit, having straightened up, murmured, 'I liked that, mistress; allow me to do it again,' and this time it was the other cheek which he saluted.

The kiss was lingering, and when it was finished he did not withdraw his mouth, but trailed it gently down towards her lips. For a moment Celia allowed him free rein, then smartly withdrew her face, raising her hand to touch her cheek where the kiss still lingered, sending unexpected tremors through her whole body. 'You should not have done that, sir. I gave you no licence to do that.'

'I know.' Kit was leaning back now against the thick hedge behind the wall, his eyes on her. 'I could not help myself, nor dared I ask permission. You might have refused it, as you might refuse this.' And he picked up the hand with which she had stroked her cheek, and which now lay lax beside her, and kissed it—first the palm, which he turned towards him, and then the pulsing wrist above the palm.

A *frisson* of delight shot through her at this second wicked invasion. Celia looked wonderingly at Kit. He had bent his head to kiss her hand and now he looked up at her, eyes mischievous, so near to her that she could see the hazel flecks in their green— and there, in the black pupil—was that a miniature Celia?

What was she doing? Dallying here, quite alone, with a man whom Barbara Palmer had hinted was a conqueror of female hearts, as doubtless they all were at King Charles's court.

'And you shouldn't have done that,' she said severely, and oh, how weak that sounded.

'I know,' he said again. 'But confess you enjoyed it.'

'If I did, and I'm not saying that I did, then I should not have done.'

Kit threw his head back and laughed at this equivocating answer. 'So, you did enjoy it and, dedicated to the truth as you are, you do not deny it. I know, as I know that the sun rises and sets, that you could not deny me, but offered me a sophistry instead.'

'I offer you nothing, sir, and will accept no further kisses from you, either,' said Celia smartly, rising and shaking her skirts. 'And I suppose the whole court is wondering how far you have got with me, and Lady Castlemaine is probably taking bets on the matter by the fashion in which she spoke to me.'

This was so near to the unpleasant truth of his own situation regarding Buckingham and their bet that Kit shivered. The game of dalliance and opportunity which he had begun so light heartedly beside the river seemed tawdry. Even the ducks rejected him and it for, excited by the raised voices of the humans above them, they were swimming away.

'So, Sir Christopher Carlyon,' said Celia, 'you had best return me to my father and confine your attentions to those who would welcome them.'

Kit sighed, made a small face, and took her arm again, which nearly overset Celia, his touch having so strong an effect on her. He must never know that, she thought, no, never, and when he said into her ear, 'Confess again, it was not so unwelcome as you proclaimed it, mistress. I felt you tremble beneath my touch,' she shook her head at him. She did not deceive him, for Kit was a man who could read his fellows by observing their smallest movements, and he had read Celia's response correctly, however much she might deny it.

He must be rebuked, and quickly, for that.

'Oh, sir, you mistook repulsion for attraction.'

'Not so, mistress, but, even if it were true, then attraction and repulsion are allies, as your studies should have taught you. Where one is found then the other is not far behind.'

'You would chop logic with the devil himself,' exclaimed Celia a little angrily, to have him answer, eyes dancing,

'Why, you are no mean mistress of that art yourself, lady.'

Kit was a little astonished at his own response to the cool girl beside him. He had begun to make gentle love to her almost out of habit, but where normally such an approach paid useful dividends almost immediately, with Celia, nothing of the sort. She had repelled him, even though he was certain that she had not found his idle kisses distasteful.

He was not used to being denied, especially by someone to whom he was becoming strongly attracted, and now, beside the bet, he had another unworthy aim. And that was to have her begging him for his caresses, pleading with him to consummate what had begun between them. He had never before wanted with such passion to bring a woman to lie in his arms and be pleasured. He wanted, nay, needed, to see those clear shining eyes turning to him in love and trust, not in despite.

The very thought was, to his horror, sufficient to

rouse him. She was walking beside him, calm, controlled—and he, what could he do but walk beside her in a stew of desire?

He stole a look at her perfect profile, beautiful in its severity. She was as little like Barbara Palmer's voluptuous easiness as a woman could be. Worth the winning? Oh, very much so, far beneath him though she was in rank, and now the thought of his bet with George seemed grosser than ever. But he was trapped in it and, after a strange fashion, so was she.

Kit had been to another astrologer, naming himself plain John Clarke, and had given the man his birthdate and asked a question of him, saying, 'I desire a woman most desperately and she hath no knowledge of my desire, and were she to know would reject me. Make up an horary and tell me whether I shall succeed with her.'

The man had not demurred, had sat down, and Kit had agreed to pay for an afternoon's work. At the end of it the astrologer had looked at Kit, puzzled. He said, 'This is passing strange. I have not seen the like before. I would see the lady's horoscope, too.'

'That is not possible,' Kit had said shortly. 'Tell me what you see. I may be able to understand the sense of it.'

The astrologer had shrugged before answering him. 'You will achieve your wish, good sir, but only after a fashion that will not be understandable to you. From denial and affirmation will come fulfilment. You and she are surrounded first by blood and then by fire.'

Kit had stared at him. 'I came here to have an

answer to a mystery, not to be shown a new one. Cannot you answer me plainly with a yea or a nay?'

The man was not offended. Clients had shouted at him before, and he had always outfaced them.

'Your success is assured, but it will not be what you expected. Whether it will please you or no, I cannot tell. Sometimes the stars are vague and, when they are, it means that it may not be a good thing for the subject—which is your good self—to know the future.'

'And shall I, then, be happy?' Kit was more impatient than ever.

'Why, as to that your stars say you are not an easy man to satisfy and what shall signify happiness to you may not to another. I will only say that what you wish now is not what you will wish by the time that this race of yours is run.'

These weaselling words affected Kit so strongly that he wanted to take the man by the throat.

'You are all the same, all of you,' he announced coldly. 'You do not know what the future holds but you use words in a double sense so that poor fools like myself think that you do. Well, you are not deceiving me, and I will pay you, but grudgingly.'

The man looked at him equally coldly and the room itself grew chilly, as though with an unseasonal frost. Kit had dressed plainly, wearing some of his servant's clothes so that he looked like one who had little money to spare, and was one of the downtrodden of this world. He had tempered his language accordingly and he had grudgingly flung a few coins in payment at the man sitting opposite to him. When the astrologer had touched them his face had paled.

'Why, Your Excellency,' he said, and bowed low.

'I had not thought to entertain such as you. Think of me tonight when you sing to the King's majesty.'

Kit's laugh had been contemptuous. 'Oh, another trick. You have recognised me, then?'

'Not I,' said the man briefly. 'I have no notion of who you are. Only, as I touched your money, I saw you and the King seated together, and you had a guitar in your hand and were singing. You were not dressed as you are now, but finely. That is all. I know nothing more—except that I doubt that your name is John Clarke.'

Kit had flung out, disappointed. The man had deceived him, had he not? But yet, but yet, there had been the ring of truth about him, and that night, when he was singing to the King, he remembered him.

And now he was walking with another charlatan, a female one and, if the man had read aright, she was bound to him. After a strange fashion, as the man had said. She did not know that yet and, for one brief moment, he wanted to say, Go, leave the court, come here no more. Forget me, forget the King, forget Buckingham. Go home to your father and be once again an innocent, for what this court will do to you, I dare not think.

But he said nothing, for the stars might not be denied and they had said that he and Celia were bound together.

CHAPTER FOUR

'AND so, dear Antiquis, if you will but hold still for
a moment we shall have you fit to appear before the
Queen this evening. For sure, you cannot come
among us in your sober greys and blues, fit though
they may be for the work for which you are
employed. There——' and she turned Celia about
'—you may now behold yourself.'

Celia was in Miss Hamilton's room being prepared
to attend the Queen at a ball where all the stars and
luminaries of Charles's court were to be present. Kit
Carlyon was sure to be there and also the Chevalier
de Grammont, at whom Miss Hamilton, the Queen's
maid of honour, was given to casting sheep's eyes—
when he was not looking at her, that was.

'For the first rule of all,' she had told Celia gravely
when she had taken her under her wing, 'is never to
let any of the monsters know your true feelings. You
are to be as proud and haughty as they are.'

She had been pinning up the gown she was lending
to Celia as she spoke. She sat back on her heels to
laugh up into Celia's austerely beautiful face. 'Not
that that will be difficult for you, Antiquis. On you
it comes naturally, as Charles Sedley hath already
discovered.'

Celia made a little face as she inspected herself in
the long mirror in the corner of the attic room which
Miss Hamilton shared with Miss Dorothy Lowther.
Was that creature in the mirror the retiring Mistress

Celia Antiquis? Miss Hamilton had made her over into the likeness of every maid of honour who graced the Queen's entourage.

Her gown was of deep blue satin, cut low at the bosom to expose the beginning of a fine pair of breasts which she had hardly realised she possessed. The sleeves were slashed to reveal an underdress of the sheerest white silk, which depended below them and ended in a froth of lace pinned back by a small brooch at each elbow. Miss Hamilton had lent her the brooches, together with another at her bosom which, she saw, drew attention to the cleft between her breasts, rather than distracted the eye from it.

Around her waist was a sash of white silk tied in a great bow at the back; the dress's full skirts trailed a little along the ground, but Hamilton, as she had asked to be called, had shown her how to loop them up, which gave a tantalising view of a fine pair of ankles.

The small circlet of pearls around Celia's neck, as well as the two drops in her ears, were her own. Hamilton had dressed her hair elaborately, freeing it from the simple knot which Celia had always affected, combing forward a fringe of curls and then drawing the rest behind in a blue bow to match the dress so that her golden locks flowed unhindered down her back.

'Can this be I?' said Celia to her reflection, to have Hamilton sigh behind her.

'Oh, they will fight over you tonight, Antiquis, Kit Carlyon and the rest—see if they don't. It was time you emerged from your demure shell. If the court sighed after you when you looked like a pretty

Puritan, think how they will behave when they see you garbed like Venus herself.'

'Diana,' said Celia abstractedly, 'I am Diana, and now I must return to my rooms to fetch my viol, for the Queen hath commanded me to be ready to play it this evening.' Unlike the maids of honour, who were compelled to share a room, she had been fortunate enough to be given a small study and a bedroom opening off it in the attics not far from where Hamilton was lodged.

'Oh, pooh to that,' said Hamilton, laughing a little. 'You must get that hulking footman of yours to carry it for you, and be ready to hand it to you when the time comes for you to play. You are a great lady now, remember, and great ladies do not act as menials, no, indeed.'

And how long shall I be a great lady, and will *he* like me now I seem but another maid of honour? For always, since she came to court, Kit Carlyon was in her mind. When other men openly admired her, praised her modesty and beauty, he said nothing, but always stood near her. He would protect her, he had said, and he had done so the other evening when Charles Sedley, drunk already though the night was yet young, had approached her as she stood behind the Queen.

'Oh, chaste Diana,' he had said, and the wine on his breath had been hot in her face as he spoke. 'Will you not forget the moon you serve and assume the sun instead? For sure, mistress, you were not made to sit apart when Cupid fired his arrows, for he has already made me your slave and I would fain claim you for my own.'

Before she could stop him he had put an arm

around her shoulders and pulled her behind the curtains which were draped about the dais where the Queen sat, so that they were hidden from the room. Celia could not escape him, nor his plundering hands. He had pulled down her bodice and was rifling her bosom.

She gasped, tried to push him off, but he was insistent, thrusting his face into hers and trying to force a kiss from her. She could scarce breathe and stamped on his foot but, although he cursed at her, she could not stop him until, suddenly, he was pulled away from her and she heard Kit Carlyon's beautiful voice, harsh, now, and commanding.

'Come, Charles, be off with you. Mistress Celia plainly does not welcome your attentions.'

Kit must have guessed Sedley's trick, to try to pin her down where she could not resist him without creating open scandal, and had come to rescue her. Her face flamed red, for her dress was now about her waist, and what would Kit think of that?

He took no note of her, but kept his eyes averted and held her attacker at arm's length. Sedley tried to fight free of him, but could not. He was both shorter and less muscular than Kit, and his drunkenness made it difficult for him to do other than struggle. He decided to use his agile tongue as a weapon instead. 'What, Kit, friend, dost want her for thyself?'

'It is not what I want, Charles. It is what Mistress Celia wants. I think that she doth not want any of us—unless the stars have told her that one of us is the man for her—which I doubt. Is not that true, mistress?'

Celia, whose fright at Sedley's cavalier handling

of her had disappeared with Kit's dramatic entrance, replied as coolly as she could. 'Why, as to that gentlemen, I am the Queen's astrologer and am not in the market to please the King's gentlemen save in the matter of conversation and the making of music. You, sir, proposed neither.'

'Another witty woman to plague a man with her conceits,' muttered Sedley morosely. 'What in the world hath come over you all that a man may not take his pleasure without a sermon to cool his appetite? Let go, Kit, I have done. I'll leave the lady to you. You deserve one another.' And he was gone through the curtains.

Kit took Celia gently by the wrist. She had pulled her gown into place again and the flush had faded from her face. He led her through the curtains, down the room, away from prying eyes into a window embrasure where they could be seen but not heard.

'He meant nothing by it,' Kit said kindly. 'He did not think that, when he treated you thus, you were other than most of the ladies here. He forgot that you were but a novice at Court.'

'Oh,' said Celia coldly. 'And were I not a novice he might do with me as he pleased?' She had recovered her composure with commendable swiftness, Kit thought, admiring her as she stood before him, as cool as though the brief altercation with Sedley had never happened.

'No,' he answered her. 'But you have no knowledge yet of how to hold such a one as Charles Sedley at bay. Let him but once understand that you are not in the market to play the games he wishes to

play with you and he will do one of two things. . .'
He paused.

'Which are?' asked Celia acidly. 'I thought that I
had come to Court to practise my mysteries, not to
evade the lechery of drunken courtiers.'

'Both, alas,' said Kit with a little sigh, thinking of
his own dark designs on her, and how this evening's
matter had advanced him further in her esteem so
that, whoever she feared, it was not Kit Carlyon.
'Charles will either pursue you relentlessly, to bend
thee to his will, or he will ignore you—for he might
guess that your will is greater than his, and he would
not be humbled.'

'So I should hope——' Celia was acid again
'—that he would give up pursuit of me. But, sir, I
have not thanked you for my rescue. I doubt that
Sir Charles Sedley intended to ravish me in the
curtains behind the Queen's majesty. . .' She saw
Kit's face change as she spoke, and gasped. 'Ah, no!
You mean that he might have done? Oh, shame.'

Kit thought of what he had done himself. Thought
of Dorothy Lowther, who now hated him, and
whom Buckingham had threatened with condign
punishment if, in revenge for the fashion in which
Kit had treated her, she told Celia Antiquis of the
bet of which the whole court knew. Since Celia had
come to live among them, and they had seen her
cool composure, they were all watching Kit's campaign against her with the keenest interest.

Unknown to her, Harry Killigrew, Tom
Killigrew's wild son, had nicknamed her the Fair
Virgin. There were few at Charles's court who had
not been given some such nickname or other.

'Alas,' he said, a trifle stiffly, 'you must be Argus

of the hundred eyes where the courtiers are concerned.'

'And you, Sir Kit? Am I to fear you? Or should you, like some of the others, be more truly named an Argus of the hundred hands?'

Kit closed his eyes. Again, he almost told her the truth, but could not for very shame. He could not bear to see her shrink away from him in hate and disgust. He had thought of trying to lose the bet by refusing to pursue her, by refusing to be alone with her, even—but he knew that he was unable to do other than be with her.

For Celia was drawing him as no woman had ever done since his lost youth, and he could not bear to be away from her. Ironically, the one man whose declared mission it was to despoil her was the one man who could make sure that no other did. Kit's physical strength, his prowess with a rapier, were so well-known that few would dare to cross him if he appeared to protect Celia Antiquis.

'Trust no one,' he said at last. 'It is the law of life, both in the Court and out of it.'

It was as far as he dared to go to warn her. He saw her face clear, and hated himself all over again. He had taken her arm gently and murmured, 'Come, we must away. If we talk overlong together, alone, tongues will wag—and Charles Sedley's tongue is both long and vicious. Let us not give him an opportunity to exercise it on us.'

Remembering this, she wondered whether Sir Charles would try to force her again this evening. She thought not, for he was a little afeared of Kit, who was her protector. Despite Kit's disclaimer, his statement that none at Court were to be trusted, which must include him, Celia thought that she *could* trust him. She was also learning the ways of the Court and the devices which the women about it employed to hold off unwanted gallants. She was not a maid of honour but, inevitably, all of the maids, except Dorothy Lowther, who seemed to have a distaste for her, had become her friends because they were of an age together.

She was clever enough to understand that she was a new toy and that in time she would be accepted, and forgotten. But for the moment she was everyone's pet and must endure that, however little she wanted the honour.

Walking along—behind the Queen, but before the maids—into the great room where she had first seen King and Court, she made a resolution. She would not become proud and challenge the gods. She would try to remain humble, so that when she returned to real life and the Strand again she would not hanker after what she had lost.

In the meantime, she would enjoy this strange life, and Kit's company, and she looked for him, to see him in the circle around the King, Buckingham at his side. She saw that the candles were all aglow, that the great glass doors were open to the fading light, that the sky was pale pink and pearly grey, with streaks of mauve and lemon in it. She saw—for tonight her sight seemed to be wondrous clear—that the men were handsome, especially Kit Carlyon, and the ladies were fair, and Celia Antiquis, improbably, was one of the fairest of them all.

Kit, looking across at her, saw her in her newly found beauty, saw that her eyes were glowing and that her lips were parted. Oh, she was an innocent nymph among the blasé ladies of the court, and he feared for her, and for himself.

He heard the King say, 'Sir Kit, you have brought your guitar I hope, and Mistress Celia has brought her viol. Buckingham has his fiddle and tells me that you have already been practising with her, and that you have a new song to entertain us with. Before the dancing begins I would wish to hear it. Music on a fair night is something nigh to heaven.'

As the King commanded, so his courtiers must perform. Yesterday afternoon Kit, Celia and Buckingham had sat and made music together with such innocent joy that it was an impossible thought that he and George had bet upon despoiling her chastity. The King had not been present but Buckingham had spoken to him later of their harmony together, and here was yet one more occasion to bring Celia before the court to display her prowess in another field than that of astrology.

'As you wish, sire,' he said, and there was something in his voice which touched the King, who stared at him a little and said, 'Fie, Kit. Doth ill humour ride on thy shoulders? You are not usually loath to amuse us with your singing.'

'A passing malaise, sire. 'Tis nothing. I shall joy in the doing when the music starts, for sure.'

'Come, then.' And the King clapped his hands and retired to one of the great chairs of state set out for him, his Queen behind him, and his court—the most polite and refined court in Europe. So said the Chevalier de Grammont, who now sat himself at Miss Hamilton's elbow, while the servants brought forth the musical instruments, the stools and the stands, so that Charles might enjoy one of his favourite diversions—listening to music performed by his friends.

Had the Celia Antiquis who had lived so quietly before George Buckingham and his friend had invaded her home ever thought that one day she would be called on to entertain a monarch? Celia, trembling slightly, refused the stool—she felt happier playing when standing—and joined Kit and Buckingham on the small dais where music was often performed. She bowed when Kit and the Duke did and heard Kit say, 'We shall begin with one of Shakespeare's songs, sire, but you must give us grace—we but played it for the first time yesterday.'

It was 'O Mistress Mine', the first song she had ever heard him sing, and they had mastered it yester afternoon, so that Celia forgot her fear of failure in the performance. Then they played his own song, which she was not sure that she liked, clever though it was, for it said that love was fleeting, never long, and she could not believe that it was true for everyone. Was it true for Sir Kit? Did he mean what he sang? Did he think that love *was* never long.

And when it was ended, and the applause was long and loud, Buckingham called from where he stood, for he had followed Celia's example, only Kit sitting so that he might play the guitar more easily, 'Now, friends, let us play for thee an old song which Kit hath found. It is not a love song, faith, but is passing sad, and the music so fair that it draws tears from one's eyes. Let us be melancholy together, for it is called 'A Farewell to Arms' and was dedicated to the late Queen Elizabeth of blessed memory, in honour of one of her old soldiers and deals with the passing of time. It is a fit song for Kit to play, for he, too, is an old soldier who has served his sovereign.'

It had grown quite dark while they had played and Kit had sung. The candle flames flared and guttered in the slight breeze which came in through the windows to cool the unseasonable warmth of the late May night. They began to play and, as Kit's voice soared into the air after the opening instrumental passage had ended, silence fell among the spectators, for the melody, as Buckingham had said, was a moving one, and Kit's voice matched it.

Celia could see his face as he began to sing. She did not need the sheet of music propped before her, for she had rapidly learned the song, falling prey to its beauty as Buckingham, and now the court, had done. It had been written for the lute and a high voice, but between them Kit and Buckingham had transposed it for the three instruments and Kit's baritone.

'His golden locks Time hath to silver turn'd,' sang Kit, whose own chestnut locks had strands of silver in them. The song dealt with the passing of youth, but added that duty lived when all else had gone.

And when he began the second verse, 'His helmet now shall make a hive for bees. . .' his eyes looked into Celia's, green met grey and, at their meeting, each of them was aware that they loved the other. Only the necessity to continue playing without disgracing herself prevented Celia from falling into one of her prophetic trances. She held it at bay by concentrating on the music.

Kit, who was unaware of what was happening to Celia, felt the words of the song and the plaintive music begin to work on him, and he knew that before him, playing for him alone, oblivious of Buckingham and the court, was his own true love at last—whom he was sworn to despoil.

Strange that a song which was not a love song could so affect him! He could not bear to keep his eyes on Celia and, when he turned his head to look away from her, another lost, loved face rose before him, a face belonging to the days when he had been a soldier, before he had abandoned his own helmet.

He was, at last, saying goodbye to that face as he sang. The poignancy of the words and the music, and of his singing, were such that when his voice faded into silence and his head dropped, for tears were in his eyes, silence fell on the room for a space, before scattered applause slowly broke out.

'Faith,' exclaimed Charles, who had been as rapt as the rest of his court. 'They knew how to write songs in the old Queen's day. That must be thy end, my friends. It were a shame to try to cap such a performance. Mistress Celia, I would speak with thee, for thy virtuosity was the most to be remarked. Kit and Buckingham have often played together, but you have practised with them but rarely and are to be the more commended.'

Celia walked from the dais, conscious of the many eyes on her, to bow her head before the King, who was taking a ring from his little finger and handing it to her.

'A reward for thee, mistress.'

It was a simple ring of thin gold, with a tiny diamond set in it. He took Celia's right hand and slipped the ring on to its third finger.

'You honour me too greatly, sire,' stammered Celia.

'Nay, mistress, that were not possible. Now, enjoy the evening, for thou hast earned it. Kit will partner thee in the dance. I do command it.'

Kit, who had also stepped down from the dais, having handed his guitar to his footman, Buckingham following him, was visibly taken aback. He had inwardly vowed that whatever happened he would not now pursue her further. More, he would avoid her. He met the King's eyes fairly and squarely, saw the sardonic amusement in them and, bowing low, said, 'As Your Majesty commands,' in his coldest voice. Taking Celia by the hand he led her away, the lubricious eyes of the whole court following them.

Celia, quite dazed by all that was happening to her, and still affected by the music and the stunning discovery that she loved Kit Carlyon to distraction, pulled away from him a little and said in a low voice, 'I do not know how to dance, Sir Kit. I would not wish to spoil thy evening for thee.'

She felt a strange reluctance to be with him. She wanted to hug her secret to her, to come to terms with it. For how could humble Celia Antiquis, only present at Court by the oddest of chances, hope to win the heart of one of the King's favourites? The three weeks she had already spent at Whitehall had plainly shown her that that was what he was.

From the chatter of the maids of honour she had discovered that he was poor, that all that he possessed were a few barren acres in the north and the one thousand pounds a year which was the salary of one of Charles's Gentlemen of the Bedchamber— and which was rarely paid, the king being so poverty-stricken. Even so, he was far above her and she must not dream useless dreams. And he had told her so meaningfully to trust no one.

No matter. She had vowed never to marry and she might as well love Kit Carlyon, knowing she could never have him, as another. She looked shyly up at him, wondering whether her face and body betrayed her feelings to him, to see him looking as grim as he must have looked when once he had been a soldier; all his usual careless charm had vanished. And, thinking that, the room vanished again, and she was in the dark, bending over someone. As once before there was blood upon her hand, and then everything slid away and she was in a bed, by candlelight. She was looking at a ring on her finger, and it was not the ring which the King had given her, but Kit Carlyon's beautiful ruby, and then such desolation swept across her as she had never known. . .

She was back in Whitehall again and Kit was supporting her, saying, 'Room for Mistress Antiquis, she is faint, needs air,' and he was guiding her to the open doors, through a line of staring courtiers, and sitting her on one of the stone benches outside the doors, where the court gallants sported on fine afternoons.

'Now, Mistress Antiquis,' he said kneeling beside her. 'Tell me what happens to thee when your eyes inform me that you are no longer with us.'

'Nothing. I felt faint, that was all,' Celia lied, for she did not want to confess that not only did she occasionally have trances in which she saw strange and puzzling visions of the future, but also that lately these trances had increased and he always figured in them.

'Now, why do I not believe thee, lady?' Kit's voice was soft, but dry, and now he straightened up. 'But since you say so, then Amen to it.'

He did not believe her, that was plain, but no matter. Celia shivered. His eyes were on her, but they were not cold, and in the dark their green flashed fire.

'I would walk,' she said abruptly, 'not sit.' When the trance passed she felt a need for action.

'Then Amen to that, too,' returned Kit, almost lightly, and he offered her his arm. There were other couples strolling on the grass who had left the light of the great room and were content to hear the music of the dance while walking in the open.

Informality reigned at Charles's court and unmarried young women took liberties not granted them elsewhere, Celia knew. Only here at Whitehall might she walk at night with a man and remain unremarked. Or comparatively unremarked, she thought wryly.

They passed Barbara Palmer, arm in arm with Harry Killigrew, whispering in his ear. A strange sight that, and one at which the King would not be best pleased, Celia thought. She was beginning to know the intrigues of the court. She stole a glance at Kit, who remained strangely silent.

He continued to walk until they had passed all the others who had sought the peace of the night and at last they were alone together beneath the moon and the stars.

'Celia,' he said abruptly—no Mistress Antiquis, nor Mistress Celia now. He turned her towards him and, against everything he had vowed, but he could not help himself, he bent his head to kiss her lightly on the cheek.

It was not enough; it would never be enough. Goodbye honour and goodbye truth. Goodbye to all his resolutions to keep away from her, forfeit his ring, lose Latter rather than hurt her. He would be one with Rochester and the others who never let such trifles as honour and unspoiled virginity deter them from pursuit and conquest.

He gave a little groan, pulled her close into the circle of his arms, and kissed her with all the fire and passion at his command, full on the lips. His right hand rose to cup and cradle her head when he felt her sag against him.

For a moment Celia had felt fear when he had first pulled her to him. The fear was succeeded by something quite different, a wicked desire—it must be a wicked desire—for him to kiss her, which he had done. The sensation of his lips upon her cheek was so sweet and powerful that it ran through her whole body and, oh, she had wanted more still, which she had received.

This time, when his mouth met hers, her own untutored lips opened to receive him. Time, as in her trances, disappeared. All else disappeared save *him*, and when his hand rose to cup her breast she felt not revulsion, as she had done with Charles Sedley, but a sweet delight. Her whole body throbbed in a strange rhythm. What had the stars said when she had consulted them, asked about Kit and herself?

They had paltered with her, as they sometimes did, given her an answer so strange that she could hardly understand it. They had said that he and she were bound together, that each would get what they so dearly wanted of the other, but after such a fashion that they would not recognise it. As to love or marriage, which she could not really expect from him, they offered nothing. Her trances spoke to her of blood and pain, and so did the stars.

But this was not blood or pain; this was joy unconfined. Her hands found his face to caress it as he was caressing her. The music and the night had done their work upon her and upon him. They had deprived Kit of honour and Celia of caution, for she now knew that she loved him.

When he pulled down the neck of her dress, as Charles Sedley had done, the more easily to caress her body, she did not resist him as she had done Sedley, but welcomed him instead. She was a bird in his hands, fluttering, trembling, unable or unwilling to use her wings to fly away.

What ended this passage of unrestrained love-making neither of them fully knew. One moment Celia was shivering and crying beneath his hands and Kit was joying in the knowledge that she was his, it seemed, for the asking, then Celia gave a strange cry and pushed him away. She had been sensation, merely, ready to surrender to him, but suddenly, over his shoulder, she had seen the moon.

Diana's sign, and she was Diana. Was she mad that she half lay in a man's arms, ready to offer him her maidenhead beneath the sign of the very goddess who ruled her life and hopes? The stern principles which had guided her life until she had come to Whitehall reasserted themselves. Never mind that *she* loved *him*; the song he had sung earlier was in her ears again: 'Love, alas, is never long.' He would love her, and then, and then. . .and then nothing.

'No,' she said, pulling up her dress, turning away from him, for, after all, he was only doing what Charles Sedley had done, and as lightly as Sedley had done it. 'Oh, no. I must not. . .you must not. . . It was so sweet, but it is wrong,' she added hurriedly, lest she distress him, for she saw by his expression that he had been even more lost than she.

It was true. Kit, for a moment, had felt her warm against him, her surrender obvious; he had become roused to a degree which was almost painful and to have her refuse him at this last gasp was torture itself. He retained just enough self-control to allow her to escape him, to say to her sorrowfully, 'Oh, Mistress Celia, forgive me. I should not have treated you so, nor will do so again. The moon and the music have both betrayed me. I would not hurt you, no, never. I said that I would protect you and lo, I am worse than those who might exploit you, for I have promised you otherwise.'

But, said a small voice, you still have not told her the truth about the bet. Be brave and do so. He *could* not. Bad enough that he should have so forgot himself as to put them both into such temptation — worse to have her turn away from him in dislike, as she must, when he told her what he had done before he knew her.

'Flee the court, Mistress Celia,' he said hoarsely, his face averted. 'Thy goodness is temptation itself to men who have forgotten that women possessed it. And let us flee the moon, the stars and the night, and return to the haunts of men. I said trust no one and, see, I have proved that you should not.'

'But when I said no, you stopped immediately,' replied Celia. They were already retracing their steps and were among the strolling crowd again, almost at the doors of the room. 'And I, I lost my head, too. I allowed you to begin what I must have known would finish as it nearly did. You see, you are not the only guilty one.'

'But I am experienced as you are not. I took advantage of you. I shall not do so again, I promise you.'

It was the end, he swore to himself. He would make no further attempts to be alone with her. He would lose the bet by default. Buckingham would not let him withdraw, but he could not compel him to try to win it. The only flaw in that argument was that he had fallen in love with the astrologer's daughter. There was nothing he could do about that, save worship her from afar, which was not enough, for he wanted her so dearly, not only for her body, but for her mind and soul. He, who for years had seen women as incidental to his life, playthings, the one woman having been lost, was netted at last.

He was the plaything now. Nothing could save him but the love of the woman beside him, and that he could not in honour hope for. He had nothing to offer her. The thing which might free him from the wheel of service to which he was bound at Court was the prospect of Latter, a home and a small estate of his own at last, to which he might retire with wife, children, dogs and horses.

But to win Latter he must betray Celia, and in

any case what was Latter worth if gained at such a dishonourable price?

They were in the public room again. The dance was on and they had not been long gone, but knowing eyes followed them. Both felt a profound weariness.

'I would fain retire, Sir Christopher,' said Celia, as though being formal with him would blot out those few moments of mad desire which they had shared beneath the moon. 'It hath been a long day and a tiring one.'

Kit bowed gravely, matching Celia's own formality. 'I bid thee goodnight, then, mistress, and a fair night's sleep.'

Which is more than I shall enjoy, he thought wryly, watching her move away from him to speak to Miss Hamilton, to shake her head in refusal of Hamilton's attempts to have her stay, finally to leave by the door through which she had earlier entered. God grant that she never finds out what a double tongue her supposed protector possesses!

CHAPTER FIVE

CELIA bent over the horoscope which she was constructing. She had not only cast two elections for the Queen, but she had also obliged several of the maids of honour who wished to know what the future might hold for them. The only maid with whom she was not on friendly terms was Dorothy Lowther but, seeing that she did not much care for Mistress Lowther herself, that was no matter.

She had seen and spoken to Kit Carlyon on many occasions in the three weeks since the night he had begun to make love to her after they had played and sung for the King. They had never been alone since. She had sung and played the viol with him and with Buckingham on several afternoons and they had been friends together. She did not know quite what to make of George Buckingham. There was, on occasion, something sly about him. Kit had told her to trust no one; and so she did not trust Buckingham, but he amused her.

Tomorrow it would be the end of the first week of June when, she had told the Queen—who had told the King—the stars said they could expect news of the English fleet which had put to sea in late April to fight the Dutch. There was an air of suppressed excitement about the court. The Duke of York and some of the courtiers had left before Celia's arrival to join the fleet and since then there had been nothing but rumour. On June the second

Mr Commissioner Pepys had burst into Lady Castlemaine's lodgings when she was entertaining the King and Court, Celia and Kit among them, with the news that the two fleets were in sight of one another, gunfire had been heard in London, and then even that had died away, and still, no news

Other rumours were also disturbing. The plague, instead of going away, or remaining among the confines of the poor, had spread into the City itself, and the numbers dying from it had grown week by week. There was some talk that if it continued to spread the Queen would leave London, which would mean that Celia could return home, as her duties related only to when the Queen was at Whitehall.

For the moment, though, neither what was happening to the fleet nor the progress of the plague greatly affected the tenor of life at Whitehall. It was interesting to be at the heart of things, to see the King and his ministers daily, to know, before the commonalty, what was happening in the great world. Perhaps the weather, for it was the hottest June ever known to living men, caused more conversation and distress than either the Dutch war or the plague.

Willem had called yesterday to tell her that her father, whom she had visited on several occasions since coming to Whitehall, was unwell. She had, for one dreadful moment, thought that he meant that her father had contracted the plague, but, no, the wasting sickness which had afflicted him for more than a year had gained such a hold on him that he was declining daily, Willem said. She had gone to the Queen and asked for leave to go home. The Queen, as was often true with great ones, Celia was beginning to discover, showed much verbal sympathy but could not spare her until the week's end, even though the horoscopes Celia was casting for her could have been as well done at the Strand as at Whitehall.

Willem had given her a letter from Robert Renwick. He congratulated her on her advancement but also said that when she returned home, as she must when the Queen left London, for everyone knew that if the plague grew worse the Royal household would begin to disperse into the country, he would be happy to resume his suit to her, and hoped that by then she might have a better answer for him. 'Thy most humble servant and admirer, Robert Renwick,' he ended.

She had almost forgotten him in the excitements of life at Court. That afternoon she had arranged to sing and play with the Chevalier de Grammont, as well as Kit. Buckingham was absent on some business for the King, for which she was half glad. She liked Grammont, with his attractively broken English, and to be with Kit was always a pleasure.

He had never, since that one evening, attempted to make love to her again. There was no denying that he wished to. Occasionally she caught him looking at her with such an expression that she had no doubt of what it meant. She had to suppress the stirrings of her own heart. That was the poetic way of putting it, she had discovered, for it was her body which yearned for him, and had done so since the first moment when she had seen him with Buckingham at her home in the Strand.

She admonished herself sternly, for she had put down her quill and was staring mindlessly across the

room through the window at the cloudless
Mediterranean-blue sky—they had prayed for rain
in Whitehall's chapel last Sunday, lest the harvest
be ruined. That a man should render Celia Antiquis
mindless!

Resolutely she brought her attention back to her
work until it was finished and the last words sanded.
She rose, picked up her papers, tied them together
with a blue ribbon and placed them on a side-table.
Later that afternoon she would present them to the
Queen when she waited upon her. In the meantime
there would be music—and Kit.

But there was no Kit waiting for her in the small
room off the gallery where they practised. Only
Grammont and, surprisingly, Buckingham, who had
returned from his errand and was already playing a
melancholy air on his fiddle. She thought she had
contained her disappointment but something about
her must have betrayed it, for Buckingham, lifting
his head, laughed mockingly at her. 'No, he is not
here, mistress, but contain yourself. Presently, presently, he will come. Old Rowley demanded a game
of tennis—he needed to be beaten, he said—and
took him off to the court. Where I doubt not that he
will suffer a royal beating for delaying Kit's meeting
with his mistress.'

'I am not Kit's mistress,' replied Celia coolly,
taking up her viol and beginning to tune it.

'Oh, I spoke but in the figurative sense.'
Buckingham was airy. 'The whole Court knows of
thy chastity and Kit's worship of it. Why do we
worship that which we would most like to destroy is
a question I often ask of myself, and rarely find an
answer.'

Celia knew her Buckingham by now and how far she could go with him. 'Why, I suppose that the questioner hath a lack in himself, that he finds the question unanswerable. Or perhaps the question itself is void of meaning, and should not have been asked.'

'Should write plays thyself, Mistress Celia,' said Buckingham, 'thou art so witty,' before changing the sombre music he was performing into a wild jig.

Grammont, who had been following his original tune, called reprovingly, 'I know not that melody, George, and you have not given me the written music whereby I may play it.'

'Oh, I always enjoy requiring people to play tunes which they do not know,' was Buckingham's riposte. 'Witty Mistress Celia, the voice and votary of Diana herself, tell me, would you not like to play a new tune with Sir Kit?'

Celia, her viol tuned, had followed him into the jig, and for a moment contented herself with mastering it before looking across to him, to say, in a pause in her music, 'If a new tune hath a proper line, Your Grace, then I will gladly learn it, whoever I am required to play it with.'

Buckingham laid his fiddle down, and walked across to where Celia sat. 'Your Grace, Your Grace,' he said softly. 'My name is George. Say George, Mistress Celia, say George to me, with that melting glance you give Sir Kit, or I will require a forfeit from you. No, on second thoughts, I will take your disobedience as read, and claim the forfeit regardless.'

He put out his long hand, a musician's hand, as beautiful as Kit's—but she did not want his hand—

tipped her face up to him and, bending, kissed her on the lips. A light kiss, a butterfly's kiss, but she did not want it; she wanted to scrub the lips he had kissed to remove it, but she could not, for he was Duke and she was unconsidered maiden. She endured it and because, despite his lack of consideration for others, he was sensitive to others, the Duke knew of the endurance.

Looking beyond her, he saw Kit enter, and the devil which often moved in him moved again. Malicious mischief worked in him, so that he kissed her again, then raised his eyes to see on Kit's face confirmation of what he already suspected.

'Thy mistress pines for thee,' he flung over his shoulder at Kit, going to pick up his fiddle again, 'so I thought to console her. She will not say me George. Tell me, Sir Christopher Carlyon, does she call thee Kit?' And his light laughter followed them as he began to play a bawdy ballad whose words were fit only for a brothel, knowing that Kit would be aware of what he was doing, but Celia not.

Kit wanted to kill him. For one blind moment, as he had entered and saw the Duke's mouth on Celia's, the red rage had him in its grip. As the Duke had moved away, he had seen the stiffened outrage on Celia's face, which had had two contrary effects on him. The first was relief that she did not wish to endure the Duke's advances, the second was that he wanted to strike the Duke for daring such an outrage on her, his love.

Self-control won, as it so often did with him. He was also saved by Grammont, who exclaimed in a light, rueful voice, his kind eyes on Celia, '*Pardieu*, George, have we come here to make music, or to make love? I had thought the first. Let us return to where we began.'

'Oh, willingly,' sang the Duke to his merry music before gliding back into the melancholy piece he had been playing when Celia arrived. 'Let but Mistress Celia call me George and all will be well. Say George, mistress, say George,' he sang in time with his tune.

Celia looked imploringly at Kit, and then at her tormentor. She rose, still holding her viol, bowed low in the Duke's direction. 'As my master bids me,' she murmured. 'I will call thee George, but not before the King, I beg of you.'

Buckingham, still playing, began to laugh. 'And I shall call thee Celia, but not before the King. Thy mistress is a witty bird, Kit, and is about to soar into the heavens and sing for thee, I hope. Say Kit, say Kit, Celia,' he sang, 'when next you speak to him before me.'

Oh, if only this would end, thought Celia. Why was he baiting her so? He had been kind to her since she came to Court, having failed to tempt her when he had visited her in the Strand, before he had brought Kit with him. Why was he now so cruel? For his eyes on her were inimical, and she could not think why.

Kit knew, and the knowledge pained him, pierced him to the heart. The Duke thought that Kit was succeeding where he had failed and that the ring would not be his. To the Duke, worse than losing the ring was the thought that Celia might fall to Kit, having held him off, for being with her had renewed his own desire to have her, and he was doing his wicked worst to create friction between them, so that Celia might be shy of Kit and Kit would fail.

Worst of all for Kit was the thought that, out of sheer wanton mischief, the Duke might tell Celia of the bet rather than have Kit win her, even if he lost the ring in the doing by rendering the bet void. So unreliable, so mercurial was the Duke, that he was capable of anything.

For the moment, though, he ceased his baiting and concentrated on the music and, thereafter, lost in the sounds they were creating, the four of them spent a pleasant hour. Kit, despite, or perhaps because of his fears, was in particularly fine voice. The Chevalier persuaded Celia to sing to their playing, which she did in a small, sweet and true voice. It was not fitted, as she had admitted, for a large room but, playing as they were in a chamber, it was perfect where a larger voice would have overwhelmed them.

'Is there no end to your talents, mistress?' observed Kit softly in an interval in their playing.

'A small one only,' she said, shaking her head at him, at ease since Buckingham had left her alone. 'I make no claims to being a nightingale.'

'A lark,' said Buckingham, who had overheard them. 'Shalt be a lark, and Kit shall be an eagle. What do eagles do to larks, Kit?' It was plain that, music-making over, trouble-making was going to succeed it.

Grammont ended that. He put down his viol and thrust an arm through Buckingham's. 'Come, my friend, you promised me a game of tennis if I consented to join you in music-making. That I have done and I call upon you to fulfil your promise.'

'What and leave the song-birds alone?' riposted Buckingham, who had an urge to see how far he might go with Kit and Celia, and was reluctant to leave them together. He feared that the bet was almost won, since he did not believe in any woman's chastity, For they are all whores at heart, he had often said. He had bet that Celia would hold Kit off, but he did not believe that she would or could.

'Song-birds sing best when left together,' averred Grammont with a grin, drawing the reluctant Duke out of the room and winking at Kit as he went.

Celia did not see the wink, but began to rise, to leave. She was fearful of remaining with Kit, fearful to be away from him. He put out a hand to stay her and said, 'Would you like me to kill him for you?' and Celia knew that it was Buckingham he meant.

Her hand flew to her mouth. 'Indeed not. I would not have you hang.'

'No chance of that.' Kit was brief. 'It would be done in proper form. A challenge and a duel, an affair of honour. Say but the word. He could not stand against me in a contest with either pistol or rapier.'

'Nay.' Celia was agitated. 'I would not have you do such a thing. If you could defeat him so easily, then it would be murder, whatever the law says. No, he doth not hurt me, for I do not value what he says. Do not destroy your honour by sacrificing it to destroy him.'

'My honour.' Kit's smile was twisted. 'Well, well, if that is what you want, mistress. I am yours to command.'

'That is what I want, Kit. Believe me.'

'Always,' he said. 'And now, mistress, another

song? Let us sing one last piece together before we part. The Queen is leaving Whitehall soon, the King will follow her and I shall be with him, and our summer of music will be over. Seize the day, mistress, for it may not come again.'

He had used similar words to Dorothy Lowther and the memory saddened him. Were there any new words he could use to tell her of his love and that it was true? Fresh-minted words, perhaps, with no tainted memories clinging to them. He had never before regretted how idle his previous passions had been. She brought a clean soul to him, but what was he bringing to her?

Celia agreed, sat down again, and Kit began to play a new song he had written for Tom Killigrew's latest play. It was for two voices. A lover told his mistress of his love, but she refused to believe him because he had told the same story to so many before her.

'My love at thy feet, I do hereby place,' sang Kit, at the end of the first verse, to have Celia sing back, above her viol,

'Oft repeated words so soon lose their grace. . . .'

They sang no further. Kit swung around on his stool to slide from it and fall on his knees before her, to clasp her round her knees, laying his bowed head there, saying, 'Oh, God, Celia, I cannot go on. It is too like our own situation. Forgive me, but if I may not love thee, then allow me to worship thee, my chaste Diana.'

Celia put down her bow and her viol so that she might stroke his bent chestnut head. She could feel the warmth of him, could feel him trembling against her. She could scarce stand for her own trembling.

He looked up at her and said, 'Oh, if I had aught to offer thee but poverty and ruin I would ask for your hand, but I have nothing—only a few barren acres and this post of the King's, which might cease at any time if the whim took him. I can live from hand to mouth, but I cannot do that to a wife and family. Oh, Celia, my love, my dearest love, how strange to find you now when I thought I should never find another. I am wrong to accost you so, to no purpose. It hath been torture for me to be with thee. . .but not now, not now. Like this, I am at peace.'

'And torture for me,' murmured Celia, still stroking his head, looking at him as he spoke with such great eyes, so full of love that he groaned at the sight.

They stayed thus for some moments. The scent of Celia filled Kit's nostrils, as his filled hers. Lost in time, Celia felt the trance almost on her, but resisted it. Kit's presence, she knew, was provoking it, and why that should be, she did not know.

He released her at last. Strangely, loving her so this afternoon had not physically roused him, but quietened him, as though his renunciation of her had brought him a new serenity. Physical desire for her would return, he knew, but not here, not now.

They stood apart and he gave her one last kiss, upon the brow. 'Remember me,' he said, 'when you leave Whitehall,' and said no more of love.

'We shall meet again before I go,' faltered Celia, loath to lose him; it was like losing life itself. She wanted to say, I would sooner be poor with thee than rich with another, but she could not. She was a true modest maid, and Whitehall had not yet ruined her.

'Oh, indeed, mistress, as friends, I hope.'

'Better that, sir, than nothing.' But, oh, she was grieving inside. To lose him was like a little death.

He bowed to her, and she curtsied to him, and he was walking away from her. Soon, she would be home again, and Whitehall and the court would be forgotten, and he would be a memory for her, as she for him.

Laying down her viol, walking slowly back to her rooms, Celia was certain only of one thing. It was the love of her life who had walked away from her, and now she would truly be Diana's maiden, for there would be none other for her after Kit, she was sure.

Her rooms seemed desolate. She shivered and sat down, tried to think, then placed her hands on the table, saw that they were soiled and decided that, as she had been summoned to be present in the Queen's quarters this evening and it was likely that the King would be visiting, she needed a bath. It was harder here than at home in the Strand to keep herself spotless, despite the presence of a bathing-closet, but there would be, she thought, few there at this hour. She would be alone and the idea pleased her.

She rang for her chambermaid and ordered a bath to be filled, then fetched towels and clean underlinen and a loose gown to wear over them when she had finished, deciding to change into her court dress at the last moment before attending the Queen and presenting her with her elections.

The bathing-closet was along a privy corridor and inside it the baths were arranged behind a glass partition before which a couch was set where bathers

might recline while they waited. The baths had
gauze curtains around them to protect the modesty
of the bathers, and the chambermaid first helped
Celia into the bath, then drew the curtain and
retired, leaving her alone to enjoy the warm water,
but not her thoughts.

Celia was not alone for long. Her progress to the
bathing-closet had been watched by Dorothy
Lowther and Barbara Palmer. Each of them, for
their own reasons, had no wish for Kit Carlyon to
succeed in his campaign against Celia. Dorothy had
complained to Lady Castlemaine that Buckingham
had threatened her with condign punishment if she
betrayed the bet to Celia, and Barbara had first
laughed at her and then thought that she might use
her.

Lady Castlemaine's hatred of Kit was of a different order from Dorothy's. She had tried to make
him her lover and he had refused her. 'I serve the
King, my master, in everything,' he had told her,
and since then Barbara had been the traditional
woman scorned. Now she saw her chance for
revenge, and the two women made for the bathing-
closet to sit on the couch and begin the work of
losing the bet for Kit Carlyon. Had they known that
that afternoon Kit had finally walked away from it,
at great personal cost, they would still have worked
their spite on him, if only to hurt Celia, whose
resolute innocence was an offence to them both.

Celia heard them enter and thought nothing of
it—she had grown used to the semi-public life of the
court—until suddenly, in the midst of an animated
conversation about the absent Lord Rochester,

whom Lady Castlemaine also hated, her own name came floating over the partition.

She stiffened and sat up. She tried at first not to listen; thought, indeed, of pulling back the curtains and letting the speakers know that she was there. Except suddenly she heard Kit's name also mentioned and in such terms that she sat in the cooling water in an agony of shame and distress.

'Poor creature!' half laughed Dorothy Lowther. 'To make such sheep's eyes at him, with her pretence at virtue, when the whole court knows of Kit's bet with George Buckingham, and how he has vowed to take her maidenhead since she refused George's assault on it.'

'Indeed,' replied Barbara, her velvety tones contrasting with the Lowther's screech. 'And is it true— Jermyn swears it is—that Kit hath promised George his ruby ring if he fails, the one Cellini is supposed to have crafted? And that George will give Kit his fine manor of Latter if he succeeds?'

'Quite true.' Dorothy was casting mocking glances in the direction of the drawn curtains. 'And it is also true, for George told me so himself, that Kit hath a cunning stratagem to win her and Latter—by leading her on to think him a very *preux chevalier*, a spotless knight, by holding off and saying such things as "Oh, your virtue, Mistress Celia, is so great that I must respect it," and "Trust me, my sweeting, I will protect thee from the naughty gallants of Old Rowley's court," while all the time *he* is the gallant from whom she most needs protecting!'

The two women began to laugh, while Celia sat in silent humiliation, thinking of all the sidelong glances which she had received since she came to

Court, of the many two-edged statements which had come her way and which she had taken at face value.

Worst of all was the thought of Kit, whom a moment ago she had been loving for his honourable treatment of her, his refusal to continue to make love to her that night, when all the time it had been a trick to lure her on until he could take her maidenhead without a murmur of protest from her — rather, her willing collaboration. His honour. They had spoken of his honour, but he had none, to bet upon a maiden's virtue.

Silent tears ran down her face as the conversation continued, leaving her in no doubt as to his perfidy. She thought of what George Buckingham had said to her earlier that afternoon, and saw the double meanings in it. Grammont, too, had connived at leaving them alone, no doubt to give Kit the greater chance to win her.

But always she came back to Kit, and then she heard Barbara Palmer say something which had her thinking again.

'I suppose the biggest bribe for Sir Kit in all this was Latter. It is well-known, even the King knows, that he would dearly like to leave the court and be a country gentleman after all his wandering round Europe and the Turks' territory. Think you he will achieve his aim?'

'Oh, aye,' said Dorothy, sneering. 'The poor fool accepts all of us, and him, at face value. Why, he's such a whore-son cur he took me against the wall on a bet from Buckingham that he would have me before any other did when I new came to Court this spring.'

Celia heard no more. She shut out the muttered

voices and the laughter and further unpleasant gossip about the amours of others. They had spoken true. She thought of how Kit had said that he had nothing to offer her but barren acres. To discover the truth of him was such a blow that it was as though Celia Antiquis had died and gone to hell and someone else had taken her place. She would have her revenge on him and on them all. How, she knew not. She remembered what the horoscopes had said of her and Kit, that they were bound together and would so stay, but not in a fashion that they would at first understand. Well, she had been bound to him, but no more. The horoscope was wrong.

She would shame him—and time and chance would show her how to do it. She would punish Buckingham, as well, who had half-pretended to be her friend, as Kit had promised her that he was her true love. She should have known better; she had heard his song and what it said, its mockery of all that love meant. *That* was the true Kit Carlyon—the one who had pleasured Dorothy Lowther against a wall! No wonder she had given sideways glances at Celia from the moment she had arrived at Whitehall.

Most of all she mourned for the man whom she had thought that she had known. The man who had spoken gravely to her of serious things, who had made music with her, who had held off the night when he might have taken her, who had spoken that very afternoon as though he were renouncing all efforts to make love to her.

A trick, a trick, a very trick! All designed to make her surrender the more complete. She would play her trick on him when the time came, for had he not taught her by his own corrupt example how to play

tricks on others? The moon goddess would tell her
what to do when the time came, and she would do
it. She would humiliate him as he had sought to
humiliate her.

The water grew cold before the gossipers went—
to laugh in the corridor, clinging to each other,
shaking with indecent joy at the cream of the jest.
'For,' said Barbara, weak with mirth, tears running
from her eyes, 'if we have not set a mine beneath
Kit Carlyon which will explode on him with such
suddenness that he will know not what hath struck
him, then my name is not Barbara Palmer and I am
not Old Rowley's whore!'

CHAPTER SIX

CELIA was as coolly beautiful as ever. No one could guess at the passions which seethed beneath that smooth brow. She wore a new gown of moon-coloured silk, especially made for her, and on it was pinned a brooch shaped like the moon's crescent which Adam had given her to celebrate her apprenticeship to Diana when she was a child.

She had dressed her hair loosely, allowing it to hang down her back, with a long rope of pearls twisted through it. The pearls were Hamilton's—which she had previously refused to borrow, but she wished to look her best. Her presence was something remarkable, as though what she had heard in the bath-closet had strengthened not weakened her. She was placed beside Dorothy Lowther in the line of ladies behind the Queen and Dorothy Lowther was dismayed at her serenity. Could it be possible that the venom which she and Castlemaine had dripped to poison Celia's mind had not, after all, been swallowed? Impossible, but nothing about Celia betrayed the shock which she must surely have felt on hearing what a blackguard was her supposedly faithful cavalier.

Keeping calm before Dorothy Lowther and the others was easy. It was seeing Kit and Buckingham which Celia feared. But when they entered, talking together, fear disappeared and a burning rage took over. Yes, Kit would suffer—as she was suffering.

She had heard of the dreadful tricks which Lord Rochester had played on everyone and she had been glad that he was away with the fleet and was not there to plague her. But Rochester had not been needed; Kit Carlyon had stolen her heart away, it was lost forever, and it had all been a lie, a terrible lie to deceive Mistress Celia Antiquis, the astrologer's daughter, fair game for a gallant of the court.

Still she smiled, and curtsied low to the King when he spoke to her, and called Buckingham Your Grace when she spoke to him before the King. Turning away from the King, Buckingham mouthed 'George' at her. She had thought that she could not bear to look at Kit, but she could, and she marvelled at the sight of him that, knowing what he was, he could so touch her heart.

He was wearing green and gold. He never wore much in the way of jewellery; she supposed, from what she had heard, that he had little, but tonight he wore an emerald in the lace at his throat, and a pearl in his left ear. His chestnut curls, new-washed as her hair was, seemed burnished in the candlelight. His height marked him off from the others and his presence was such that Buckingham, Duke though he might be, paled before him.

Traitor, though, and trickster—to steal the heart out of a girl's breast so that he might take her one priceless possession, her virginity. Would he have held her against the wall to do it? This treacherous and exciting thought made her cheeks burn, so that Buckingham, who had inveigled himself to her side, whispered in her ear, 'For whom dost thou burn, fair Celia? Is it for him?' and he glanced sideways at Kit, who was looking sterner than usual.

Yes, she burned for him. Vile though he was, he had touched her heart, nay, had stolen it from her breast, and how to avenge herself she did not know, but God, or failing Him Diana, might help.

The King sat down to play Bassett. He did not encourage gambling overmuch at Court, however much was done elsewhere, but the Queen enjoyed playing for low stakes so he and the Queen, and a favoured few, Kit and Buckingham among them, played for pennies.

The game had hardly begun before the double doors at the end of the room, away from where Celia stood among the maids, were thrown open, and a man, preceded by a footman who tried to announce him, came into the room in a great pelter, shouting, 'Let me to the King! I have news for him, news of the fleet!'

The cards were forgotten, the King started up and the rest followed suit. A passage was made to him, through the ranks of the courtiers, and the man, weary and battle-stained, who had ridden from the coast to bring the message, struggled through it to fall on his knees before the King to tell him his news.

'A victory, sire, a most notable victory. The Dutch fleet all sunk and their admiral, Opdam, gone to his proper doom—blown into fragments even as his ship exploded. Ten thousand men dead.' The detailed despatches would arrive the next day, he said.

Celia shuddered a little, but the room exploded like Opdam's flagship; men hugged one another; the news left the room, travelled into London itself, where, all thought of the plague forgotten, bonfires were lit and the bells were rung far into the night.

At last Londoners had something to celebrate, and celebrate they did. It could no longer be grumbled that victories had disappeared with Old Noll Cromwell's death.

Kit had seen Celia shudder and, leaning across Buckingham, he said gently to her, 'Art dismayed by the victory, mistress?'

She answered him fair, because she would not have him know that she had found him out. 'I was thinking of the dead,' she said simply. 'Victory is sweet, but there will be English dead as well as Dutch. No death is good, except that we may rejoice that we lost less men. But still we lost men.'

She spoke truer than she knew. On the morrow, when the despatches arrived, King and Court would grieve for the loss of Charles Berkeley, Lord Falmouth, the charming favourite. But that was still unknown and wine was being poured, toasts were being drunk, and the King left to find Mr Chancellor Hyde and Lord Albemarle, both of whom had prayed for victory but had feared defeat.

In the ruck Celia came face to face with Lady Castlemaine, whose eyes swept over her in a dislike which she could not suppress. Why this was so puzzled Celia—it might even have puzzled Barbara herself. Vice, faced with virtue, was often put out of countenance, and Barbara knew virtue when she saw it.

'Stay, mistress,' she said, for Celia was about to leave. The party had grown noisy and wine had flowed in sufficient quantities to loosen both tongues and morals. 'Enjoy the revels. Thy cavalier is here and will lend thee his arm—if thou requirest nothing else.' And her smile was lewd.

Celia might have escaped to her room and safety, had not Buckingham chosen to join in the game.

'Amen to that, Lady Castlemaine,' he said, light eyes glittering. He had drunk more than a little before the news had arrived and was now highflown, though beside him Kit was still sober. He invariably drank little, having seen what drink was doing to those around him.

'Tell me, Celia—and say George when you do— we are celebrating the victory of one campaign, pray tell us whether we may celebrate the victory of another. When thou and Kit meet, tell us, then, who is the victor, who the vanquished?'

He had spoken into the strange silence that sometimes fell on noisy parties. Every head in the room was turned towards him. Celia could see Dorothy Lowther, her face eager, hate written on it, hate for both Kit and herself. She could see Buckingham, who did not know whether or not he wanted to win his bet—and Kit, on whose face a strange agony was written. And every face, even kind Hamilton's and Grammont's, was waiting greedily for her answer.

She was Diana; she was the moon. She needed but a bow in her hand, her hounds about her, ready to tear apart the man who had shamed her, to be a subject for a great master to paint. She knew, suddenly, how to gain her revenge, provided she could speak after a fashion that would mock and yet compel belief.

'Why, George,' she exclaimed, and trod on the word, so that heads not already turned turned at the sound and at the knowing familiarity in her voice. 'Dost thou speak of the bet between Sir Kit here and thyself, touching my virginity and its surrender?'

In the brief pause she made she saw Kit's face grow white and joyed at the sight. Oh, let him know that she knew of his perfidy and that she was stone towards him.

She saw surprise on Buckingham's face and pressed home her advantage. 'What, silent, George and silent, Kit, together? Fie, fie upon you both! Did you think that I knew not of it? There are no secrets in a court—e'en a novice like myself knows that. Why, as to the encounter between us, I know not who was the victor, who the vanquished. Let Sir Kit keep his ring and gain Latter, for he carried out with me that which he said he would, but he keepeth not me. I would not have him. For sure, I wonder what the whole business is about, seeing that I thought so little of it, and all of you so much. He—and it—pleased me not, however much he may have pleased others.'

She had her revenge. The coldness of her voice, her rejection of dalliance, her dismissing of Kit and the Duke was so complete that silence stayed for a moment until a great laugh broke out. But not before she had seen Buckingham's anger that he had lost both the bet and her, and Kit's dismay at her lie.

'No,' Kit almost shouted. 'No, it is not true. Upon mine honour, I never lay with her. She is maiden yet. Why. . .?' He began to ask her why she had said what she had, but his voice was lost in laughter at him—even Buckingham had begun to laugh.

'Success,' he roared, clapping Kit on the back, 'and ne'er a word from thee. Latter is yours. I cede thee the ring and the game. The lady's word is good enough for me.'

Kit had tried to deny what she had said, then saw her face as stone before him. 'You have won the bet. Latter is yours,' she answered him, as he again began to deny what she had said, again to be met with mockery and amusement from all around.

'Oh, Kit, Kit,' laughed Buckingham. ''Tis too late to play the gallant knight; the lady hath blown thy claims to virtue. Thou sly dog, to win her and to say nothing. And thou, lady, may I not wrestle a fall with thee, now Kit hath had his turn?'

She had known that this was coming and was ready for him. 'Nay, George—Your Grace, as you must be again. Tomorrow I leave the court and, since the Queen goes into the country, my duty here is done. My farewell hath been made, to you and to him.' And she bowed in the direction of Kit. Turning her back on them all, she began to walk away from them, out of the door and out of Whitehall, to return to the life where she had been merely the astrologer's daughter.

She had gone but a short way down the corridor towards the stairs when a strong hand caught her by the shoulder and whirled her around. It was Kit, and, if her face had been stone, his was grey granite.

'Why?' he exclaimed again, as though it were the only word he knew. 'Why did you lie to them, throw away your reputation? You know it is a lie. I have shown you nothing but respect. . .'

He faltered at the sight of her unchanging steadiness. 'Respect?' she said. 'What respect did you show me when you bet upon my virtue with yon weathercock? You knew nothing of me, whether I was knowing or innocent, but still you bet. You have lain with me a dozen times in your heart, do not deny it, and that others think that you have done so in truth is nothing to me. Keep thy ring, take Latter and go; do not trouble Celia Antiquis more. I meant what I said. I want none of thee, Sir Christopher Carlyon. Rejoice that the court thinks that you have notched up one more conquest and do not invite their laughter by denying it.' She turned away from him and resumed her slow walk along the corridor.

Every word which she had spoken broke her heart, and every word was a lie. The love she had borne for him she bore for him still. If he had wanted to lie with her, and had dreamed it, why, faith, she had felt the same for him.

Kit caught up with her, to question her again. He was, astonishingly, she saw, between rage and tears. And so was she, so was she.

'Why call yourself a whore before the world? Why? Why? I know I bet upon thee and should not have done so—I regretted it the moment I saw you. I saw thou wert spotless and you still are. . .'

'You never said a word.' Celia was steadier than ever. 'A true man would have told me of the bet, and begged my pardon.'

'By my life, I *could* not once I knew thee. I wanted thy esteem as well as thy love.'

'And the others? The others you bet upon with him. Were they not deserving of your esteem? Have you left no broken hearts about this court? Why should you care that one woman lies to give you a conquest which you did not make? Whose esteem were you seeking by holding off?'

For a moment her voice faltered, and Kit saw it, even in his misery, and said quickly, 'And you—you felt something for me. I know you did. And now, this afternoon, when I walked away from all I have done, and vowed to live a better life in future, you make a mock of me before the court, for that is what you have done.'

'Why, had we lain together,' said Celia, 'would that news have come better from you than me? Go to, go to, I must go home and forget King, Court and all of you.'

'No,' he said, and was upon her. 'I have a mind to make thy lie come true.' And now he had pinned her against the wall, his mouth was on hers and his strong body was mastering hers. 'Give yourself the title of whore, mistress, and pay for it.'

For a moment, as his mouth ravaged hers, his hands as well, Celia thought that she was truly lost—and did not know whether she was glad or sorry. Then Kit gave a broken cry and stepped back from her, hands held high. 'I cannot. No, I cannot. Not even to pay thee for thy lie. I did the first wrong when I bet upon thy virtue and it is I who must pay for that. Go, Mistress Celia Antiquis, but I do not think that you will forget Kit Carlyon in a hurry—as I cannot forget you.'

He turned on his heel and almost reeled down the corridor, leaving Celia to make her way downstairs alone, to her rooms, to spend her last night in Whitehall. She could not weep, which might have brought her surcease from pain, as all feeling seemed to have left her. She had trampled on her love, and publicly at that, and the world would not go back again to the moment before she had gone to the bathing-closet and heard what she had heard.

* * *

She had thought, only twenty-four hours ago, that leaving Whitehall would be painful. So it was, but not in the manner which she had expected. Then it had been leaving Kit, while believing in him and yearning for him. Now. . . But she put the thought away, and the anguish which went with it, into a cupboard which she had created in her mind. She would forget him.

Packing to leave took some time. Her chamber-maid wept a little. Celia had been a considerate mistress and the groat which she clutched in her hand was no recompense for losing her. There were other farewells to be made. She had to take leave of the Queen, who had stared a little at the composed face of the girl who had publicly branded herself whore—for the tale had reached her, told by a gloating Dorothy Lowther as she had prepared her mistress for bed.

'I will see you again, perhaps,' the Queen said. 'When the plague is over and we come again to Whitehall?' It was a question, not a statement.

Celia bowed and shook her head as she rose. 'I think not, Majesty. By your leave, I think that I was not made for kings and courts.'

The Queen did not deny her, but merely said, 'As to that, mistress, we may not always choose our destiny—it compels itself on us.'

She was thinking of herself as much as Celia. She was living in a strange land, tied to a man who did not love her, however kind he always was to his undesired wife. God would give her no chick nor child, no matter how many times she conceived, and she had come to terms with that, as she knew the girl before her would come to terms with her own

destiny which, given her age, had not yet worked
itself out.

Then there was only Hamilton to say goodbye to,
for Hamilton had been kind, and after that there
were the stairs to walk down and the corridor and
the path which ran to the river—the gravelled walk
down which she had come and on which she had
strolled with. . . No, leave that. That was over and
gone.

At the bottom of the stairs she met Dorothy
Lowther. She stopped and the footman behind her,
carrying a few parcels in which her personal effects
were packed—the majority of her belongings had
already been taken to the wherry which awaited her
at the foot of the river steps—also stopped.

'So, you leave us, mistress. You have much with
you, I see, but the most important thing of all you
have left behind.' Her smile was a Gorgon's grin,
one of delight, for in a sense she owed Celia. Had
she not publicly dismissed Kit as a tedious lover,
hardly worth the loss of her maidenhead? But she
could not forbear a taunt.

'True,' returned Celia, as cool as she had ever
been. 'But I take much with me, and that more
precious than anything I may have lost.' She would
not, at the last, lie to Dorothy Lowther.

'Oh, and what is that, Mistress Celia?'

'A better knowledge of life, Miss Lowther, and of
what my fellow human beings will do to gain their
ends. Even the stars had not told me the full extent
of that.'

'And did the stars tell you that you would lose
your virginity at Kit Carlyon's hands, and confess it
to the world in public?'

'The stars told me many things, Miss Lowther, but not always in a fashion one might easily understand.' As she spoke she had the trance again, briefly, and she saw Dorothy Lowther, lying on a bed, dead. There was blood on her gown and her face was distorted.

Celia could not help herself. Recovering, an infinite pity filled her heart. She held out a hand to the other girl and said impulsively, 'Oh, pray be careful. The future holds many things for us and, if we have not a care, they may be mortal.' The vision had not told her how Dorothy had died, only that her death had been painful.

Dorothy had seen Celia's face change before her warning. She stepped back, eyes fearful. 'Oh, 'tis you who must have a care, mistress,' she shrilled. 'It is not long since they burned witches. Whitehall is well rid of you.'

Celia's smile was sad. 'I but thought to warn thee.' She bowed. 'I must leave you; my wherry awaits me. My father is ill and needs me by his side.'

'Well, neither Whitehall nor I need you by our side, so go, mistress, go and do not return. I would not see you more.'

The thing which lived inside Celia and at times told her what she did not wish to know, either through a trance or a voice which sometimes spoke, told her that she would never see Dorothy Lowther again but that she might see Whitehall, although that message was not plain.

Why could not the voice, or a vision, have told her of Kit's falseness before she had given her heart away? Why show her only vague pictures of a future where she would see him again, a future which was lurid, shot with blood? The visions might be false. She had experienced one at least where she had seen danger in strange circumstances, and then the danger had not come to pass because, knowing it was there, she had taken action to avoid it. So the future could be changed. She had warned Dorothy for that reason, but Dorothy would not heed. Somewhere, that bed, that fate, awaited her. She would plot against others once too often.

Stepping into the wherry to make the journey to the Strand, she could not help but think of Kit, and wonder what he was doing on this fair morning. A breeze had sprung up, it was not so oppressively hot, and the journey downriver was pleasant. There was, she saw, little water traffic and, nearing home, she also saw that the streets were strangely empty. It was not until she was on the Strand again, and saw a house marked with a red cross, that she knew that the plague, forgotten while she was at Whitehall, had almost reached to the Palace itself and was destroying London.

Kit Carlyon had not yet climbed out of the drunken stupor into which he had fallen somewhere around midnight. After he had left Celia he had felt such pain, such disgust at himself and the cynical world in which he lived, that he had come to understand why Rochester and George Villiers, Duke of Buckingham, drank so hard.

It was not only to escape that world, it was to escape themselves. Both men had claimed that their best poetry came to them when drunk, but that was not the whole of the matter, he was sure. They wanted oblivion, and that was what he had wanted.

He had gone back into the room where Celia had made her mock of him in the strangest of fashions; by claiming he had conquered her, that she had known of the bet even as she submitted, and that she had found him wanting as a lover, she had demeaned him, not herself.

Even as he drank heavily, he who rarely drank and pitied those who did, he asked himself when and how she had found out about the bet. Someone must have told her—or had she overheard some of the lewd jests on it which ran about the court? No matter. She *had* found out, and had then destroyed herself and him. She would not, he saw, be any man's pawn. She would be her own woman, as a man was a man, and had so proved.

The knowledge made him drink the harder, for he knew what he had lost. He might have walked away from her the other night, renounced her, but always, at the back of his mind, there had been the hope that he would somehow be able to win her, to have her for his wife. That hope might have been fantastical, but it had been a hope, and now it was gone.

He remembered Buckingham coming to him as the drink took him almost into the Nirvana he sought and saying, 'Why so glum, Kit? You gained Latter and, for a brief space, the girl. It should not worry thee that an untutored wench did not value thy caresses. Perhaps another might teach her better. Shall I try to supply that lack?'

He had reared up, reeling and gasping. 'Damn you, George, you would jest at a man's funeral.'

'Thy funeral!' Buckingham had begun to laugh. 'Art run mad, Kit? You have gained everything and drink as though you had lost all. I'll see the papers drawn up which will give thee Latter in the morning. Enjoy your prize—it is worth the winning.'

'I want not Latter, for I did not win it.' He was on his feet, face flushed, hardly able to stand, one thing and one thing only burning in his brain. 'Damn you, George, and damn the lying bitch she is! I did not sleep with her, George. I did not win the bet. She is virgin still, and why she lied I know not. I held off and my reward is she makes a mock of me.'

'Oh, come, Kit. What ails thee? Enjoy Latter, it is fairly yours. What woman would label herself whore when she is not? Why, those who *are* whores do not claim to be so, but deny it most vigorously though the whole world knows the truth. The little Lowther, for instance.'

Kit said an ugly thing about the little Lowther. Perhaps it was she who had told Celia of the bet. But no, she would not—she feared Buckingham too much.

He had collapsed on to the table with a groan, the sound of Buckingham's laughter in his ears. What ailed him, that he should run mad because a cold-faced woman without a heart had treated him badly? Why, the Kit Carlyon whom he had been would have laughed in her face afterwards and, instead of releasing her on the stairs, would have taken his fill of her on the spot and tossed her away, for others to use.

He knew, he knew! He was no longer that Kit Carlyon. He had met a woman who was peerless, with whom he could talk, laugh, make music as though she were a man, and yet she was a woman, too, a prize so well worth the winning that the thought of her drove him mad. And if he had vowed to betray her, he had not done so. But she had betrayed him and thrown his love back in his face. . .

At that point he had lapsed into unconsciousness and only came to shortly before noon, to find himself in his own bed where Buckingham had had his lackeys carry him.

He staggered to the window to look out of it at the brilliant day, the sun hurting his eyes, and cursed the indulgent self-pity which had caused him to break a lifetime's rule and sink himself in drink. He would not so behave again. A man had to look life in the eye, not lie down and be destroyed by it. Such a thing would be hard to do, but he would do it.

The first thing to face was that she had gone. He knew that she was due to leave in the forenoon and the clock on his tallboy told him that noon was on him and the afternoon approached. Then it would be night, when he would have time to examine the ruin which Kit Carlyon had made of his life and try to rescue something from the wreckage.

CHAPTER SEVEN

THE house on the Strand, which had always seemed
airy and full of light, now seemed small, cramped
and dark. Celia had grown used to the spacious
rooms and high ceilings of Whitehall. Willem was
there to greet her, Mistress Hart by his side. Her
father had not been able to rise that morning, they
said, their faces anxious. He was yet abed.

Useless to try to justify herself, to say, They
would not let me come before today; small folk like
ourselves mean nothing to the great. Celia cast off
her cloak and, still in her Whitehall finery, for she
had been told to wear it to say farewell to the
Queen, walked upstairs.

Her father was lying in his four-poster. Against
the wishes of Willem and Mistress Hart he had
ordered the curtains to be drawn back and the
windows be open so that the fresh air of the day
blew in. He was propped against great pillows and
he motioned her to come and sit beside him.

'Welcome, my dear,' he said, and her heart mis-
gave her at the sound of his weak voice. 'Willem
said that they would not release you before today,
and therefore I prayed to God that He would not
take me before you came. I have much to say to
thee.' And then, anxiously, 'Thou art well, my
child? You look pale.'

'Nothing,' said Celia as lightly as she could,
although the sight of him smote her to the heart. 'I

found it difficult to get used to the late nights at Court, and to rising late. It is a life which would tire a horse.'

Adam gave a feeble laugh at that. 'I see that they did not rob thee of thy spirit. Come, sit on the bed beside me, so that I need not raise my voice. The sickness has had me in its grip since you left, and now its grip has tightened so that I am not long for this world and must prepare to meet my maker, the great architect of the universe. Before that, I have somewhat to say to thee.'

His voice failed him suddenly and Celia, seizing his hand, said, 'Oh, Father. Do not distress thyself. Rest a little before. . .'

'Nay, nay.' He reared up in his anxiety. 'I must speak now. I may have no tomorrow. Celia, I am afraid for thee. I leave thee a woman alone. I know that I have given thee the tutoring of a man, but the world is full of wolves. You have a man's mind, but not a man's strength. You are full old to marry, being almost twenty-three, and I reproach myself that I have not seen you married before I came to this pass. Robert Renwick is still of a mind to wed thee, and you have not yet given him a final answer. Relieve my mind, daughter, so that I may die happy, by telling him that you will accept him, so that I will know that you are safe when I am gone. Promise me!' He gripped her hand with such strength that she almost cried out.

What could she say but yes? Had not Kit proved false she would have refused, in the hope that he might yet offer for her truly. But he would not now that she had flouted him so publicly. And the wishes of a dying man were sacred, or so the Church said, and not only was he dying but he was her father and she owed him her duty.

Whatever it cost she would be Robert Renwick's wife—and it would be at great cost. She had pledged herself virgin even before she met Kit and, after him, virgin she would have wished to stay. She had no desire to be wife to any man; she had wanted to be free Celia Antiquis, to be free as a man might be; but that was then, this was now.

She bowed her head so that her father could not see her tears. 'Yes,' she said, her voice grave and low. 'Yes, Father. I will do your bidding. I will agree to be Robert Renwick's wife.'

Adam sank back on to the pillow from which he had raised himself in his agitation.

'Now, I die happy. Thou art a good child, Celia. The best. I would not have thee unprotected when I am gone. Master Renwick will protect you, I know, and will be a good father to thy children.'

Children! Robert Renwick's children! The children she had wanted were Kit's. Grave, fair-haired girls, and tall boys with curling chestnut locks and green eyes. But they were dream children, never to be known on earth. Mistress Renwick's children would be dour replicas of a dour man who knew not music and was, Celia already knew, suspicious of her knowledge, and would not wish her to use it.

Any other dream which she might have had had died at Whitehall. Her duty was to reassure her father who, she was sure, had not long to live. Seeing him resting against his pillows, giving him the composing draught which Willem had prepared at his orders, she told herself that her life was now of the earth, that Diana must be forgotten, and that domesticity must take her over.

Walking downstairs she shivered a little, but she shut the door of the cupboard in her mind again, and vowed never to think of *him* but only of her duties—first to her father and then to the man whom her father had chosen for her to marry.

Adam did not linger long. A doctor arrived to make sure that it was not the plague from which he was suffering. He had a cloth soaked in vinegar before his mouth and nose, but left it off when it was plain that Adam had no temperature, no buboes or boils on him and no other signs which meant the plague.

'He is not long for this world, mistress,' he told Celia when they had left the sickroom.

'Yes,' said Celia. He was telling her nothing which she did not already know. He was giving her instructions as to how she should treat her father, but she paid little heed. Either Adam would tell her what to do or she would use her own knowledge. He recommended bleeding and she did not tell him that Adam deplored bleeding. 'For how,' he had often said, 'can it be good to weaken a man when the illness is upon him?' He had a hard commonsensical attitude to life and to illness which he had passed on to Celia, saying, 'Observe, always observe, take nothing on trust. Believe not the books, but rather your eyes.'

Before the doctor arrived, Adam had talked to her of many things which he had observed since Celia had gone to Whitehall. 'Item,' he said, 'we have a plague of rats, large black ones, and I have had Willem kill all he finds with a spade. I know not why there are so many. Perchance it is the un-seasonal heat. I have known no June like it in all my days.'

Celia returned to his side after the doctor had gone, droning his admonitions as far as the door. Adam was still conscious, still lucid in his speech. 'The doctor hath said that the plague grows worse, which is only telling me what I already know. I can hear the death carts rumbling by and, before I was confined in here, I could see the doors with the deathly red crosses on them, signs that the plague was within. "Bring out your dead," they cry. Well, I shall join them. For if it is not the plague which carries a man away, it is another thing.'

Useless to deny him, to offer him false reassur-ance. He spoke often to her and said once, 'I have been thinking on something which Dr John Dee said in the old Queen's day. That were we to send a mirror to the stars and turn it on ourselves, so far away are we that we might see therein what had happened in the past, or mayhap the future. He was not certain which. I wish I had such a mirror, Celia, so that I might see whether or no I leave you safe.'

Celia thought of her trances, her visions of the future, all clouded though they were, and answered him simply. 'I do not think it a good or a right thing to know the future, Father. We might not like it, and then, seeing that it will come, we should never know a happy moment.'

'I have made you a wise child,' he said. 'I think you learned something at the King's court, Celia, by the face you have brought home. Wisdom and sorrow reside in it.'

She did not deny that and, in the five days which

it took him to die, she said nothing of what had happened to her, nothing of Kit or the Duke, but merely told him of the King and Queen, and said again, when he admonished her, that she would marry Robert Renwick when he asked for her. As he would, her father said, because he had sent for Renwick and told him that he would make Celia swear to marry him on his death.

On the fifth day, Adam died, peacefully, his hand in Celia's, and Mistress Hart and Willem sobbing at the bed's end, for he had been a kind and considerate father and master. Celia thought it strange that Robert Renwick had not come to see her father. Willem had told her that he was on an errand for a great man; he was not sure of his name and doubtless had little time to spare, even for the deathbed of a man whom he had called friend.

Tearless, for she could not yet believe it true, Celia walked downstairs into the parlour where they had entertained the Duke and Kit. Mistress Hart was seeing to the laying out, and the pair of them would arrange the funeral. Celia was numb. So much had happened to her in such a short time, and none of it happy. She had lost her love and her father, and would shortly gain a man whom she did not want.

It was fate, she later thought, which brought Robert Renwick to the house within an hour of Adam's death. The afternoon was fine and stifling and she was sitting in the parlour with the windows open, a fan in her hand. Mistress Hart had finished her duties upstairs and was now washing herself carefully as Adam had always commanded her to do after she had tended someone sick, dead or dying. 'You do not want the miasma on your hands,' he always said.

Willem answered the knock on the door and brought Master Renwick to her. Celia rose to meet him.

He was finely dressed in a fashionable brown silk suit. He wore a new wig, very black and curling, which did not suit him. He looked every inch the rich merchant he was. Celia thought, mistakenly, that he had come to court her, not knowing that Adam already lay dead upstairs.

She was soon to be disabused. He did not even ask after Adam and forestalled her when she was about to tell him of his death.

'Oh, madam,' he began, and his voice was iron, the voice which he used to his apprentices, not at all like the voice which he had used to her when he had proposed marriage. 'I am sure that you will know why I have come.'

'To see my father,' she said, 'but——'

He did not let her finish. 'Later, madam, but you and I have a reckoning first. I made a proposal to you when last we met and you turned me away most foully. And, in doing so, you lied to me, madam. I told thee I would make thee a good husband, but a bad enemy. I see you remember, madam, by your colour.'

'I lied not,' began Celia, her heart beating wildly, for his mien was such that she was afeared of him.

'You did, and you lie still. You told me that your heart was whole, that the court gallant who came here meant nothing to you. If so, madam, tell me this: why is there a ballad being hawked about the streets telling of the astrologer's daughter who visited Whitehall and who lay with the gallant who bet on her virtue so that he might win a rich prize? You are that woman, madam, and no decent man would ever touch thee now. Thy father wishes thee to be Robert Renwick's bride, but fie upon the pair of you.'

His face was red with rage as he lashed her with his tongue. 'You are damaged goods, madam, and I want none of you. He has taken thy maidenhead which should have been mine. For shame, thou wanton, thou trull. If thy whore-son lover doth not want thee, then neither do I. All London sniggers at thee and thy antics. The balladmongers have sung of thy wantonness from street to street.'

Celia stood mute. What could she say? To tell him that she was innocent would be useless. He would spit in her face, for had she not proclaimed her lack of it publicly? She could not claim otherwise now.

She tried to speak, but at first could not. She had not thought that they would make a ballad of her shame. Was it Kit, Buckingham, or another? No matter; the deed was done.

'I told you,' she said at last, as firmly as she could, 'before I left for the court, that I could not marry you. What I do, or have done, since I refused you is nothing to you.'

He was consumed with baffled desire, for after Adam's promise to him he had been sure that Celia would be his. Lust denied drove him on; he was frantic at the loss of what he thought had been reserved for him.

'Thou slut, that can scarce speak for very shame.

I shall make you pay, both of you. You and the man you lay with, who made you whore, be sure of that.' He was advancing on her, hands outstretched. 'Why should I deny myself? You are any man's, madam, and I would have my way with you now, make you whore, indeed, who would have made you wife. A wench who has fornicated with one man outside the law may do so with another. You need no marriage lines from me, nor payment neither.' Then he was upon her.

Celia retreated from him and said, nay, almost shouted, 'For shame, Master Renwick, for very shame. Would you vent your lust on me in a house where my father, whom you called friend, lies newly dead?'

He did not hear her, or chose not to hear her. He pushed her towards the wall, pinned her there and began to tear at her clothing. Celia's strength gave out—she was lost, a trance suddenly upon her. Robert was gone, the parlour was gone and she was in the dark, blood upon her hands, and there was thunder above her this time. It rolled on and on.

She was back in the present again. The thunder was someone beating on the door. It was Willem calling to her. 'Mistress, you are there, I know. Mistress, answer the door.' And he began to hammer on it the harder.

Robert released her with an oath and began to pull up the breeches which he had dragged down. Celia sank to the floor, but only for a moment. She. . .they. . .could not be found thus. Willem's arrival had saved her, for the time being, at least. Even Robert could not continue with Willem at the door. She opened it to let him in. His face was anxious, for he had heard Robert's raised voice and had feared for her, although he could not have believed that Robert would have been on the point of raping her.

'I thought,' he said doggedly, not looking at Robert, 'that Master Renwick would wish to pay his last respects to your newly dead father, his old friend.'

Robert shook his head to clear it and turned to follow Willem who was indicating the door, the worried look still on his face. Robert flung over his shoulder at Celia, 'Aye, I will go. But do not forget what I said, mistress. I will take my payment when the time comes. Fortunate for thy father that he did not live to see thy shame.'

He was gone. Celia sank on to the settle, crying great tearless sobs. Of all the dreadful events of this dreadful week this was perhaps the worst. Later she heard Robert descend the stairs and leave, banging the front door behind him with such force that the whole house shook. She was well rid of him, but the knowledge did not comfort her. For she must live with the knowledge that now not just the court but the whole world knew of what she had proclaimed so boldly.

She raised her head. Her indomitable, unconquerable will moved in her as it had always done. She would outface the world as she had outfaced Kit, Buckingham and the rest. How she would live and what the consequences of her act would be, she did not know, but she knew that, somehow, she would come through this and in doing so would be the stronger.

* * *

Robert Renwick had been in a stew, a fever of rage, since he had been told of and had then heard the street ballad about Celia. His honourable offer had been refused and then the trull had lain with another whom she hardly knew—a fly-away gallant of Charles's dissolute court who had taken her for his idle pleasure and now, presumably, seeing that she was home again, had cast her off. He would have his revenge on them both, as he had sworn, but on the man first. He moved swiftly. It was a pride of his that in all his doings he let time wait not on his feet.

That night, dressed plainly, a velvet cap pulled down over his face to obscure it, he took himself to an inn in Alsatia, the slum in Whitefriars where London's thieves congregated. Not even the fear of the plague, rife there, could keep him away.

The tavern-keeper recognised him, not as Robert Renwick, master goldsmith—for that man was unknown at the sign of the Black Bull—but as one Jude Scrivener who occasionally came to talk to some of the rogues and cullies who used the tavern as their place of employment.

He took his ale to a rough table in the stinking den, conquering his aversion to it, and when a pair of thieves whom he knew entered he raised a finger to call them over, and tossed a coin to them when they did so. They carried the ale they bought with it over to his table and sat down opposite to him, grinning.

'Aye, master,' said the larger, who sported a black eye-patch. 'What can we do for 'ee this time? What noble piece do you wish us to lift for 'ee?' He winked grotesquely with his one visible eye. The other said nothing, clutched his tankard and waited to be told what his new mission was.

Robert Renwick, who was Jude Scrivener, not only a respectable master goldsmith but also secretly a fence, a man who, because of his knowledge, could tell the thieves who stole for him where to find the treasure he wanted, smiled savagely at them.

'No treasure for me this time,' he said. 'I have another errand for thee, a different one. You are as apt as the bully-boys in Alsatia, I am sure. The braggarts who swagger around with rapiers but know how to use a club even better are no better than thee.'

One-Eye, for that was his nickname, went quite still. 'Oho,' he said softly. 'You wish us to do over an enemy, master? It will be a pleasure.'

'Discreetly,' said Robert. He had barely touched his own drink and wanted only to finish his mission and be gone. 'However it is done, I do not want it tracked back to any of us.'

'And the man you want us to. . .tickle, master. Who is he and how shall we know him?'

'Oh, you will know him. His name is Sir Christopher Carlyon, one of the King's Gentlemen-in-Waiting. I want him watched and followed. He is not to be touched unless he approaches the astrologer Antiquis's house in the Strand. Then you may do with him as you wish, short of killing. Best not to kill him—we want no hue and cry over a favourite of the King.'

'A dangerous man to quarrel with, perhaps, master,' whined the second man, who had not yet spoken.

FREE! THIS CUDDLY TEDDY BEAR!

You'll love this little teddy bear. He's soft and cuddly with an adorable expression that's sure to make you smile.

PLAY THE MILLS & BOON LUCKY STARS GAME!

Scratch away the silver panel. Then look for the matching star sign to see how many gifts you're entitled to!

 WORTH 4 FREE BOOKS, A FREE CUDDLY TEDDY AND FREE MYSTERY GIFT.

 WORTH 4 FREE BOOKS, AND A FREE CUDDLY TEDDY.

 WORTH 4 FREE BOOKS.

 WORTH 2 FREE BOOKS.

YES! Please send me all the free books and gifts to which I am entitled. Please also reserve a Reader Service subscription for me. If I decide to subscribe I shall receive four superb new titles every month for just £10.00 postage and packing free. If I decide not to subscribe I shall contact you within 10 days. The free books and gifts will be mine to keep in any case. I understand that I am under no obligation whatsoever. I may cancel or suspend my subscription at any time simply by contacting you. *I am over 18 years of age.*

12A4M

MS/MRS/MISS/MR _____

ADDRESS _____

_____ POSTCODE _____

  mps MAILING PREFERENCE SERVICE

◄ **POST THIS CARD TODAY!** ►

◆ TEAR OFF AND POST THIS CARD TODAY! ◆

Mills & Boon Reader Service
FREEPOST
P.O. Box 236
Croydon
Surrey
CR9 9EL

NO
STAMP
NEEDED

'Nothing to that if you do your task secretly and well.'

'And how long will we watch and wait, master? And the payment?'

'Until I tell thee to cease. But I do not think it will be long before he approaches the house.'

'And if it be day, master? We cannot do him in the day, in the Strand.'

Robert gave a knowing smile. 'I do not think that it will be day when he visits the astrologer's daughter.' Robert thrust his hand into his breeches pocket and passed money below the table to One-Eye. 'Night covers many misdeeds. If he comes not to the house within a fortnight then you have my permission to wait for him one evening and do as you will with him wherever he is. Remember, surprise will be all. This is no soft boy—he was a soldier once and is a hard man.'

'Hard or soft,' said One-Eye, winking again, 'Wat and I know the tricks of our trade as well as you know yours, master, I dare swear.' He saw Robert's face change and added hastily, 'Never fear, master, we'll not betray thee. You pay too well for that!'

'Leave me in a short while,' ordered Robert, 'and there will be more money for you when the deed is done. Trust me, friends. I have never cheated thee yet.'

They knew that, and it kept them loyal. Robert was as shrewd in his role of thieves' employer as he was in his other as solemn master goldsmith, that respectable pillar of society, whom some said would be Lord Mayor of London on a day not too far distant.

THE ASTROLOGER'S DAUGHTER   145

CHAPTER EIGHT

'COME, Kit,' shouted Buckingham. 'Leave off that glum face. What's one wench more or less? All cats are the same at dusk, friend.' And he gave Kit a great blow across the shoulders.

They were walking in the gardens by the river. The Queen and her court had left for Salisbury. There was talk of King and Government moving to Oxford, since the deaths from the plague had risen to new heights that week and had even dimmed the euphoria of the naval victory over the Dutch. Many of the wealthier citizens had already fled London, although it was not in their districts that the plague raged. The King did not wish to desert his capital, but his Privy Council and the ministers near to him were putting pressure on him to do so.

Word of Adam Antiquis's death, and that it was not from the plague, had reached court. No one knew where the news had come from. Buckingham had shaken his head when Jermyn had grinned at him that it was his minions who were keeping watch on the doings of the astrologer's daughter and had brought him the news. He was lying, as he always lied—the lie being more interesting to him than the truth.

The urgent curiosity which always drove him had driven him to put a watch on Celia. One of his many retainers told him all that passed and he knew nearly as much of her comings and goings as he did of his own. Some time that game would pall, but not for the present. There was too much amusement to be gained from it, for the game between Celia and Kit was not finished—he was sure of it.

Kit shook off Buckingham's arm, placed round his shoulders after the blow. Buckingham took no offence but merely said, 'Cheer thyself, Kit. There's Castlemaine still ready to try a fall with thee and, for real desperation, there's the Lowther.'

Kit grimaced and tried to reply lightly, but could not. He felt as though some light which had entered his life, a light which might have led him to better things, had been extinguished. He had seen in Celia the possibility of salvation—a wife, children, a settled home, all things which he had possessed long ago, but which had been lost long ago.

'You say the father died a week since,' he finally offered abruptly.

'Aye, and the wench is alone in the house, Kit. Go there and try another fall with her. Why not?'

'She would not speak to me,' replied Kit shortly, 'and why should she? I behaved most foully to her, as did you.'

'True, but she has had her revenge on us both most sweetly. She robbed me of Latter to give to you and, giving in to you, she branded thee clumsy. A cunning whore, Mistress Celia. I had not met her like before and do not hope to do so again. I fancy trying a fall with her myself.' He looked sideways at Kit and laughed to himself at the menacing expression which passed across Kit's face.

Oh, he pines for his doxy and hates the thought of anyone else having her! Whatever *she* had felt about the loss of her maidenhead, friend Kit had enjoyed himself when he had relieved her of it and wishes to enjoy himself again! Buckingham said nothing of that, however, directing the talk to other things, and laughed when Castlemaine approached them, using her fine eyes to try to enchant Kit. Kit gave something which was almost a grunt and, turning on his heel, left them.

Buckingham called after him. 'Go to Latter, Kit. Visit thy new estate. That should cure thy megrims.'

Go to Latter! He had as lief go to hell, thought Kit, as he strode along the gravelled walk, brushing past friends and enemies alike. It was his week for duties in the King's bedchamber and for the moment he could go nowhere. He had gained Latter unfairly, on a lie, and Buckingham refused to believe the lie was other than the truth and had already made the manor over to him.

'A fair place,' he had said, 'large enough for a gentleman to live there comfortably, set in seely Sussex—beautiful, but a nuisance to me. It is divorced from my other lands, came to me by an odd inheritance. Easily got and as easily passed on. I lost it fairly. Do not grudge me the paying of my debt.'

Lost it fairly! Kit writhed at the memory. Oh, if only he had shown no scruples before she left and had finished what he had started against the wall, making her, in truth, the whore she had claimed to be. But no, he could not. Spotless she was, though spotted she had proclaimed herself. Besides, it was not in him to take a woman against her will.

He was by the river where they had sat together to watch the same ducks which hurried and scurried along the water before him. He had been happy with her. If he had gained Latter by any other means he could have taken her there as his bride and lived out his days in happiness and obscurity, making music for her and their children.

He threw himself full length on the grass, to lie on his back and stare up at the heavens, the passing clouds, whose movement made him feel that he sailed on a great sea. When his week of service was over, and before the Court moved to Oxford—for he was sure it would go there in the end—he would repair to the house in the Strand to see her again. To find, perhaps, absolution; to explain that he had begun the bet idly, thinking her merely another trull who had held off Buckingham on a whim.

No, that would not do! He could imagine her looking at him gravely before saying, 'Oh, Kit, do you dismiss all women so easily? I am not the only woman who wishes to keep her virtue and does not wish to cheat her present or future husband. You should never have bet on a woman whom you did not know to fill an idle moment. It was a wrong thing to do.'

Face it, Kit, face it, he told himself. No lies, no self-pity. You but did it to win Latter, and a haven. The woman you intended to despoil meant nothing to you.

And now she did. She meant everything. She was the sun in his sky, or the moon which she had proclaimed herself, he did not care which. He knew that, if she were his wife, she would be his mistress, his lover and his friend. He burned with passion for her, but he burned also to walk with her in the garden and talk with her—and he had lost her. Latter meant nothing to him.

Kit rose. He would go to see her in two days' time when his duties were over. He would go in the evening, when the heat of the day was over. He would beg her forgiveness, he would——

He did not know what he would do or say. He would leave that until he met her and looked in those great, grave eyes and hoped to find pity there. He wondered how she fared, what she was doing. . .

Celia was numb after the shocks of Adam's death and Robert Renwick's perfidy. Mistress Hart and Willem sustained her. She had no relatives in London, and when she examined Adam's papers, after he had been buried with all due solemnity, not thrown hugger-mugger into a pit as the plague victims were, she was astonished to find from them that his true name was Arthur Archer, and also the name of the village in Leicestershire which he had left to come to London. She supposed that there might be relatives there.

Celia Archer, she thought wryly, that is my true name; it did not have so noble a ring as Antiquis. But for the moment she would retain the one which she had known all her life.

She must make herself a new life, too. A life without Adam—and without Kit. She had never really planned on a life with Kit, but at the back of her mind had always been the impossible dream— what if. . .?

That dream was dead. They had shattered it between them. It had never truly possessed life. It had died aborning. And there was work to do. She had a living to earn. She would carry on her father's business and would do, as well, those things which he had not really wished her to do. She would become a wise woman, would aid women in trouble—women who could not conceive, women who conceived overmuch, and women in childbirth who could be helped by her herbs and simples.

The week flew by. Robert did not appear again, but on the Wednesday, two days after Adam was buried, Mistress Hart came into the parlour, her face distressful.

'It is not that I want to do this thing, Mistress Celia, but my son John. . .' She hesitated, wringing her hands, for she had loved Celia and revered Adam but, as she was about to say, she had other duties, too.

'Yes, your son John,' prompted Celia, wondering what new blow was about to strike her.

She did not have to wait long. 'My son John wishes me to accompany him, his wife and children into the country. He is leaving London for my elder son, Thomas, is dying of the wasting sickness at his farm near Reading and hath written asking John to come to take it over. John, being but a butcher in a small way, is only too thankful for the chance, but. . .' And Mistress Hart stopped, to start again almost at once. 'His wife Alice is ailing since their last child came—seven in nine years, a cruel thing for a woman—and he wishes me to go with him, to look after them all. Blood is thicker than water, he says, and he hath the right of it. Loath I am to go, but I must, Mistress Celia, and I would go with your blessing.'

Another loss. For Mistress Hart had been with them for many years, not wishing, as a widow, to be a burden on her son, and now she was to go. Celia's world was falling about her, but she must be brave.

She bade Mistress Hart not to repine. 'For you have your duty, as the Bible says, and it is to thy family and not to me. But, oh, I shall miss you sorely.'

'And I you, Mistress Celia.' The two women were sobbing in one another's arms. 'And the worst of it is,' the housekeeper faltered, 'is that John wishes to leave on the morrow, for we not only gain a competence, he says, but a blessing, too, that we may 'scape the plague, which threatens all our lives.'

So there was another link with the past gone. Would Willem come in and say that now Master Adam had gone, he too wished to leave? He did not, instead he came to her saying, his honest face troubled, 'I thought it best to tell thee, Mistress, that I count my home here with you. You will need a strong arm to protect you and, though I grow old, I count myself a man who can still defend those whom I serve. Master Adam was troubled that he was leaving you alone and defenceless and now that Master Renwick hath cast you off. . . Yes, mistress, I know of what is said of you, and I do not believe it, whatever that double-dealing peacock thinks. You would not betray yourself with any man and if you said you did, the which I have been taunted with, then I do not believe you. Everything about you says otherwise. I am proud to serve thee.' He fell on his knees before her and kissed her hand.

'I know thee as a woman who knew thee as a babe. You are the daughter I lost when this same plague took my wife and children many years agone and Master Antiquis saved me from the sin of self-murder and thus from falling into the pit. In serving you, I pay my debt to him.'

All was not lost. Cast thy bread upon the waters: for thou shalt find it after many days, the Bible had said. Adam had cast his bread and it was returning to Celia at a time when it was most needed. With Willem by her side she would brave the sneers and the sly laughter which followed her when she went abroad and in time the gossips would find another target for their mockery. Her story would become an old one and forgotten.

The thought buoyed her up in the early days after Adam's death. She did not hire another house-keeper. She and Willem between them would be able to do all that was necessary and the work would keep her busy and prevent her from falling into the pit of self-pity. Mock they might, but Adam's clients came to her and, as she had hoped, on her first day a child came to call her to the bed of a woman sick after childbirth, and she was able to ease her pain. Some came to her for nostrums to help them with-stand the plague but although she made up pouches of herbs for them to wear or place among their clothes, she always told them what Adam had done in similar case: 'These might help, or they might nct, but at least there can be no harm in trying.' She recommended cleanliness as Adam had done, but most scoffed at this advice.

She sent for Willem one evening and said to him, 'The house is too large, Willem, and I would have a smaller, but it is for you to advise me whether that is a good decision or a bad. I do not think I shall have the income which my father did and the difference between a smaller place and this would leave me with some treasure to put by against hard times.'

'You do not intend to marry, then, mistress?'

Celia shook her head. 'No, that way is barred to me. I have no desire to be the chattel of a man who marries me for what I have, and that is the only fashion after which a man will come wooing me.'

She said nothing of Kit, or the court. She would not go back there and had decided that when she left the Strand she would be Celia Archer, pupil of the late Adam Antiquis, and thus she would tell no more lies—she was sick of lying after her one great lie. She tried not to think of Kit, but he would come to her on the oddest of occasions—doing her laundry, or when she read her father's books. She would see him standing opposite her, strong face turned towards her, the chestnut hair curling on his shoulders, the green eyes burning at her. He was a ghost who would not leave her alone, who haunted her whether she would or no.

She was working one evening in the early dark, a candle burning on the table before her, listening to Willem go about the house, closing the shutters and locking the doors before repairing to the kitchen where he lived. There was a door at the side of the house which opened on to a lane which ran beside it, and Willem liked to think he guarded it. Lanes in London, in the dark, were dangerous places, best avoided, and Willem had no mind for a house with one young woman and an old servant in it to be broken into. The plague had made men lawless, he said, and, now that the whole of London was in its grip, men were as like to die from marauding bullies come out of Alsatia to rob the deserted houses which plague had robbed of inhabitants as from the plague itself.

All was quiet until she heard noises from outside and the sound of Willem unbolting the side door and leaving the house. After that she heard nothing until Willem, running and breathing hard, came into the room to say, 'Mistress, you must help me. There is a man outside sore injured and in need of help. I heard his attackers running away, but I do not like to leave him.'

Celia rose and followed him. She saw a man half lying on the step before the door, half of him lying in the alley. She bent down to touch him, a little fearful that Willem might be mistaken, that he had collapsed when stricken by the plague. Only as she straightened up a little, after touching his face gently, she could see, by the light of the candle which Willem had carried with him from the kitchen, that there was blood on her hand. . .

She was in one of her trances and yet not in it. She had twice had this vision when she had been with Kit and, full of a great fear, she bent down again to turn the man's face towards Willem's candle.

As her trance had suggested, it was Kit, his face swollen and bruised, blood running from a wound on his temple, the chestnut curls dabbled and matted with it. There was blood on his fine coat and he lay quite still, with no sign of life about him. A dreadful fear that he was already dead seized Celia. She gave a low moan and picked up his wrist to find the pulse in it, the pulse which told that life was still in a man, as Adam had said, to find it beating steadily.

'I know who it is,' she said to Willem. 'It is the

court gallant who visited me before Father died, who came with the Duke of Buckingham. I do not think he has collapsed with the plague—see, he has been cruelly beaten. We must take him into the house.'

'He is a big man,' said Willem doubtfully, looking at Kit's long length stretched along the ground, 'but we will try, mistress.'

Together they wrestled Kit to his feet and their pulling him about disturbed him. He gave a low groan as they placed his arms around each of their shoulders and he returned to consciousness sufficiently for them to half drag, half walk him into the kitchen, where he collapsed again to lie sprawled on the floor.

Willem stared at him. In the greater light of the kitchen they could plainly see that he had been most brutally treated. His face was swelling, one eye was black and, by the state of his clothing, he had been heavily clubbed about the body. 'No getting him to bed in this condition, mistress, I'd best fetch Job Potter to help me.'

Job was their neighbour and he and his wife had been among the few people to be kind to her after the ballad had been sung about the City streets. She did not say Willem nay and, after he had gone, she sat on the floor and taking a damp cloth began to wipe the blood from Kit's face and hair. She wondered what he had been doing in or near the Strand to be attacked. Had he come looking for her, and why? Useless to speculate, as Adam had often said, about that which we may not know, but can only guess at.

She was still occupied with this when Willem

arrived with Job, who also stared doubtfully at Kit and his fine clothing. 'You're main sure that he has not taken the plague, Mistress Celia?' was all he said.

'He hath not the plague, I would dare swear,' replied Celia. 'I would have him taken upstairs to Father's bed and only you and Willem can do that for him. But, if you are doubtful, I give you leave to examine him for the signs of the plague, for I am sure that you know them as well as I do.'

'Aye, I will that,' Job grunted. 'And if he hath the plague, why, then, your house must be shut up, the cross put on it and the authorities notified.'

He knelt down by Kit and with Willem's help stripped the clothes from him and began to examine his trunk and groin for the signs of buboes, boils or any other signs of the plague. As Celia had expected they found none. Besides, with his clothes gone, the marks of the beating were strong on him. Celia ran upstairs to fetch one of Adam's fine linen bedgowns to place upon him before they carried him to Adam's bed.

'Damn those who did this,' was all Job said as he straightened up. 'London is a foul city since the plague came, with every man's hand against everyone else. They are saying that those who have the plague run into the street to spit into the faces of those not so afflicted, so that they, too, may die. And the bullies from the dens of St Giles and from Alsatia roam the streets murdering and robbing. Strange,' he muttered, peering at Kit's great ruby ring, still on his finger. 'They did not rob him. He still wears his jewellery.'

'I think that I interrupted them at their wicked

work,' said Willem while they dressed Kit in Adam's
gown. Together he and Job carried him to where
Celia had never expected to see him—to the room
where her father had lived and died—to lie, deeply
unconscious, in Adam's great four-poster. He had
groaned once as they hauled him upstairs but when
he was finally placed on the bed he lay there
unmoving, his face ashen, as white as the pillows
against which it was propped.

'Bad blows about the head and shoulders, those,'
Job observed, inspecting him. 'You will need all
your arts to keep him alive, mistress,' was his final
offering to her before he left.

Celia feared that he spoke true. She ordered
Willem to bring her a bowl of warm water, cloths
and linen to bandage Kit's head and the other
wounds which she found upon him. His torso was
beginning to display the marks of heavy bruising and
she did not like it that he showed no signs of
knowing where he was or what was being done to
him as she administered to him as best she could.

He had been a ghost, who now was with her. But
the ghost had more life in him than the living man.
The chestnut curls were dull, the green eyes were
closed and the beautiful singing voice was mute—
and she feared that she might never hear it again.

Yet he was hers as he might never be again, living
or dead. Had she conjured him here, by thinking on
him? And when she had seen him like this in her
trances, although she had not known him then, had
she laid a sign on him that he might come to this
place to be beaten nigh to death so that she might
tend him?

Oh, she hoped not, she truly hoped not. She

would carry out an election to discover what might happen to him, whether he might live or die. She had hated him for treating her and all women in such despite but, laid low as he was, she could not but pity him. She tried to think that she did not love him, that her love had dropped dead when she had discovered how he had deceived her, but if she were to hold to the truth, to purge the great lie which she had told, then she must be honest and confess that she loved him still.

CHAPTER NINE

'GOD's blood, this is not to be borne! Who hath written this mock of her and me? For sure, I'll have his blood!'

Kit was in a fever of rage. No one had dared to tell him of the ballad but one day, going into his room, all of a sweat after a hard game of tennis with the King, he found lying on the broad windowsill one of the crude sheets circulating around London. Below the bawdy words mocking at Celia and himself a stave of music was printed—it was written to be sung to a tune already popular.

Someone had left it there for him to find and the sweat turned cold upon him as he read it. Did she know of this? Worst of all, could it be that she might think that he had written it? She knew that he wrote songs and she would know that someone from the court had written this, so why not Kit? For revenge, if nothing else.

He crumpled the paper fiercely in his fist and then, just as he was, dishevelled, stinking from the game, he went in search of Buckingham. He found him in one of the privy gardens, immaculately dressed, holding court, his sycophants about him.

Kit thrust the paper in his face, regardless of protocol. Buckingham was supposed to be his friend; had he done this to Celia—and to him? What was friendship to George? Celia had called him

160

weathercock. In later years, the poet Dryden was to call him worse.

'Is this your handiwork, George? Is it?'

Buckingham took the paper disdainfully and looked at it with an expression equally so.

'Oh, this. Yes, I have heard this sung. Who gave you this, Kit?'

'A friend or an enemy left this in my room for me to find. Does it matter? You have not answered my question.'

'Well, I left you not the paper.' He looked Kit full in the eye as he spoke, which meant nothing; Buckingham looked everyone full in the eye as he betrayed them. 'I am thy friend, Kit. Such a question doth not deserve an answer.' Buckingham gave Kit his shoulder instead. 'Shame on thee, Kit. There were nigh an hundred present that night when Mistress Celia told us of thy triumph. Why be ashamed of it now, man?'

Kit wanted to kill everyone. Most of all he wanted to kill himself, who—and Buckingham was right about that—had brought her to this pass by betting on her virtue.

And now her name was bandied about the streets as whore and trull. He must see her, he must, to tell her that he had not written this thing, had not exposed her to the world's mock. Vilely though Kit Carlyon had behaved towards her, he was not so vile as this, to take his revenge after such a fashion.

He flung the crumpled paper at Buckingham's feet, and said, in as cold a voice as he could muster, 'I do not know what to believe any more, George. I suppose that I must accept that what you have said is true.'

'Oh, better so,' returned Buckingham carelessly, 'for we are old friends, Kit, and go back to the days when we scoured Europe in rags, eh? Find out who did this and kill him for me.'

The red rage was on Kit again, but he had no one towards whom to direct it. 'Oh, depend on it, George. If I find him he shall die slow.' He walked away rapidly, almost running, for he could not bear himself, or anyone else for that matter, and must be alone for a space before he visited Celia.

Buckingham watched him go. The game was shaping even better than he had expected. When he had written the song and passed it through one of his agents to the printer he had hoped that it might start the hare running again, and so it had. The hare was almost running down the walkway!

He had taken even more of a hand by slyly remarking, in front of Dorothy Lowther, that the cream of the joke about the song was that Kit, one of the chief actors in it, still did not know of its existence, that his mistress was the butt of London.

She had taken the hint to some effect, he was sure, for she was still voicing her hatred of Kit daily, and had somehow made certain that he learned of the song. He must reward the whore after some fashion, for Kit was about to chase after his mistress to assure her, doubtless, that it was not he who had betrayed their amours! Oh, there was more to come from this; it was a better entertainment than a play, for this was life, and life was always better than its mimicry—either on the stage or in a book.

Kit might wish that he were living in a book, since real life had become so unendurable. He must wait, as Robert Renwick had thought that he would, for the evening and the friendly dark to come before he visited Celia.

To go to her in the day meant that he might be seen and more gossip would roar around London and the court. Unaware that two groups of spies were watching both him and Celia, he changed himself into something decent, but not gaudy, for he had no wish to play the fine court gallant with her. Sobriety might convince her of his innocence.

All in black, with silver trimmings, the chestnut locks new-washed to rid him of the stench of the game, his best rapier of Damascene steel by one side and a dagger at the other—for he had learned to fence with both sword and dagger in Italy— Kit set out for the Strand as dusk fell.

The boatman took him downstream to disembark at the steps on the Strand near to Celia's home. He ignored the wherry which followed him, which One-Eye had hired when his watch at Whitehall told him that Sir Christopher Carlyon was making for the City.

'To visit his doxy at last, as Jude Scrivener prophesied,' he said coarsely to his aide. 'Darkness having fallen, a new kind of darkness might fall on the good Sir Kit.'

Kit was tracked as he walked along the Strand to Celia's home. There were few in the streets, the plague kept most indoors, and even the prophets of doom who ran about the city shouting 'Woe! Woe! The new Babylon is doomed by a just God,' had retired to their haunts. He had reached the small lane which ran by the Antiquises' home when One-Eye and his companions struck.

They caught him by the throat from behind, an

old trick which left the victim voiceless as well as helpless, and dragged him into the alley to thrash him senseless. 'Not to kill him,' roared One-Eye at his subordinate, who showed a distinct desire to slaughter a fine gentleman when he had one at his mercy.

George Buckingham's spy watched them from his post which gave him sight of the house and of Celia's and Willem's comings and goings. He would have something meaty to report to His Grace tonight, and no mistake! For he had recognised Kit at the moment when One-Eye took him by the throat.

Kit was aware of very little. One moment he had been walking along the Strand hoping to see his beloved again—for she was his beloved, he now recognised—and in the next he was strangling, stifling, the world growing dark, before a brutal blow on the head deprived him almost completely of his senses.

Not quite, however, for as he fell to the ground, instinct taking over, his hand went to his rapier, to be clubbed away by one of his assailants—he had no idea of how many there were. Pain and confusion followed. Then the worst pain stopped but a general pain remained. He had been hurt—how badly, his failing senses did not tell him.

He tried to drag himself towards the Antiquises' home—again he was driven more by instinct than by any use of reason. He no longer knew who, what or where he was, only that he needed refuge. For a moment after Celia and Willem had found him and dragged him indoors he was aware that he was being helped and tried to speak, except that the effort was so great that the next thing he knew he was lying on a hard floor and someone was stripping him. He tried to speak again, failed, and the world fell in on him again. He returned to semi-consciousness, to know that—— What was it he knew? Was he in a bed? Or was he lying on a battlefield?

Conscious thought stopped and he was dreaming or, rather, he thought that he was living in the past, but was not aware that it was the past, or that it was a dream, only that there was a woman with him and. . .the woman was Anna.

The woman's arms were around him, she was holding him up, wiping his face. It must be Anna, but somehow he knew that it could not be Anna. There was something wrong with his sight. A minute ago he had seen her, but now he could not. He could only feel her gentle hands, soothing his pain.

He turned his head, or thought he did, to where the woman might be and said, strongly he thought, but in truth it was a whisper, 'Anna, my darling, is that you, Anna?' and then fell into the dark again. . .

Celia had seen Kit struggle towards consciousness as she tended him. He was restless, moving his head from side to side as she applied a soothing lotion of herbs to his bruised face which was swelling rapidly. He grasped weakly at her hand, looked at her with blind eyes and whispered, 'Anna, my darling, is that you, Anna?' Then his eyes rolled into his head and he fell forward so that she was compelled to catch him and lie him down against the pillows.

Willem, who had been holding the bowl and had heard Kit whisper, but did not know what he had said, murmered anxiously, 'Can you manage him, mistress? Let me help you if he grows fractious in his delirium.'

'He is peaceful at the moment.' Celia leaned forward to wipe Kit's face again. It was easier to tend him now that he was lying unconscious and spent in Adam's bed. She had heard the woman's name and a pang smote her.

Who was Anna? Was she one of the women about the court whom she had not met? He had called her his darling. She might have known that Kit Carlyon would have a darling and that the darling's name would not be Celia! But she must forget that, for it was plain that he was sorely hurt and must be cared for as gently as possible. Neither she, nor Willem, who had often helped her father, thought that any bones were broken — but the head wound was a bad one, and was keeping him from recovering his consciousness. Head wounds were strange and dangerous things and men often died from them quite suddenly, although occasionally death was slow and the patient never fully recovered himself.

The seat of reason, Adam had said of the head, and when that seat was shaken and damaged only a very wise man knew how to help the patient recover it. God grant that Kit was not so badly hurt that he slipped from life without a murmur — other than his words about Anna.

Celia made a swift resolution. She would not allow her emotions, either of love or anger towards Kit, to prevent her from being a good nurse to him. He must not be left alone. Either she or Willem must tend him and they would take alternate watches as she had seen her father do with his patients. Neither Adam nor she had a licence to practise medicine, but astrologers were unofficial doctors, particularly among the poor who could not pay an official one. The astrologers did not call what they did practising medicine; it was healing through their arcane astrological knowledge, they said, and Celia wished that she had Kit's birth horoscope so that she could help him the more easily.

As it was, she would have to cast an horary for him and trust that the auguries would be hopeful. She left the bedcurtains drawn, bade Willem stay to watch him, and then went down to change into clean and simple clothing; to wash her hands after tending him—as Adam had instructed; to eat, although the food stuck in her throat. Adam had always said that the nurse must be as strong as he or she could be and transmit that strength to the patient.

At the door she cast a last glance at him. He was lying immobile, propped against the pillows. The ashen look on his face was disappearing, and there was a flush present which she did not like. But no matter of that. The doctor dealt with what he saw and not what he wished to see. Self-deception was the worst of all things, Adam had often said, benefitting neither agent nor patient, and she must remember that and all his other wise words. Every now and then Kit twitched and shuddered so that Celia wondered whether he was dreaming; once he cried out and plucked at the bedclothes.

If he was restless, although apparently asleep, she would have to quieten him with a tincture of poppy, but she hoped that would not be needed. Meantime she must prepare herself for her vigil, for she would take the night hours, those being the ones in which a patient was the most at risk.

* * *

Kit was in a place which he had not thought of for many years. He was on a wide beach, walking with Anna. The sea was tideless. He knew that it was the Mediterranean, that sea in the middle of the earth, which once he had never thought to visit.

It was six long years since he had fled Worcester field and England to leave his bedridden father behind. He had been the last child of his father's old age and his second marriage, and his mother had died within six months of his birth, her duty done. Her marriage had been an arranged one to get Sir Christoper an heir in the place of the one who had died at twenty-one of the sweating sickness while with the court at London.

He had shown Kit a distant affection, and what would have happened if the Civil War had not broken out was not to be known. Kit was seventeen and went to war in his father's place. Sir Christopher was nearly seventy and could not do his duty to his King, so he sent Kit instead. Father and son never met again after Kit rode out to join King Charles's army with a small band of ill-armed tenants. The Carlyons were not then poor, but Cromwell's triumph at Worcester made them so. Sir Christopher, ailing and near to death, was compelled to make a forced sale to a Cromwellian merchant, leaving himself only with the manor house and the little piece of scrub around it.

He died knowing that Kit had no true inheritance, for the forced sale brought only a derisory pittance, but sale it was, which meant that, years later, when Kit returned with his king, the Cromwellian merchant kept it. Only those who lost lands by confiscation could claim them back. The Captain submitted that Sir Christopher had sold him his lands willingly and there was none to give him nay.

Kit, living on the Continent after escaping England, knew nothing of this. He stayed for a little time with the King, but grew restive under the unwilling charity meted out by the courts of Europe to the unfortunates who had lost lands, home and King to the Protectorate. Charles granted him permission to leave to become a soldier and he travelled into Italy to join a company of mercenaries who hired themselves out to protect merchant adventurers against the predatory Turks, acting as pirates on the sea and land, claiming all that they could capture as theirs.

And then, at last, in southern Italy he found a haven and a home in one of the small ports along the rocky coast. By now he had a little band of his own and was hired by an ageing merchant to protect his modest fleet of ships on a trip across the Aegean sea.

Kit had learned seamanship and the management of ships, as well as gaining proficiency in Italian. He liked Italy and the civilised arts of living in the peninsula. It was there that he began to play the guitar and to sing—Italy was a land of music. His success with the merchant led to his permanent hire and the merchant took him to his home in the little settlement high above the small port, where his company had its headquarters, and there he met Anna, with whom he walked along the beach.

He had married her shortly after meeting her. Eighteen years old, dark and fiery in appearance and temperament, she had taken one look at Kit and determined that he should be hers. Kit's

passionate response to Anna had been no less imme-
diate and Anna's father, growing old, was pleased
to allow their marriage. His daughter had gained a
protector who would be well able to look after her
when he had gone. Kit had assured him that he had
no wish to return to England—news of his father's
death and the loss of his inheritance had reached
him while he was still in France with King Charles.
There was nothing left for him in England; he had
come to love Italy and had found there the love of
his life

And now he was to accompany his father-in-law's
fleet to a North African port with an important
cargo, leaving behind Anna, her father, whose
health was beginning to fail, and his six-month-old
son whom Anna held in her arms as they walked
along the strand for the last time before Kit set sail.
The Italian love of children was something which
Kit appreciated and after a time he took small Cecco
from Anna's arms and carried the child himself,
looking tenderly down at his son's green eyes and
the curling chestnut hair which had begun to succeed
the sparse blond locks of the newly born baby.

All through his lonely boyhood and youth he had
been starved of affection and now he had found it in
abundance in Italy. He was astonished at the passion
of his own nature—he had thought himself cold.
Italy and Anna had taught him that he was not. She
was speaking to him.

'Ah, Cristoforo mine, I wish that you were not
leaving me. Can you not stay? I know it is stupid of
me, but I have a fear of this voyage.'

He leaned over and kissed her.

The Kit who lay in Adam Antiquis's bed was both

remembering and reliving this little scene. It was as though he were there and not there. He knew it was the past and yet it was more present to him than the life which he had been living at Whitehall since King Charles II's restoration. He even remembered that he had met another woman whom he now loved as passionately as he had loved Anna, but with a seasoned man's love, not the love of a young man scarcely out of his boyhood.

In his dream Anna and Celia had become mixed. When he looked away from Anna it was Celia he saw, her smooth fair hair and grave grey eyes, not Anna's wild curls and passionate black orbs. Who was it with him on the shore and by the bed in which he lay and dreamed of the lost past? Anna, or this other?

He answered Anna because she was looking at him and waiting for him to speak. 'It will not be for long that I am gone,' he had said, and the Kit who was dreaming could have wept at what he was saying, 'and your father has promised me that when I return he will teach me to run his business and we shall hire others to go with the fleet so that I need not leave you, or the business. And we shall build a house high in the hills and found a family which will rival the Medici in Florence!'

He was teasing her and she knew it, and threw him a glance so passionate that he almost wished that Cecco was not with them so that he might take her in his arms and make love to her on the sand, the sound of the sea strong in their ears and the wild birds calling overhead.

The scene was as fresh as though he were genuinely experiencing it, as though it were not past and gone, and as though what had come after it had never happened. He had never told anyone of his life in Italy. He had tried to forget it because living in the past would have unmanned him, and he could have sworn that he could not even remember Anna's face and yet here she was, walking with him—and how could that be?

For a moment the seascape shimmered before him; he was no longer holding his son; Anna was not there. Someone was speaking to him, and Anna, Cecco and the south Italian beach were all whirled away into the dark into which Anna and Cecco had disappeared so long ago. Was it important that he should respond to that voice?

'Anna,' he whispered and for a moment she was before him, then a man's voice spoke and she disappeared again. Someone was holding his head and spooning something into his mouth, and after that he knew nothing—either of Anna, Cecco, or the man and woman who were tending him. The kindly dark swallowed him, and he was at last at peace.

Willem, who had been holding him up, looked across Kit as he laid him down. It was the following morning and he had fetched Celia, whom he had relieved of her vigil a bare hour agone, from her bed, because he felt that Kit was failing. He was growing visibly weaker and, when Willem spoke and tried to rouse him, would not respond. Celia had come into the bedroom in her night rail and had ministered to the injured man, finally fetching a tincture of poppy which she had prepared before she had gone to her rest and had poured it down Kit's throat to relieve his distress.

He had tried to sit up and began to speak in a strange language to the woman, Anna, and to someone called Cecco with such grief in his voice that Celia knew that she must relieve his pain if he were to stand any chance of recovery. The poppy took him in its arms and rocked him to sleep, as Adam had once described its effect, telling Celia never to give too strong a draught or the patient might die.

Well, she had given Kit a strong draught to relieve him of his misery—but what draught could she take to relieve hers?

She left Willem with an injunction to rouse her if Kit's condition troubled him, and she looked at the sleeping man with such an agonised expression that Willem could hardly bear to gaze on the face of the mistress whom he loved. Like Celia, he wondered who the woman was who haunted the man on the bed.

He said to Celia as she stood by the door, 'He called on you, mistress, several times when he was rambling in his mind. He spoke of this Anna who troubles him and then, at the end, he called out your name again quite strongly, almost as though he knew that you were tending him. But the head wound has addled his wits, and he knoweth not what he says.'

Celia spoke the thought which she was trying to dismiss. 'Suppose he never recovers himself? Father said that head wounds were parlous things, and he hath a bad one.'

'Nay, mistress,' replied Willem firmly. 'Never think the worst 'til it hath happened. Have hope that all will be well under your ministrations. Perchance later he will be himself.'

But he was not. Neither that day, nor the next. Whatever they did for him, he knew not who they were. His eyes were open, he looked at them, but he seemed blind, except that once, with the curtains drawn and the cruel sunlight of that hot and doomed summer shining into his eyes, he threw his arm across them to escape its radiance—so, Celia said, proving that he could see, even if he knew not what he saw.

It was almost, she thought despairingly, late one night when she was sitting by his bedside wearing her night rail, that he did not want to see her. He walked with Anna and Cecco on a seashore, by what he said—and sometimes with her. Once he was in the privy garden at Whitehall with her, reliving the time when they had examined the sundial together, early in their acquaintance.

She had put her hands gently on each side of his head and turned his unseeing eyes towards her and looked into their brilliant green depth, saying, 'Kit, look at me. Who do you see?'

He had twisted his head away and answered her almost pettishly, 'Nothing, I see nothing,' as though he were happier walking with his ghosts by the sea.

Once he said, 'Oh, I love thee, oh, how I love thee,' although whether he said it to her or to the woman Anna she could not tell.

Tiredness of mind and body enveloped her. That afternoon, as she had left the house after a brief sleep to go to market, the dead cart had come by. She had seen it often and often but, perhaps because of Kit's parlous state, it had not had the emotional effect on her which seeing it that morning possessed.

She had looked at the heap of corpses sprawled in it, the rictus of death on their faces, limbs disarrayed, haphazard, with the cry, 'Bring out your dead,' ringing over their unheeding ears. The death toll had grown so high that the bodies of the victims were being thrown into common pits, pell-mell, with no mourners, those who tended the pits frantic to cover the bodies in them at all speed so that the contagion should not spread from them to others— or to the diggers themselves.

The sight made her more worried than ever over Kit's condition. Suppose that in his weakened state he somehow contracted the plague? There were on many doors in the Strand now the red crosses that showed that the plague raged inside them. Doctors, she was told, were refusing to visit the plague-stricken and the exodus from London of those who could afford to leave it grew daily. Grass had begun to grow in the streets and the unnatural heat worsened the sense of doom in the city.

'If only it would rain,' Celia found herself saying. She tried to imagine it—tried to call up the scent of fresh rain on grass, the blessed cool of it. She would never complain about rain again. Like Adam, she began to think that perhaps the heat and the plague were associated. Certainly she thought that it was the heat which was bringing the black rats above ground and had them running about the streets instead of hiding from men as had been their customary habit. It was the heat which had made her throw off her stifling clothes to put on her nightgown and sit in that.

A movement and a cry from Kit broke her sad reverie. She moved from the bed to see what ailed him. He looked up at her when she approached, a puzzled expression on his face. He had been walking with a woman in his delirium, but who the woman was he did not know. Only that it was someone whom he dearly loved.

There was a woman by him. He could smell her subtle scent, feel her gentle hand as she bathed his face. A plait of soft and sweet-smelling hair fell across his face, and a *frisson* of delight ran through him.

Celia, who had wetted his face to relieve his fever, was astonished to find that it had almost gone and that he was cool again—although he was still in the grip of the delusions which had afflicted him since he had been brought to Adam's bed. He put up a hand to stroke her face and then, quite suddenly, with a strength which she thought that he had lost, he caught her by the wrist and pulled her towards him.

'My love,' he said, 'come lie with me,' and his hand stroked the breast so close to him. The delight was now Celia's. She looked straight into his tortured face as his hand clenched on her, and she thought that if he were asking for comfort then she would give it to him.

Was it Celia Antiquis who lifted the bedclothes and slipped into the bed to lie beside Kit Carlyon, to take him in her arms, to cradle his head, with its damp chestnut curls, on her breast so that he lay there passive and quiet as he had not been since Job and Willem had brought him upstairs?

Was it Celia Antiquis who, when he dreamily

turned his head to suck at her breast through the light cloth of her gown, held it there until she felt his breathing change and for the first time he fell into a natural sleep?

Was it Celia Antiquis who remained in the bed, with him warm against her, his body—despite its illness—hard as hers was soft, rejoicing that she had given him peace, that he no longer roved in his dreams, but gently breathed on her bosom. She thought that she would not sleep, and she did not, but fell into a doze.

At what time of night was it that Kit awoke, still lost in the land of dreams in which he had lived since being assaulted in the alley, to find that he lay in the arms of a warm and loving woman who stroked his head in his sleep? Did it matter that his natural instinct was to lift himself above the woman, to begin to kiss and caress her in that sleep of dreams where he was now, not with Anna, but with Celia whom he thought that he had forever lost?

It was a dream, of course, for Celia was gone, but the dream was so satisfactory and pleasant that he did not want to wake from it as he put his mouth to the sleeping woman's and began to kiss her and to caress her soft, warm body with his hands.

Celia awoke from her doze, a doze in which she was dreaming that she was in Kit's arms, to find that that was where she truly was, and that he was slipping the nightgown from her shoulders. For a moment she flinched from him, looking into blind eyes which did not know her. His fever had gone, it was plain, but Kit Carlyon was not in this world but one of his own, a refuge from a reality which had become too harsh to bear.

There was a moment when Celia could have slipped from under him, escaped from him, kept the maidenhood which she still possessed, even though she had publicly denied it. What kept her with him she did not know. Perhaps it was because she loved him, and might never have him otherwise. Perhaps it was because if she gave him what he wanted then he would not have gained Latter on a lie and could live there in peace. Perhaps it was to help to heal him, to bring back his confused senses.

Perhaps it was all of these things—or none of them. Just the instinct of a woman with the man she loved, an instinct as old as time, that had been with men and women before they were truly men and women and would be with them—if the race were to continue—as long as men and women lived on earth together. Or was it the love of God? Or simply that the horoscope which Celia had cast had told her that she and Kit would come together after a fashion which was past understanding, and this strange meeting supported what the horoscope told her?

Whatever it was, thought vanished, and she was with Kit in his dream world where he was pleasuring his true love Celia who had come back to him, calling her name as he did do; where for a moment as virginity was lost she felt a brief pain, but he was being so gentle with her in his lost world that even that did not last and together they scaled the heights which men and women, occasionally—certainly not always—reached.

Afterwards there were tears in Kit's eyes—as there were in Celia's. In his dream Kit knew that there was something he must do. There was a ring on his finger which he must give away in exchange for what he had just won. The love of a virgin who had given herself to him as sweetly as a woman might.

He lifted his hand, slipped the ruby from it, took the woman's left hand and slipped the ring on its third finger. He thought that he said, but was not sure, 'With this ring, I thee wed,' and, having spoken, he laid down his head again on her soft bosom and fell into a deep sleep.

After a time, Celia slipped from the bed where she had been blessed as few women were, and wondered who Kit had thought that he had lain with. She was not sure that he really knew who she was, even though he had called her name in their final transports. The first thing she was sure of was that he was at peace. The second thing was that he could no longer stay with her. She did not want him to awaken and remember—and then deal with her out of shame for what he had done, or pity for her. He was Anna's, and had never been hers. She had been the subject of a bet for which he had, perhaps, felt a little remorse, and she had given him, as much as she could, a certain healing.

For a time he had been hers, but no longer. He must go back whence he came, to be healed by the grand physicians of King Charles's court—if it were that he could be healed. He had given her what she had wanted since she met him—himself, and together they had celebrated in innocence, like Adam and Eve before the Fall, what in knowledge could not be.

She would send him back to the court and, if he recovered, he might perhaps have a dream of a shared love—and wonder where his ring had gone.

She would take the ruby he had given her as an exchange for Latter, for she had whispered that in his ear as he had fallen asleep. Perchance he would remember and be glad, even if he forgot Celia Antiquis, the astrologer's daughter.

CHAPTER TEN

WILLEM knew his way about Whitehall a little. The last time he had visited it, it had been busy—men and women everywhere. Now, it was deserted. The porter at the gate had told him that my lord of Buckingham was still in residence, but was preparing to leave. The King had already gone to Salisbury and after that would make for Oxford, from where he would govern the country—plague-stricken London was not safe to live in.

He looked doubtfully at the litter on which Kit lay, still unconscious, Celia having dosed him with a small draught of poppy to keep him peaceful on the river journey back to Whitehall.

'You are sure he hath not the plague?'

'My life upon it,' replied Willem firmly. 'I would not palter with the plague. He hath a head injury, as is most plain to see.' And he pointed to Kit's bandaged head. 'He is asleep because those who have tended him when he was not fit to be moved have given him the poppy. He is His Grace of Buckingham's friend and is to be delivered safe to him.'

'Wait, then,' said the porter and called a footman, who had been lounging in the corner of the room and now looked resentfully at Willem, who was making him work by sending him to Buckingham's quarters.

It was some little time before he reappeared.

Buckingham was quite alone, no attendants with him as was usual, strolling behind the footman as though receiving the unconscious body of a lost friend was all in his day's work. He walked over to where Willem stood, the litter on the ground, the two labourers hired to carry it standing to one side, indifferent.

Buckingham looked down at Kit, gave his odd secret smile and drawled at Willem, 'I have seen you before, fellow.'

'Aye, Your Grace.' Willem was not insolent, but was not far from it.

'Mistress Celia Antiquis's man.'

'Aye. Her faithful servant come to deliver your friend, who was attacked and left for dead in the alley outside her home. He hath recovered his health but not his wits and is fit to be given into the care of those who know him and may help him to recover them.'

Buckingham raised his eyebrows. 'Mistress Celia hath nursed him?' he asked, as though he did not already know what his spy had told him of the attack on Kit and Celia's care of him.

'Aye, and having delivered him, now I may go.'

Buckingham whistled a little at this sturdy independence and, capricious as he was—for today he found it amusing, whereas yesterday or tomorrow such behaviour might have gained punishment—he decided to reward it. He pulled a coin from his breeches pocket and tossed it on the ground before Willem.

'Here's for you, then.' And he turned and ordered the two labourers to follow him with the litter.

Willem debated whether to leave the coin where

it lay then decided that it might be unwise to do so,
grunted, and made off with it, his duty done.

Buckingham, who had thought the coin might be
refused, turned to watch him accept it and leave. He
whistled again. The commonalty grew impudent,
but money would always tame them! Now to see Kit
to a decent bed, fetch a surgeon to tend him. His
coming journey must wait, which would annoy his
servants. No matter to that—what were servants for
but to be annoyed by their masters and then do as
they were bid?

As he turned away, something struck him. He
bent down, picked up Kit's hand to inspect it. The
great ruby had gone. His spy had told him that Kit's
assailants had had no time to rob him—so where
had the ring gone? He replaced Kit's hand carefully
and tucked the blanket which covered him over the
bereft fingers—another interesting puzzle for him to
solve.

Later, the surgeon departed, he sat by Kit's
bedside. His friend had emerged from sleep to stare
at the surgeon and himself—and know neither of
them. So it continued for the next few days. Kit rose
and walked again, but as though he were in a dream.
Occasionally it was plain that he listened to someone; occasionally he spoke the word 'Anna' in a
questioning voice, and once he looked at
Buckingham when he came in to see how he was
and addressed him in Italian, a language of which
Buckingham knew a little. At other times he called
on Celia, once turning in the bed as though to find
her, a hand out, questing.

He wondered sardonically whether Kit Carlyon
would ever find himself again. The doctor, a pedan-

tic man, said that he had met such cases before, that one had remained wandering in his wits perpetually and that another, more fortunate, had recovered them.

'Fortunate for him if he recovers soon,' he said heavily. 'The longer he wanders, the less likely he is to be himself again.'

'Soon.' Buckingham was suddenly impatient. 'He must recover soon. I must be off to Salisbury.'

Since he had left Celia's house, Kit had wandered perpetually on the seashore, sometimes with Anna and sometimes without her. Once or twice he had walked again with Celia in her garden; once he was in bed with her enjoying such raptures that he awoke, roused, but could not remember why he should be so nor with whom he had been. Dimly, at the moment of waking, he knew that such moments were important to him, more important to him in some ways than the interludes on the beach, but he felt uneasy with the grave-eyed nymph who walked by his side. When he was fully awake he could not recall the women with whom he had been, and stared at Buckingham and the doctor before turning his face away and refusing to speak to them.

When Kit recovered himself, more than a fortnight later, it was quite sudden. He was half seated, half lying, dozing in a great chair by an open window, his man with him. He was on the beach again. Lately Anna had not walked with him. On the last occasions on which she had she had become insubstantial, whereas Celia had become the more real.

It was as though the sea, the sun and the small cloud at the corner of his vision were becoming transparent. What if they became completely so—what would he see then? And what am I doing here? This has not been my home these eight long years? As he asked these questions it was as though a great bell tolled in his mind and a kaleidoscope of incidents from his past swam before him.

He was at Worcester field again—beside him, a cannon ball had taken the head from the shoulders of one of the tenants who had marched with him to the battle. He was on a ship, fighting across its slippery deck. He was on horseback, cutting with his sword at someone who was below him. He was in a bright room, staring with shock at a grey-eyed woman who was holding him in despite. And, lastly, he was in an alley, God knew where, being struck at again and again; his senses were failing. . . He cried out, and was awake, broad awake.

He was sitting in his room at Whitehall Palace. A man was shaking him, he looked up and it was Caleb.

'How came I here?' he exclaimed, and looked around him, Anna and the beach and all the other dreams fading from his mind like shadows, gone now that he was himself in the full light of day again. 'Caleb! Where have I been?'

'Oh, praise be to God, Sir Kit, you are back with us again!'

'Back again,' he repeated stupidly, shaking his head to try to clear it. 'Why, have I been away?'

He knew as he spoke that he had travelled a long distance in space and time. His last memory was of leaving Whitehall to go to find Celia, to apologise to her, to tell her that he loved her.

So how came he here? he asked himself. Caleb,

satisfied that Kit was safe to leave, ran into the corridor to call a footman and bid him tell His Grace of Buckingham that Sir Kit's wits were no longer wandering.

Kit heard him in some wonder. His last memory, although he did not know it, was of some month agone, and the time he had spent in limbo was unknown to him, vanished. He knew that he had dreamed of Anna, and of Celia, but vaguely, after the fashion of a man who had been dreaming and who, on awakening, felt the dream fast fading from him.

After a little time, during which Caleb brought Kit French brandy to drink—for on recovering he had lost what little colour he possessed—Buckingham came in. He was plainly dressed, as though for a journey, and wore no wig but a silk turban twisted around his head.

'So, you are back with us.' He was abrupt, almost severe, as though Kit had been fooling for the past weeks.

'I had not known I was missing.' Kit tried to rise but felt his weakness and said, startled, 'I have been ill?'

'Ill and out of your wits,' agreed Buckingham. 'What do you remember?' His eyes, hard and keen, were on Kit. Kit felt as though Buckingham were sitting in judgement on him. His head had begun to ache vilely. 'Nothing,' he answered, mouth twisted a little wryly. 'I remember that I left Whitehall in the evening, and then. . .nothing. My head hurts. Was I attacked?'

'You do not remember the attack?' Buckingham was clinical.

Kit had a vague memory of pain. 'No. I was on my way to see Mistress Antiquis, but all I can truly recall is taking the boat to carry me to the Strand, and after that nothing.' He looked feverishly at Buckingham. 'I must see her, George. I must. I behaved most vilely to her last week. . .'

'Last week!' Mercurial as ever, Buckingham began to laugh. The judge, the doctor, were gone; he was the bawdy jester of Charles's court again.

'Why, you have been a month anonymous, my friend, wandering where you might, anywhere but where you actually were. The King and Court have left Whitehall, and I have been waiting for Kit Carlyon to be himself again. I am for Salisbury, and you, when you are fit to travel, my friend, must go to claim Latter before you visit King or Court again.'

'Ah, Latter,' replied Kit. He wondered why the sound of it did not cause in him the feelings of pain and distaste which he had felt before his illness. On the contrary, he was eager to see it—he had been given permission to go there. . .by whom? he wondered hazily. 'Yes, I will go to Latter, but not before I have visited Mistress Antiquis in the Strand to ask her pardon.'

'Ah, yes, that,' murmered Buckingham, turning away to look out of the window, a wicked smile on his face. 'When the surgeon says that you may, and then to Latter. I will give your regrets to the King and tell him you will visit Whitehall when he returns and you are truly healed.'

'And you have caused me to be looked after, George? You are a true friend.'

'Oh, am I not.' Now Buckingham's smile was wry. 'Well, you are yourself again and I shall leave, knowing that.' He put out his hand and Kit clasped it in gratitude. Buckingham made him a great leg and walked out of the door, laughing to himself. 'Oh, go to the Strand by all means, Kit Carlyon, and pray God that you enjoy what you find there!'

The game was not yet over, and George Buckingham had still a hand to play. Mistress Antiquis was still there for the winning. His spy would keep him informed of all that she did and, as for Kit—he must visit the Strand and ask her to cast him an election or a horoscope. He laughed silently all the way down the corridor and back to his rooms to prepare himself and his train to leave.

It was a week, an impatient week, before Kit was allowed by the surgeon to visit the Strand. He had discovered the loss of his ring shortly after Buckingham left him. The thieves who had attacked him must have made off with it and the thought pained him. Anna had given it to him on their wedding-day, and now it was gone.

Or so he thought, but on the first night of his recovery he dreamed again—a fair dream, a dream which he remembered, a peaceful dream which soothed his soul. He was in bed with Celia, and even in his dream that surprised him and, after he had made love to her, he had given her his ring, slipped it on her finger, told her she was his wife, and then he had awoken, trembling. He thought that after he had given her the ruby she had given him some instruction, but he could not remember what it was. For sure, he had thought, as sleep left him, the ring is not lost. Waking told him that it was.

Two nights later, he dreamed the dream again, the same at all points, and he awoke at the same moment. He was impatient with himself. Impatient to see Celia, to ask for forgiveness, perhaps for more than forgiveness. . .

This hope buoyed him up as he made his unwillingly deferred journey to see her. Dressed in sombre magnificence, with Caleb and a footman behind him—for they had told him that the City streets, ravaged by the plague, were now dangerous for the well-dressed on their own—he made his way up the river steps to the Strand to find that nearly every house on it had a red cross on its door. Pray God that she still lives, was his inmost thought. To recover himself, and find that his love was gone— God could not be so cruel. But he knew that He could.

Praise be to Him. The houses on each side of hers had the fatal cross, but hers was virgin. He hammered upon it, hardly able to bear the delay which would follow before Willem came. But no one came. The house was shrouded and silent. He made his way down the side alley, where he had been attacked over a month agone, to find that the garden was neglected and there was no sign that any lived there.

Desolate, he walked to the front again to try one last despairing fusillade on the door. A dog ran down the deserted street, followed by a shambling man who stared at him as he stood there in his misery. Celia was gone, or dead, and he had no means of knowing which supposition was true. For the third time his life had disintegrated around him. The Lord his God was a cruel God and had no mercy on the poor sinner who was Kit Carlyon!

The old man stared at him and Kit asked, his voice cracking, 'Pray, sir, can you tell me what hath happened to Mistress Antiquis and her household who dwelled here? For there is none else to ask, the plague having taken her neighbours. Did the plague take her?'

The old man looked at him. 'Nay, sir. Mistress Antiquis left this house before the plague arrived in the Strand, taking with her her servant and many of her goods and chattels.' He paused, and then forestalled Kit's question. 'I have no notion of whither she went, save that it was somewhere in London— or perhaps it wasn't. I know that her housekeeper retired to the country, and so may she have done.'

'No more than that?'

The agony on his face was such that the old man said gently, 'Why, fair sir, I would help you if I could, but I cannot. I think Job who lived next to her knew, but Job and all his family were taken away in the death cart nigh on a sennight, now.'

And that was it. She had gone. And where she had gone, he might not know. While his wits were straying, she had strayed from him. Buckingham had suggested that he had been nursed for a week before he had been left on a litter at Whitehall. Had Celia cared for him? Or had it been another? He would never now know.

It was only as he was returning home that a thought struck him. An unwelcome thought. He remembered how ambiguously Buckingham had spoken to him of his visiting the Strand. Had he known that Celia had gone? Surely not. Even Buckingham, capricious as he was, would not have treated a friend so cavalierly. He had been kind to him over Latter, and he must repay that kindness. Latter was where he must go. He did not ask himself why he thought this, who before his illness had almost vowed never to go there, but go there he would.

To heal, Buckingham had said. Well, his body would heal—but would his mind and spirit? He would grieve for his lost love, whom he had thrown away before he met her when he had made that accursed bet.

On the morrow, Kit packed and left for Latter.

From the moment when Willem returned after leaving Kit safely with the Duke of Buckingham, Celia had determined to leave the Strand with all speed. Even before Kit had arrived she had resolved to sell the house. Its actual sale would have to await the end of the plague, for during it there was neither buying nor selling. She had enough spare money to buy or to rent a dwelling where she might continue her work, and she would sell the house when the times were more propitious.

She had said goodbye to Job, unaware that she was seeing him for the last time and that she was leaving the Strand before the plague arrived to sweep away most of its inhabitants. She had considered going to Reading and asking Mistress Hart to take her and Willem in for payment received, but had decided against that.

She needed occupation, and there would be nothing for her in Berkshire. London had been her home, and was where a female astrologer and wise woman might practise her mystery. She would go where she was not known, but where Adam's name would be. She had already determined that she would be Celia Archer, the late Master Antiquis's assistant, and those who came to her might make what they would of that.

Willem came to her a week after she had sent Kit back to his own kind to be cared for.

'I have found somewhat for us, mistress, but you must approve of it. It is in the Hamlets nigh to the Tower itself—in its shadow almost—Swain's Yard off Tower Street. It is humble, but it is among those who might wish to visit you and we shall not be spending our treasure on a house which we might not wish to keep.'

Celia smiled at the we. She and Willem were a family now—he was all the family she had, as she was all his. She needed a strong arm to protect her, and Willem was strong, even in middle age.

'Well, very well,' she said. 'Take me to it.'

It was a humble enough property after the grand house on the Strand, but Mistress Archer might set up her signboard there. The plague was raging in the Hamlets, too, but the plague was everywhere; it was impossible to escape it, and she must take her chance, as the rest of London did, that she might, somehow, escape it.

She and Willem packed to leave. Job came to see them off, his honest face sad. 'God be with thee,' he said, and she answered him in kind.

'And with you, Job.' But they both knew that in the plague-stricken London of 1665 there could be no certainty of the future. Only the past was real, had happened, and might be visited. In the present one lived—and endured.

Unknown to her, the Duke's man still continued his watch on her. He had sent word to his master of Mistress Antiquis's move and of her new abode, of which Buckingham had not told Kit, preferring the amusement of allowing him to visit the Strand on a fruitless errand. When he came back to London, with the plague safely ended, why, he might visit the alley off Tower Street—or he might not.

Always Celia hugged the memory of her night with Kit to her. It was only in the third week after he was gone that she came to understand that she might have more tangible evidence of her bedtime discourse with him than her memories alone. She was not blessed with her monthly flowers when they should have come, and she was unblessed with other symptoms which, when she had tended women who thought that they were breeding, had always told her that they were.

Never once, on that ecstatic night, had she thought of such an outcome—which was foolish of her, she knew. She had made love on one occasion and one occasion only and, as the result of it, Celia Antiquis was carrying her lover's child. The lover who had not known with whom he was lying, but who had given her such pleasure that the memory of it was enough to dim the pains of bringing a fatherless bastard into the world. Even more must she be Mistress Celia Archer, unknown to those around her. It was imperative that Robert Renwick should not find her to persecute her as a bawd who had lain with a man who had not cared to marry her.

She would have Kit's child to remember him by. She could no longer be Diana's votary but, casting the child's horoscope using the night on which he was conceived, she found that he would have a long and prosperous life. He had been conceived under the sign of the crab and would likely be born under the sign of Aries—which was much to be hoped. He—why did she always think of the child as he?

There was no answer to that, but not for one moment did she think that she was carrying a girl— although the notion of a girl child was an appealing one. One strange consequence of carrying a child was that her trances, once so frequent, came no more. She remembered having them, and that they had become ever more frequent before the night when she and Kit became lovers. After that— nothing. Was it because she was no longer a virgin? She rather supposed that it was. The prophetesses of old had been virgins and to defile them was said to destroy their powers.

She had not felt defiled after her lovemaking, but she had lost her power all the same. To gain a new one, she suspected—for she found, once she had moved and began to practise as an astrologer and wise woman, that she was more in sympathy with those who consulted her, more able to feel and to know their inmost thoughts. She had lost, and she had gained—which, she supposed, was as Adam had often said: the law of life.

Was it the law of Celia Archer's life that she should renounce her lover, whom she had only met because of his faithlessness towards all women?

She thought that it was. If she could not have Kit, she would have nobody—except his child. Here, in the shadow of the Tower, still near to the ever-flowing river which carried everything away, as Time did, she would be free of the past at last. She would think only of the future in which she would have her child, and surely 1666 could not be so cruel to her as 1665 had been!

CHAPTER ELEVEN

'A TOAST to the bride and groom!' Everyone turned towards them in the late August sunlight of 1666; heads were thrown back and the sherry wine which kind Mistress Archer had provided was drunk down with a will.

Celia's year and more had passed and been kind to her. Her housekeeper, Mistress Bethia Ward, had been hired to replace Mistress Hart shortly before Celia's baby had been born, Willem approving her. He had approved of her so much that, before the year was out, on a day in early August, he had asked her to marry him and, despite the difference in their ages—her thirty-five to Willem's fifty-five—she had accepted him.

'So, God willing,' Willem had said when he told Celia of the news, 'there will be another child in the house. That is, if you wish to keep us here, Mistress.'

Celia, who had been casting a horoscope for one of their neighbours who made pots and pans and wished to know what the future of his business would be, had risen from her chair to throw her arms around him. 'My home will always be yours, I hope, and now you will no longer be lonely.'

He was gruff. 'True, mistress—but you will be so, I fear.'

Celia rose to lift her baby from his basket which stood on an oak chest, brass-bound, which had been one of her father's treasures. 'Nay, I shall not be lonely now that I have young Adam to keep me company.'

Adam had been born on a blustery day in April, the child of Aries for whom she had hoped. He had been a large baby and was still large, a happy child of whom there could be no doubt as to his fatherhood. His first blond baby hair had gone to be replaced by chestnut curls as the blue eyes of babyhood had been replaced by Kit's brilliant green orbs. He had a smile for everyone and, as Willem said, was 'Forward in every way, mistress. Like his father, I'll be bound,' which had Celia frowning.

She had ignored the comment and merely said, keeping her smile intact, for thinking of Kit made her sad, 'And now that it looks as though the plague has gone, we may celebrate your marriage in style.' While the plague had raged few people had liked to visit or celebrate for fear that guests brought the plague with them, but though there were still deaths from it they were few, and dwindling each week, and those who had fled had returned and the City was itself again.

Nigh on a hundred thousand had died, it was said, and there were empty houses everywhere. But the house in the Strand had been sold and with some of the money Celia had bought the land at the back of her new home, and Willem had created a garden there to rival the one which they had left behind.

It was in that garden that the celebration of his wedding had been held. He and Bethia had been married that morning in St Dionis Backchurch in Fenchurch Street, since that had been Bethia Ward's church since she was a babe herself. Afterwards the guests had come to Mistress Archer's home and had eaten and drunk from trestle tables laid out in the garden, for the day had been fine. Celia had played on the viol and Master Treharne, one of her neighbours, had brought his fiddle, and there had been impromptu country dancing on the grass.

Later, Willem and Bethia were to go upriver to an inn on the Thames near Hampton, where they would take a few days' holiday. Mistress Church, Bethia's friend, would come to look after Celia and Adam while they were away. The occasion was bittersweet. So many whom Willem and Celia might have asked had disappeared, stricken by the plague. Willem's first visit to the Strand, to sell the house, had revealed that of all their late neighbours few were left, and Job Potter and all his family were gone.

The bride and groom were sent on their way, to take the boat from the stairs below Tower Bridge, and the last guests had departed. Mistress Church and Celia began to clear up the remains of the meal. Presently she left Mistress Church to wash the pots on her own while she sat and fed young Adam in the garden.

She was sitting there in the happily mindless neartrance which breastfeeding Adam always induced, when she revisited, as she was wont to do, the lost past. It was not to mourn it, but to experience again one of the happy hours which she had spent with Kit before she had discovered his perfidy over the bet. . . .

They had been walking in the picture gallery at Whitehall. The sunlight came through the high windows and painted strange shapes on the floor. They had stopped to admire one of the portraits of

King Henry VIII, grossly magnificent in his Tudor clothes, his little piggy eyes staring cunningly at them. He was very different in his red-gold looks from King Charles II's swarthy grandeur.

Celia had remarked on this to Kit, who had said, laughing a little, 'Well, the relationship is a very distant one, after all. When I was at the French court, the old men there said that he was exactly like his grandfather, King Henri IV of France, in every way—looks and temperament both.' He did not add that he was also like him in collecting mistresses and in his ability to inspire loyalty in those near him.

Looking from Henry VIII's portrait to Kit, also magnificent in scarlet and gold—it was one of his weeks for attending the King, and he would shortly have to leave her to do so—Celia had thought how little she really knew of him, and how much he knew of her. She was aware from what was occasionally said that between Worcester field and the Restoration in 1660 he had lived a roving life around Europe and the Mediterranean, not wishing to be a charge on a king who was himself a pensioner.

Whereas her own life, by contrast, was an open book to him—and a simple book at that. Was it that strange life which had given him his air of control and authority, remarkable even in a court where most men possessed something of the air? She had not thought him over-handsome when she had first met him but, knowing him better, watching the play of light and shade on his mobile features, she thought that his face was better than handsome, it was powerful and compelling. The maids of honour, except for Dorothy Lowther, all seemed to like him, but she also thought that he was a man to be feared if he were crossed or angered.

It was his voice, however, which pleased her the most. Speaking or singing, it was a beautiful instrument which, when he sang one of the many love songs favoured by the court, could draw a woman's heart from out her breast. She could understand the legend of Orpheus better now that she had heard it, could believe that when he sang he could put a spell on any who heard him. Looking at Kit the other night she had known that, for better or worse, she loved him, and for the first time she wondered how many of the women of the court had fallen under that spell.

She had shivered a little, and had even lost the thread of what he was saying. They had moved down the gallery and come at last to the brilliant sunlight, dazzling after the shade; he had handed her on to a bench and then had sat, not beside her, but at her feet, stretching his long length on the grass to look up at her.

All about the lawn the ladies and gentlemen of the court disported themselves in the sun. For the moment none came near them.

Remembering, she wondered dreamily whether they had jested about the bet and whether Kit Carlyon was succeeding in his objective.

At the time knowing nothing of this, she had looked at him with longing, and thought how different he was from the rest, never importuning her or making lascivious innuendoes—for this little scene had happened before he had rescued her from

Charles Sedley and passion had overwhelmed them both.

'When I am gone,' she said suddenly, 'I shall remember this,' and she waved a hand at the fair scene before her.

'And will you remember Kit Carlyon, Mistress Celia?' he enquired lazily.

She smiled down at him, into green eyes looking up at her, and, oh, yes, she knew that she was flirting with him, but she could not resist it. For the first time she was discovering love—and it gave her a power over the loved one as he possessed a power over her. It might be madness to love Sir Christopher Carlyon, the King's friend who, despite his poverty, was so much above her, but it was a sweet madness.

'Of course,' she said demurely, adding with the charming simplicity which had won the heart of the man before her—although she was not to know that then—'I don't think that I shall ever forget you.'

It was not an answer that the blasé female members of Charles's court would have offered him. In one swift movement, after it had been given, Kit sat up and transferred himself to the bench to sit by her side. He plucked a buttercup from the grass as he did so, saying, 'Sweet weed, I dedicate it to thee,' his green eyes casting their magic on her.

He held it to her cheek, saying, 'Shall we play country games with a country flower, fair Mistress Celia?' and saw at once that she did not understand his mild innuendo. 'Country games', like 'country matters', in the parlance of the court meant the game of love—in bed, as well as out.

'A country flower in a town garden,' she answered

him, smiling shyly, not quite sure what she should say. Kit smiled back, leaned forward and, lifted her blonde tresses to tuck the flower behind her ear. Doing so brought him nearer to Celia than he had ever been before.

It was the first time she had ever experienced the living warmth of a man close to. Lightly she felt him brush her cheek with his lips, a kiss so slight that she hardly knew that she was experiencing it—almost thought that she had imagined it. As he drew away from her, they were eye to eye, and now it was her hand which stroked the cheek which he had kissed and his hand which lightly touched her chin.

He was going so gently with her that her heart yearned towards him.

Now, in the present, remembering, she asked herself whether it had been a clever trick—to woo and win her so slowly that inch by inch she would give way to him until the final surrender. Adam pulled hard on her nipple and she moved restlessly at the thought, and then the irony of thinking so struck her.

For, in the end, had she not freely given him all that he wanted without reservation? He had not needed to seduce her. She could have slipped from the bed, but had chosen not to do so—and the living proof of her love was on her knee, smiling up at her with his father's eyes.

'So sweet,' Kit had said, that afternoon over a year ago, 'so sweet, Mistress Celia. Tell me, how do you weave your enchantments so subtly that a man is snared without his knowing it?'

'No enchantments, Sir Kit,' she had replied. 'They are supplied by thyself, not me.'

'Ah,' he said, smiling at her, the fine black brows raised. 'Does that mean I enchant you, mistress?'

Celia had not meant exactly that, but chose not to say so. 'Oh,' her answer was swift, 'I meant the enchantments you share with Orpheus—your music.'

'My music.' He leaned back and began to sing softly, 'O, mistress mine! Where are you roaming. . .?' stopping to add, 'Do you remember, Mistress Celia, that I sang that when we first met?'

She could not tell him that she remembered everything which had passed when they first met, for that would be to tell him too much.

'Come,' he said, and now he touched her again, taking her chin lightly in his hand, turning her face towards him. 'Give me an answer, mistress.' He trod slightly on the word to give it, she was sure, a different meaning. He deserted her chin and had taken her hand.

She withdrew it, saying, 'Are you never serious?'

'At Whitehall?'

'Anywhere.'

Something in the way in which she answered him must have struck him to the heart, she was sure, even more sure, remembering.

He turned away from her, then finally said in a stifled voice, 'Oh, you reproach me, mistress. Yes, I could be serious, but not here. I live here because there is nowhere else for me. My home is a derelict ruin with no means of maintaining it. I think that I was not made for courts, but chance has made me a habitué of them. Had it not been for the war I would have been happy to have lived a country gentlemen upon my acres. *Then* I might have been serious.

Does that answer you, Mistress Celia? Can your stars tell me whether I shall ever have the opportunity to be serious again?'

There was so much bitterness in his voice that she hardly recognised it. She was so dismayed that she said slowly, 'I am sorry. I had not meant to distress you.'

He turned his head towards her again and the green eyes glittered coldly. 'Oh, mistress, just a passing cloud, no more. A man is not a man who pines for what is past and gone. I am here, and there's an end on't. Besides, I sit by the fairest and most chaste lady in the court and I must not tease her. Forgive me and, as token of your forgiveness, tell me that you will sing with me again tonight. The King hath ordered me to entertain him, and thy voice and mine conjoin so sweetly that it were a pity not to let them sing together like two birds on the same branch.' He smiled at her, put his head on one side, and said in mimicry of Buckingham, 'Say, Yes, Kit, Mistress Celia, I beg of thee.'

Of course she had said yes, and afterwards, alone in her room, she thought that for a moment he had shown her the true Sir Kit behind his light courtier's mask. There had been a yearning there for something lost, she was sure, and now, back in the present, absentmindedly loving Adam, she had a sudden intuition that it explained the bet he had made before he had known her. He had wanted a home in the country and Buckingham, in offering him Latter if he won the bet, had offered him that home.

More—in giving him Latter, by claiming that he had won it, had she not herself recognised that want and given him his wish? Beneath her attempt to demean him, had she not also desperately wanted to make him happy, to give him something, even if she were not then willing to give him herself. . .?

Useless, as he had said, to pine over what was past and gone. The present was her home, as it was the home of all mortal men and women—and Adam was the present.

Her musings were suddenly disturbed as the present overwhelmed her. The door to the garden burst open and an overawed Mistress Church, babbling hysterically, appeared.

'Oh, Mistress Archer, there is such a fine gentleman come to see thee, and he will brook no answer but that he sees you at once. I said that it was not convenient, but. . .'

'I never take no for an answer,' said a drawling voice which she immediately recognised as that of a very fine gentleman indeed, who pushed Mistress Church out of the way and advanced on Celia and her babe.

She had thought for one delirious moment, that it might be Kit, come to claim her, but of course it was not. It was that other—that fell man as Willem had once called him—Kit's so-called friend, the Duke of Buckingham, for Celia was sure that Buckingham was no one's friend but his own.

He waved Mistress Church aside and then bowed to Celia, elaborately and, she thought, mockingly, his feathered black hat sweeping the ground before her. He was dressed in his finest court clothing— black and gold and scarlet. His lace was a dream of lace; his shoes had the highest of red heels. His wig was obviously fire-new—a glory of frothing light blond curls, standing high above his forehead.

But he had deteriorated in the year and more since she had last seen him, she thought. He had put on weight, his colour was higher, drink and debauchery were beginning to leave indelible marks on him—but he still had the presence of the devil and no one could mistake what he was: a power in King Charles II's England.

So what was he doing in humble Mistress Celia Archer's garden? She was soon to find out.

'I heard that your faithful watchdog was leaving you for a term,' he offered her mockingly, once the bow was over, 'so I thought that I could visit thee.'

Celia began to button her dress and to lay a protesting Adam on her knee. He had an outrageous appetite, and an outrageous cry when he was deprived of his food. He favoured them with it now.

'Nay, nay, mistress,' said Buckingham, standing a little away from them. 'Feed the imp if thou would'st. I would have him silent and, sitting as you were, you reminded me of one of Signor Raphael's virgins—although you are not that now, it is plain to see.'

What could she do but obey him, to feel his eyes hard on her? Adam firmly clamped to her and sucking noisily, she said, as coolly as she could, 'To what do I owe the honour of your visit, Your Grace?'

'Oh, not that,' he said lazily, and he threw down his hat and sat on one of the benches which, less than an hour agone, had been the seat of those so much less in rank than he. 'George, Celia, say George, I beg of you.'

Nothing had changed in the time since they had last met—only his face and hers, for he said, almost casually, 'I thought thee a rare beauty, Mistress Celia, when you were truly a virgin, but as a mother you are a nonpareil. I am come to offer that nonpareil all that George Villiers may offer a woman, seeing that I am already married.'

'You do not come from him, then,' Celia could not prevent herself from saying.

His eyebrows lifted. 'Nay, mistress, for myself only—ever and always. No, I am come to offer thee security—riches, a fine home, not this.' He looked disparagingly around the little garden and the small house which was now her refuge. 'Seeing that I already have a Duchess, I would make thee my mistress, and care for you and the boy. Kit's boy and thine should be a nonpareil, too.'

She did not wish to ask after Kit, for she could not trust what he might tell her, but she could not stop her tongue, which had a life of its own.

'And Sir Christopher, does he know thy designs upon me? Is he at Court? Or, perchance, does he tarry at Latter?'

As was often his way he chose to answer her with a double tongue. 'Why, after his illness, mistress, he hied him to Latter. First he would not have it and then—he would. I wonder why that should be, mistress? But no matter, you have not answered me and I would know my fate—and thine. Come with me, now. Leave this place. It is not fit for thee, or the babe.'

'And for how long should we be thy toys, my lord Duke?'

'George, Celia. Art forgetful. Why, if you trust

me so little—and, after all, who can blame thee?—I would settle an estate and a fair income on thee and the babe, the only proviso being that you never see Kit again, save only in passing and in my presence. Did he give thee his ring, and did he know what he was doing when he did?'

The question was asked so innocently and without any warning that Celia's left hand—the right was holding Adam's head—flew to her bosom. The great ruby was on a ribbon, always worn beneath her dress. It was Kit's payment for betting on her virtue and winning, and for Latter.

'Oh, I see that he did! He knew? Or not?'

'No business of thine, my lord Duke.'

'Oh, but it is,' he said softly and, rising from the bench to stand over her, massive and powerful, one of the great ministers of State, he spoke to her slowly and patiently—but the menace of the mighty was in his voice

'You are my business, mistress, and have been since I first saw thee. I have watched over thee, mistress; I knew when your lover was attacked in an alley by your old home—which is more than he does, for he remembers nothing of what passed between you after that. I know when you came here, and what you paid for this house, and to whom you sold the one in the Strand. I know that your neighbours think you are an honest widow, although you were Kit Carlyon's whore, and will not be George Buckingham's. Why not, Mistress Celia? I am as fair a man as he, and greater. I could make thee rich, mistress, have you sleep on a bed of down, never work again, live but to please me when it pleased me to have you do so. What man could offer fairer than that?'

'I do not love thee.' Celia's voice was steady. He frightened her, so powerful was he, so ruthless, but she would not let it show. His smile for her was one of admiration.

'And you love him? What matter? I do not want your love—only you.'

'Well, as to that——' Celia was steady '—you may not have me, or him.' And she caressed Adam's head.

'And what if I broadcast thee whore, mistress? Brand thee one of the sluts from the court, cast off by her lover, and not the respectable widow which the poor fools around here think thee? What then, mistress?'

She must not show him her fear. She looked up at him—steadily, steadfastly. 'Why, thou would'st not do that, *George*, not even you would do that to someone who has never done thee harm.'

He struck one hand against the other. 'You do not know me, mistress. I would do anything, if it so pleased me.'

'So I suppose. I suppose, too, that there are many stratagems you might use to gain me, so that I might not refuse to do as you wish, but I can never truly give you myself, George.' This time she did not tread on his name. 'Being as I am, and you being as you are, to have me in that fashion—for there is none other in which I will come to you—would bring thee no satisfaction, and to ruin me would give you less.'

She hoped that today the weathercock in him which changed him from day to day would cause him to heed what she said. Besides, she did not think him truly wicked, only that he played at it, as another man might play at tennis to give him entertainment.

'Magnanimity, George, is all that I ask of thee. For myself, and for thy friend's child.'

She had him. The notion flattered him. Another day he might have thrown off what she said—either had her against her will or ruined her before the world. Today it pleased him to stand off—for the moment, at least.

'Well, well, mistress. Hast a cunning tongue. And thy babe is passing fair, as thou art. You shall live another day in peace but at my whim, George Villiers' whim, mistress—always remember that.'

He gave her a great bow before bending over Adam to place a large forefinger on his cheek. 'Tis pity his father doth not know of the treasure which he gave thee.' So saying, he was gone, to walk through the kitchen with as much ceremony as though he were at Whitehall, Mistress Church bowing and scraping before him.

At Whitehall, later that afternoon, Sir Christopher Carlyon, who had been at Court these last four weeks, summoned thither by the King, to finish his term as a Gentleman of the Bedchamber, now that the King had heard of his being recovered, met Buckingham in the Privy Garden. Buckingham was surrounded by his sycophants and pensioners and, Celia having earlier been harsh with him, he was being harsh with them to even matters.

Kit knew he had changed since he left London, just over a year agone. Whether it was living in the country at Latter, or growing older, or that the illness which he had suffered had made him examine himself and his life more critically which had caused the change he did not know. Where he had found amusement in Buckingham and the court's faithless free-living, he now found that it jarred upon him. The Merry Gang no longer seemed to him to be merry. They seemed to be careless and cruel.

He thought, and had thought for some little space, that the time he had spent with Anna in his delirium, reliving his past, had reminded him of the man he had once been and had thus sickened him of the man he had become. That, and the knowledge of the misery which he had brought upon Celia and himself by his careless folly.

And always there was the puzzle which he could not solve. Why had Celia claimed that he had seduced her? It had hurt him cruelly at the time, and the memory of it hurt him still.

He was thinking of this as Buckingham called him to his side, and of the earlier bet concerning Dorothy Lowther. He had not seen her among the Queen's ladies and had wondered briefly what had become of her. Like Celia, she was part of his past which he had lost, but whereas he had been grieved beyond measure at the loss of Celia, Dorothy Lowther's disappearance was a boon since to see her would remind him of his own heedlessness.

'Art glum these days, Kit,' was Buckingham's first comment. 'And thy guitar, where is it? I would have thee sing for us, if it be only the old song, "Golden lads and girls all must, as chimney-sweepers come to dust". Has thy tame astrologer gone to dust, Kit? Have you not found her yet?'

There was something cruelly barbed about Buckingham's words, some gleam in his eye which told Kit that he was being baited. He refused to rise and said, 'I have left my guitar in my room, George. I will sing for thee tonight.'

'Tonight, tonight.' Buckingham was pettish. 'I would have thee sing this afternoon. All the Merry Gang save thyself are absent, and you refuse to be merry and enchant me. Rochester is in the Tower again and Latter hath made thee sober. Fie upon thee. I would thou had'st not won it.'

'I cannot say Amen to that.' Kit was brief. 'The winning was cruelly done, but the prize hath pleased me. Nevertheless, if you should want it back. . .'

'Nay, nay, Kit, it was fairly won. You may go and take thy funeral face with thee, and leave it behind this night when you come again, I beg of you or I shall regret demanding that the King summoned thee back to us.'

So that was why he was at Whitehall, thought Kit wryly. To entertain weathercock George! Was that a compliment or not?

He was endeavouring to unravel that mystery as he walked along one of the main corridors of the palace to run into a busy man, carrying papers and, in his reverie, nearly knock man and papers flying.

It was Master Secretary Pepys, important as ever, joying in the knowledge that now that the Dutch Wars were won, he and all his works as Clerk of the Acts to the Navy Board had been justified. King, courtiers, hangers-on, MPs, admirals and soldiers— all, all, were Mr Pepy's acquaintances to be greeted by him. He was greeting Kit now.

'By my faith, Sir Christopher, I am pleased to see

thee returned to us, the hale and hearty again. You are fully recovered, I trust?' And he bowed his goodwill. He managed to be interested without being servile, and Kit was compelled to smile at him. After all, it was such as Mr Pepys who had seen, despite all the odds, that the recent Navy war was successful.

'Very well, sir, as you see. And you?'

'Most fit, Sir Christopher, most fit, and joying in the news that I have a long and prosperous life to come to me.' And he smiled from ear to ear.

'Indeed, and how do you know that?' Kit was both amused and curious.

'Why, sir, my wife hath visited a wise woman about her female mysteries, and the same wise woman is none other than old Antiquis's daughter— hight Archer now—and my wife, having had an election cast, hath persuaded me to allow Mistress Archer, who was Antiquis—whom I believe you knew—to cast my horoscope. Which she did, and promised me what I have told thee. . . Thou art not ill, Sir Christopher?'

Kit had first gone white, and then had seized Mr Pepys by his arm, having heard little after the name of Antiquis.

'Mistress Antiquis, who is now Mistress Archer, who once lived in the Strand? Tell me, Mr Pepys, where she hath her dwelling. Or did she visit thee?'

'Nay, sir.' Mr Pepys's shrewd eyes were hard on Sir Kit. He remembered the gossip about the woman and the bet, and wondered what interest the man before him still had in the late astrologer's daughter. 'Nay, sir, I visited her in her office at Swain's Yard off Tower Street, in the shadow of the Tower itself.

It is not so grand as old Adam's dwelling, but she hath made it fair enough.'

'Swain's Yard, in an alley off Tower Street!' Kit was feverish, yes, indeed he was, Mr Pepys noted with fascination, trembling even. 'You are sure of that?'

'Quite sure, sir.' Then Sir Christopher gave a curious cry between a sob and a laugh and was off down the corridor, almost running, as though all the devils in hell were after him.

Mr Pepys shook his head. These great ones! One more little item for him to record of their strange capriciousness. The man had had her, and then cast her off, and now was after her again. Love did strange things to its votaries, as he already knew himself, so perhaps he ought not to judge another too harshly!

Kit entered his lodgings on the run, calling for Caleb. Caleb, hearing the urgency in his voice, came running himself. 'To the Privy stairs, man, to hire me a wherry to take me to Tower Bridge steps!'

'Tower Bridge steps,' echoed Caleb stupidly. 'But you are due to wait on the King. . .'

'Aye, and I have my own affairs to conduct. The King's must wait. A wherry, I say, and at once. I will join thee in a moment.'

He was picking up his cloak and buckling on his rapier for protection—London was still lawless—and he ran—he could not walk, he was so impatient to see her again—after his servant, who was himself running.

To see her again! Perhaps in the half-hour! To have found her by such a strange chance when he and his man had walked about London trying to seek her out, but failing. He had begun to think her dead of the plague. Oh, the name had been wrong. The name! Archer! She was calling herself Archer! Had she married within the year? If she had, he was minded to kill the man who had robbed her from him! He almost stopped running, so struck was he by the violence of his own reactions.

At Latter, and even here, he could have sworn he had become accustomed to having lost her—but nothing to that, the moment he had thought she was found, he burned to be with her again. He wanted to both love and reproach her.

She had visited him in his dreams so often in the last year. The dream which had come to him in the aftermath of his illness had come again, and more than once. It had been strangely real and he had begun to think that it was an omen of the future, telling him that she was not lost to him, but that one day she would be found and would be his.

Suppose Pepys had been wrong? Suppose that he had misunderstood him? No, that could not be. He stared at the passing traffic on the river, for London had recovered its life again even if it had not replaced its lost citizens, and trade and play were all about him.

He must be steady when he saw her. But how he could be steady if she had married another? All the more reason to be steady. He must retain his calm, congratulate her and her husband and depart—all questions unanswered. Would she have changed in the year? He knew he had changed, but would she think that he had changed? Would she. . .? He stopped thinking. He would think again when he met her—if he did, and if Mr Pepys had not been bamboozling him, although he thought not. . .

Celia replaced Adam in his basket. Buckingham's visit had left her troubled. She could not believe that he would leave her alone. He had, after all, started the train of events which had brought Kit to her, and which had then caused her to lose him. If only it had been Kit who had come!

What would she say to him if he did? What would he say to her? There was unfinished business between them. The lie she had told about him, her disappearance, his fathering Adam, of which she was sure he did not know.

She was straightening her dress, smoothing down her skirt which Adam—he was a lively child—had disarranged. Adam was silent now. She stole another look at him. He was sleeping, the green eyes closed, one pink hand on the coverlet, the other in his mouth. He really was the greediest child! But he was always so loving, and so happy. Bethia had said that she had never known a child who cried so little and was so easy to please.

There was silence from the house. Mistress Church must have finished washing the pots and taken the opportunity to have a much-needed rest. She wondered whether Willem and Bethia had reached Hampton yet, and wished them well on their wedding-night. Tired herself, she began to doze. . .to be awoken by further noise from the house—Mistress Church once more emerging, indignant again at not being given a proper opportunity to announce the arrival of yet another fine gentleman.

It was Kit! She knew that it was Kit! She could hear his voice and then, like George Buckingham, he was through the door, and for the first time in over a year Celia Archer, who had been Antiquis, and Kit Carlyon were face to face.

They stared at one another. Both had changed and each registered the change. Celia saw that Kit was thinner, and more grave. There was a sobriety about him which she had never seen before. It was not only the care with which he was dressed, he who had always been careless, but something about the eyes and the set of his mouth had changed.

Kit saw that Celia, who had become rosier and more rounded, was lovelier than ever. The grey eyes were as solemn, the blonde curls were as bright, but the mouth was so tender, so loving, and Celia's expression was that of a woman, not a maiden. Kit thought with sudden desolation, It is the husband who hath done this for her—and I might have had the honour. For he had no doubt that the woman opposite to him was not a virgin—she was a woman who loved and had been loved.

Neither wished to speak until Celia, emboldened by Kit's silence—he who had never been at a loss for words—said coolly, as though they had met but yesterday, as though a long year and more did not lie between them, 'Why come you here? Hath thy master sent thee?'

Kit was bewildered and surprised by his silence, for over the long months he had thought of many things which he wished to say to his love. But now he could think of nothing. He had wanted to tell her that he loved her, that he wished to know why she had told the world her great lie—that he had seduced her. He had dreamed of taking her in his arms on sight but, faced with the living breathing woman, he was struck dumb, and her question confused him, so he could only say, 'My master? Nay, the King hath not sent me.'

'The King?' echoed Celia, bewildered in her turn. 'Nay, I meant the Duke.'

'He is not my master,' said Kit roughly, thinking, Why am I speaking of Buckingham? It is of her and me that I wish to talk.

'Yet he was here this afternoon, proposing that I become his whore—for a fair price, I admit—but still his whore.'

Celia, too, was asking herself wildly why she questioned Kit thus. Like him, she had thought that were she to see him again she would fall into his arms with relief—but not so. She was conscious of Adam, in his basket, behind her. Perchance if the babe were quiet he would think that the basket contained washing. For some reason which she could not understand, she did not wish Kit to know of Adam's existence.

'And thy husband, mistress? What did he have to say of His Grace's offer to enrich thee? Or does he not care that his wife might be another's trull, so long as the price is right?'

Her husband? What could he mean?

'Did he, the Duke, I mean, not tell you, then, before you came?'

'Tell me what Mistress Celia?' Suddenly the import of what she was saying struck him. '*Buckingham* knows that you dwell here? How long hath he known? Oh, never say that you and he. . .'

Kit's face grew first pale and then scarlet. He advanced on her.

'What, have you both been tricking me? Was he your lover all the time? Was it all a plot? Did *he* seduce you, and tell you to claim that it was I?'

'Nay, not so. I would not have him touch me—then or now. He hath spied upon me, knows all of what hath happened to me since I left the court.'

Kit felt light-headed. He was holding her now, not lovingly but fiercely. 'You speak true?' He was giddy, his world spinning about him. He did not know what to believe. All these long months since she had left Whitehall and Buckingham had known exactly what she had been doing, where she was! He had let Kit travel to the Strand a year agone, looking for her, knowing that he would not find her there. He had sat silent, laughing to himself, no doubt, when he and Caleb had tried to find her in the past few weeks.

Worse, he had spoken to Buckingham this very afternoon and he had said naught, had called Kit friend, treated him as a friend, and had betrayed him—not once but many times.

'You are speaking true, mistress?'

Not, My darling Celia, my lost love, spoken in affection, but could he believe anything any more? Had they both been laughing at him? Or had Buckingham spun one of his webs about the pair of them? By God, if that were so then George Villiers would pay a heavy price for what he had done!

He shook her a little and said again, 'And thy husband, mistress? Where is he?'

He had raised his voice and the child, sleeping in the basket, heard the raised voice and, although unused to hearing angry voices, instinctively recognised the sound as a threat and began to cry.

It was the last straw for Kit. He loosed Celia from him, whirled around to see the basket with the child in it, and advanced upon it.

'Why, mistress, it did not take thee long to forget Kit Carlyon! Whose child is this? Your husband's, or George Villiers's latest bastard?' And he bent down to lift the child up to inspect it. Its shawl had fallen across its face, the little starfish hands were plucking at it.

Kit accomplished the task which the babe could not. He pulled back the shawl to look into the waking face, to see—Cecco! Cecco of the chestnut curls, the green eyes and the fearless smile—for the babe, on being handled, ceased its crying and laughed up at his father, as Cecco had done, and put out his hands to him.

He reeled, staggered for a moment, blackness roared about him—was he back in the dreams of a year ago?—but the babe was real and for its sake he held the blackness off, clutched the child to him, to kiss it as he had once kissed Cecco, and turned to Celia.

'Mine,' he exclaimed fiercely. 'Mine—he is mine. How, in the name of God can he be mine? I never lay with thee, but mine he is. He is Cecco, come back to me.' And he half-sobbed the name. 'What witchcraft is this?'

Celia was as distressed as he. The dream that she had nourished for so long that one day Kit would return and they would both joy in the meeting—for in order to return he would have to love her—was over. The strange name he had called Adam had confounded her.

His own green eyes were hard on her, almost accusing. She said, voice faltering, 'No witchcraft, Kit. Yes, he is thine, I own it, and his name is Adam. Oh, Kit, I have no husband. For one night I lay with thee, once only when you were ill in my home, wandering in your wits after you were foully attacked. I thought to give thee comfort, and I did, for afterwards you slept peacefully, who could not do so before.'

Kit put the child back into the basket, from where, pushing his thumb in his mouth, Adam gazed at him in friendship. His father remembered his dream, that he had lain with Celia, and how the dream had returned again and again. But it had not been a dream, as Anna and Cecco had been a dream—it had happened.

'I remember and don't remember being with you.' He *did* remember suddenly the joy which he had felt in his dream when he had made love to Celia, and the consequence of that joy was lying chuckling happily behind him. Adam found life too interesting to sleep through; he wanted to be cuddled again, and chuckling always seemed to do the trick for him.

Not today, though. Kit looked at Celia sharply— for had she not just told him that she had no husband?—'You must marry me. The child needs a father.'

Afterwards he was to ponder dismally on the unthinking arrogance of that statement. No word of love, nothing but a demand for what was his. All the love and hope with which he had arrived at

Swain's Yard had flown away on the discovery of the tangled relationships which he found there.

The child needs a father. Oh, yes, Adam, she thought, so you do. But what of me, what of his mother? The subject of a cruel bet between unkind men who saw a humble virgin as nothing but a thing to despoil. I loved you dearly, Kit, and gave you peace, from which came Adam, and now you think that all you have to do is claim him.

Aloud, for she remembered Kit's ramblings when his wits were all astray, she said, 'And Anna? What of her?'

'Anna,' said Kit, staring at her, his attention drawn from Adam on whom he was casting doting glances. 'How come you know of Anna?'

'You spoke of her in your delirium. I ask you again, what of her?'

Kit felt that to speak of Anna and the past at this juncture was beyond him. 'Someone I knew. In Italy. No matter, she is dead and gone these many years.'

There was something so desolate in his face that Celia could have wept. She remembered Kit calling on Anna and speaking in a foreign language. She remembered, too, that he had called out the name which he had just given Adam when he lifted him from his basket.

Anna had been his love—nay, still was his love. Was it Anna he thought that he was lying with, the night when Adam had been conceived?

She wronged him, and was about to know that she did. He said, roughly, 'I dreamed I was with you, and I dreamed that I gave you my ring. You told me to go to Latter—was that when Adam was conceived?'

Celia unbuttoned the bodice of her dress, pulled forth the great ruby on its ribbon. 'In your ramblings you gave me this as a pledge that we were married and I told thee to go to Latter, for think, Kit—when we lay together you had truly won your bet and Latter was fairly thine, no lie about it.' She held the ring out to him.

Kit would not take it, waved it away. 'And you called yourself Archer so that the world might think you married—and widowed, perchance.'

'Nay, I called myself Archer because that is my true name. I found after he had died that my father's name was Archer. He called himself Antiquis to impress the multitude, I think. I told one great lie when I claimed thou hadst seduced me. I did not wish to tell any more.'

They were talking as coolly and passionlessly together as though they had shared nothing. As though the flame which had sprung up between them from the moment they had first met, and had brought them in joy to their strange marriage bed, had never been lit. Everything seemed to have conspired against them, not least George Buckingham, who had brought them together and had kept them apart.

'You will not marry me, then, for the child's sake?' begged Kit. It was the memory of Cecco which stirred in him, and Celia, whom he had longed to see, either to love or to reproach, or even to do both, was temporarily forgotten. He forgot that the icon which he had worshipped through the long months of parting had been her face.

The other thing which consumed him and destroyed his composure, drove out the memory of his love, was Buckingham's treachery. It was the wrong thing to have said, he knew that at once, but how to say the right thing?

It was Celia who was holding off now. All the bright and impossible dreams which she had cherished of seeing her love again, of explaining about Adam, of the joy of their loving—even though he had not consciously known of it—had been destroyed not only by Buckingham's treachery, but by his earlier presence.

'Are you sure you wish this thing, Sir Christopher Carlyon, even to claim thy son?'

Kit raised exasperated eyebrows at her coldness. He could not believe that a woman, unmarried, with a by-blow, would hesitate at accepting the offer of marriage from the one who could give her and the babe a home and a title, when the alternative was that she would work for a bare living and bring up the child in comparative poverty. Truth to tell, he was still mistrustful of her tale—remembering that she had lied about him before—and of Buckingham's involvement in it. Had that not been so, he would have taken Celia in his arms, told her of his love and his pride in his beautiful son and his desire to make her his wife.

For a moment he softened, walked over to her and was about to take her in his arms, when all would have been well, but, made desolate by his mistrust, she turned away from him.

'Oh, I know not what to say or do. I own I should not have deceived the world over our true relationship a year agone, but think that when I did so I had discovered that thou and that fell man had bet upon my virtue. I did but lie with thee to heal thee. . .' And oh, that was a lie, too, and one which she had not meant to commit, but it had flown from her in response to his coldness. 'I must think, Sir Christopher, most carefully on what I should do for myself and for the child. . .'

Kit committed another tactical error. 'No need to think what is best for the child. He is best with his father and his true name.'

'His true name is Adam Archer,' replied Celia firmly. 'There is no doubt of that, at least. When the horoscope said that our relationship would be a strange one it spoke true, for the marriage we shared was no legal one but a handfast, without witnesses, between a man who knew not who he was and a woman who knew who he was only too well.'

'I will not plead more,' Kit announced suddenly and proudly. 'You have my offer, mistress. Think on it, but do not think too long. I fain would have an answer soon. I acknowledge my debt to you. From what I have learned in this last hour, it is thanks to you that I live to make thee an offer at all.' It was nothing like the declaration which he had hoped to make to her when he had learned from Mr Pepys where she had her abode, but it would have to do.

'I will think on what you have said,' returned Celia slowly, 'and I will give you an answer in one week. But I must have that time, Kit. . .Sir Christopher. It is a decision for life, when all is said and done, and cannot be made lightly.'

Kit was almost rough in his disappointment. 'I am not asking you to make it lightly, but I ask you to make it soon. We have wasted time enough or, more truly, Buckingham hath wasted it for us. I have lost the first months of my son's life and would lose no more.'

Later, when he was back at Whitehall, dressing for his delayed appointment to care for the King, he wondered at himself. At the end he could, despite all, hardly bring himself to leave her and the child, whom Celia took out of his basket to hold to her, and who looked more like lost Cecco than ever. He owned that it was that resemblance together with the knowledge of his friend's treachery which had done the damage, but that acknowledgment could not cancel out the memory of his failure and of Celia's white, unhappy face next to his son's smiling charm.

He could not know that every time Celia looked at Adam she saw Kit, and that the love which had helped to give Adam his sunny disposition was the love which Celia felt for his father—felt still beneath her distress and resentment. Her life was compounded of 'if's. If she and Kit had met in any other way; if she had not discovered his, and Buckingham's treachery; if she had not publicly lied about his seduction of her; if his wits had not gone astray; if Buckingham had not arrived before Kit had done that afternoon. . .

If. . .if. . . There was no use in ifs. The other Adam, her father, had always said that life was to be lived as it was, not as we might wish it to be, and, at the last, she had to admit one thing. If the bet had not been made, it was unlikely that she would have ever met Kit—and loved him.

CHAPTER TWELVE

THERE was one thing which Kit had to do and it
must be done quickly. He was in a fever over it.
That evening he did as Buckingham had half commanded him and took his guitar to play and sing to
the King and court.

No one, watching him, could have known what
contrary passions were tearing Kit Carlyon apart.
He sang as he had never sung before, so that women
wept quietly and men turned away and asked questions of themselves. He sang a song of old Will
Shakespeare's which tore at the heartstrings, the
words staying in the mind—'For the rain it raineth
every day'.

His own face remained stone. The laughing, reck-
less Kit Carlyon of the past, careless of himself and
of others, had disappeared. The court had noted
the difference in him when he had returned from
Latter. Now the difference seemed greater than
ever.

Kit knew what had changed in him. Ever since he
had met Celia, and particularly after his wits had
gone astray, he had learned to feel again—not only
for himself, but for others. That part of him which
he thought had died with Anna and Cecco had not
been dead, but dormant. He was alert again to the
feelings of those around him, almost as though he
had lost his skin.

He could almost touch the careless malignancy

with which Buckingham, his friend, treated life. He wondered how much of that was owing to George's own experience's in exile and out of it. Buckingham had lost his father by assassination and had then lost his country to become a half-man, living in exile. The frantic fashion in which he and the Merry Gang pursued sensation and pleasure since the King's return to his own again—and Kit did not exclude himself from this judgement—was to make up for what they had felt lost to them, but which had been so surprisingly restored.

Whatever the reason, he knew, beyond a doubt, that when his term of service at Court was over he would return to Latter, to live there the life which he would have lived had not the war robbed him of his home and driven him from his country.

He understood Buckingham, but he could not forgive him anymore than he could forgive himself. After all, he and Buckingham had been friends since before Worcester field, had suffered together in exile and the claims of friendship should have prevented him from practising such casual cruelty. For treating Celia and himself so callously he deserved punishment, and punishment he would get.

Buckingham came over to him once his singing was done. 'I have never heard you in finer voice, Kit, and that is a rare compliment I make thee.'

Kit smiled back at him. Two could practice deceit, something Buckingham sometimes forgot. 'I treasure that, George, coming from you. I will exact payment from thee for pleasing thee so. We have not fenced together, thou and I, for over a year. A practice, tomorrow, in the Great Room?'

This was a room at Whitehall frequently used as a

salle des armes by the courtiers and was less often frequented by the courtiers than the tennis court, but was still popular.

'Oh, a pleasure, Kit. I like to fence with a master. Italy made thee so—I cannot remember that you were so proficient when young.'

'Italy made me many things,' Kit replied obliquely. 'At two of the clock then, George, alone, as we were wont when young.'

'At King Louis's court,' finished Buckingham. 'Agreed. I would not wish to look a fool before others.'

'Oh, you are never a fool, George.' Kit's voice was soft. 'You may be many things, and none of them overnice, but never a fool.'

If Buckingham looked after him with a little surprise on his face Kit did not see it, for he walked away to stand apart in a window embrasure looking out at the night, darkness falling, and the light from London in the sky.

He was joined by one of the maids of honour, one whom he liked and respected—Miss Hamilton, whom he remembered as Celia's friend.

Like Buckingham, she thanked him for his singing. Then, as he bowed his pleasure, he thought to ask her a question which had troubled him, for the memory of Dorothy Lowther and his treatment of her stuck like a burr in his mind. 'For thy thanks I would ask a small payment. Mistress Lowther is not with the Queen this year? Hath she left Court?'

The face Hamilton showed him was a troubled one. 'Nay, Kit. Dost thou not know? But why should you? You were away from Court, were you not? She is dead. She died three months agone, and it was I who found her. She was carrying a child and tried to lose it without help, but lost child and life in the doing.' Her eyes filled with tears at the memory of finding Dorothy cold on her bed, blood everywhere.

Horror took Kit by the throat. He had not liked the girl, but to hear of such an end! He was not to know that Celia had forseen it. A painful thought struck him, one which he could hardly voice. He said, throat constricted, half turned away from Hamilton, 'It was not. . .?'

Hamilton finished his sentence for him swiftly. She had misjudged him, or else he had changed in the year in which he had been away.

'It could not have been thine, Kit. It was conceived after you had left Court.'

Shameful relief ran through him. That, at least, was not on his conscience, whatever else might reproach him in the night hours. He spoke to her then of trivial things, harmless things—a coming masque at Court in which they would both appear, he playing his guitar and she, garbed as Venus, singing, as though such nonsense might hold the dark away.

After she left him he retired. Tomorrow he would teach George a lesson which he might not easily forget.

Celia was as troubled as Kit, but worked off her troubles in a different way. There was Adam to care for, Mistress Church to help, a horoscope to draw up, an infusion of herbs to prepare for a woman who was still in pain after a difficult childbirth. But always at the back of her mind was Kit's troubled and questioning face.

Giving Adam his last feed of the day, something which she had always enjoyed because her spirit roved free when she did so, was less satisfactory than usual because holding Adam brought his father even nearer.

Could she deprive Kit of his child? She remembered his face, the shock when he had first seen Adam, and then the yearning with which he had looked at him before he left. She had never thought of Kit as a father, of having an interest in children—they were something few men, and particularly great men like Kit, were interested in.

Perhaps she was misjudging him. Perhaps, behind the light-minded man who had bet on her, who had seemed to hold both men and women in such light esteem, there were depths to his nature which she had not plumbed. Yet always she came back to the one thing which troubled her. Was he simply prepared to marry her to gain Adam as a son? Was she still, for him, the unconsidered thing who might be bet on, but never seriously considered as a fellow human being?

Adam had taught her that she had not only an immortal soul, but a right to be something which only men were in her world—a free and independent spirit. Would Kit feel the same about her, or would he expect her to be his housekeeper and Adam's mother while he roved around the court finding his pleasure with other women when the mood took him? Would she still be able to use all her hard-won skills to help those about her less fortunate than herself?

She knew that Buckingham and the others took their pleasure where they found it, regardless of wife and family both—so why not Kit? No, she would not be a convenience for him. She would bring up Adam without him and his patronage. She would deny his fatherhood, even, to keep Adam— although in the face of the resemblance between them which had appeared so soon after Adam's birth, it would be a difficult thing to deny.

Thinking this, she finally laid Adam to rest in his cot by her bed, and went downstairs to mend clothes and do all the tasks which keeping a good and trim household required.

But the day and its visitors were not yet over. There was a knocking on the door and she called to Mistress Church who had gone upstairs, 'I will answer it,' and did so—to find Robert Renwick on the step, facing her, a pair of bravos at his back, one of them with a patch on his eye.

She made to shut the door. She thought that she had lost him a year agone, but he put his foot in the door and forced his way in, saying to his bravos, 'You will wait outside for me, I shall not be long.'

'That will be God's mercy, then,' she could not help saying.

It might be her own home, but Robert pushed her backwards into the parlour where she had left her work on the gate-legged table. He was as cold and commanding as ever, and his eyes on her burned with anger.

'So, mistress, I have found thee at last—thou and thy bastard. Is that why you fled the Strand? You have not fled the lovers with whom you whore. My men have told me that both Buckingham and the whore-son Carlyon have visited thee today. Which of them is the child's father—or do you not know? I will have thee branded trull and thy proper trade revealed. Did you think to escape me?'

He had tracked her down and was as obsessed as ever with destroying her because she would not have him. He laughed at her agonised expression and said, 'Do not seek to lie to me, mistress. I had thought that the thrashing your lover received would have cooled him to thee, but not so, it seems. Do you want me to see that he receives another?'

Celia put her hands to her ears to shut out the sound of his voice. She recovered herself, dropped them, and said with what courage she could muster, 'He is too great for thee to meddle with. I shall tell him of thy threat, warn him of what you propose to do.'

'Aye, and I shall deny it, mistress. Is thy credit so good that any man will believe thee?'

This struck home harder than he knew. Celia thought of Kit's agonised face, of his questioning her as to her relationship with Buckingham, of her own lie which had caused him to doubt her.

'Oh, I see I spoke true, mistress. I will not have what I want today, for I would have thee suffer a little before you give me what I wish—and that without the need to offer thee marriage. Be my whore, as you were his and the Duke's, and I will leave thee in peace. Deny me and I shall destroy thy home and thy living. It is plain that neither of your lovers wishes more for thee than I do. Such men as they do not marry such as thee.'

He was wrong there Celia thought, but did not tell him so. For had not Kit offered her marriage that very afternoon, even if it were only for the child's sake? He would protect her, she knew.

'I will give you the answer now that I will always give you, Master Renwick. I have no wish to be either thy wife or thy leman, and I shall call those whom you please to call my lovers for protection. I do not think you will flout them.'

For a moment he was minded to take her on the spot, but he was after all, a little fearful of harming one whose protectors were as great as Sir Christopher Carlyon and the Duke.

'Oh,' he said, 'I will wait until they become tired of you and throw you off, which, knowing such creatures, will not be long. I have no mind to be ruined over such as you. Remember me, mistress, for to be sure I shall not forget thee.'

He was gone. Celia sank down in her chair, but not to take up her work. If she married Kit, she would be safe from Robert and Adam would not be thrown upon the Parish as he might be if she were ruined. She rebelled at the notion. Yet she might have to come to it, to protect Adam, if not herself.

She went to bed, but not to sleep. The day's events ran through her head. For months she had lived a kind of peace, which if it were not happiness, was something like it. That peace had been shattered as one by one the men who desired her, and all for different reasons, had entered her life again. Of the three of them only Kit was the one whom she loved and would always love and she would not have him, whatever the cost, if for him she was some convenient pawn to be used. She would have his heart or nothing.

* * *

'So, Kit, art ready for the fray?'

Buckingham had knocked on Kit's door shortly after two had struck. He was wearing a light jacket over a silk shirt and petticoat breeches and was carrying buttoned foils under his arm. He seemed eager to test his skill against Kit's. Kit had not fenced for a year and for a moment wondered how much of his skill had left him. He was tired as well.

He had slept as uneasily as Celia had done, lying long awake and then dozing. In his dreams now it was always Celia with whom he walked. Anna was gone. It was as though, having revisited him when his wits went astray, she had said a final farewell to him and Cecco had gone to be replaced by Adam. It was difficult for him to tell how alike the two boys truly were; Adam's face now overlaid Cecco's. Strange to think that if Cecco had lived he would be ten years old, not a babe any more—but he would always be a babe in Kit's memories.

He had prepared for the mock fight as Buckingham had done, wearing light stockings, rather than heavy, for he would fight in his stock-inged feet. He had held his foil at arm's length and, facing himself in the long mirror in the corner of his room, had thrust it at his reflection as his fencing master in France had taught him. The master had suggested to him once, half in jest, that he become a teacher himself. 'You are the most apt pupil I have ever had,' he had told him.

Few whom Kit fenced with knew how truly skilled he was. He always held back, for he had discovered that most men did not like to learn how frail their own prowess was, and resented those who could beat them easily. Even with George he had always masked his light. Well, George was about to discover how skilful Kit Carlyon really was, and he hoped that the lesson would dent his haughty pride a little.

The room was empty and George locked the door. He had meant it when he said that he wished to be alone. He had never mastered Kit, had always felt that he was about to do so, and today, given that Kit had been absent from Court and had had little chance to practice, he fancied his skills against him.

Except that when they took off their coats and kicked off their shoes it was at once apparent to Kit that Buckingham was not in a good condition to undertake any physical exercise. He had drunk too much, wenched too much, eaten too much and slept too little. Nevertheless, for a time Kit played with him, until at the end of one passage, where the honours had been almost even, Buckingham drew back and said fiercely, 'Why, Kit, I vow thou art not trying. Humour me not. I would have thee stretch thyself.'

Kit offered his friend a face he had never seen. 'That is thy wish—thy true wish, George?' And when Buckingham assented, said, almost lightly, 'Why, then, thou shalt have it.' He understood that, rusty though he might be, his own physical strength had been honed by his life at Latter, where he worked in the fields with his men, so that he was leaner and fitter than ever. Debauchery had passed him by.

What followed was to be eternally engraved on Buckingham's memory. He was no mean performer himself, and believed that Kit had only a slight edge on him. He was to be rapidly disabused.

Kit began by disarming his man almost immediately. One moment Buckingham was attacking, the next his sword was seized and his weapon was on the floor.

He bent to pick it up, to find Kit laughing at him. 'That,' he said, 'is for not telling me where Mistress Celia was to be found a year ago when you knew that I was looking for her,' and he waved his foil at Buckingham to indicate that he should pick his own up.

Buckingham did so, saying ruefully, 'That were a cruel trick, Kit, I was not ready,' and they began again.

'Oh, and are you ready for this, then?' mocked Kit and, with a swift passade, a sidestep and a final lunge, he brought his own foil to lie on Buckingham's breast—where such a ploy with a naked rapier or small sword would have brought about Buckingham's death. 'And that,' he said, 'is for not telling me that you visited Mistress Celia yesterday and tried to make her thy doxy.' When Buckingham resumed as they dropped back, he added, 'And now for another lesson,' and this time after a rapid exchange he executed the infamous *coup de Jarnac* whereby the attacker, bending, turning aside the other's weapon, swept his low in such a fashion that he cut the hamstring of the person whom he was attacking, rendering him lame and incapable and ready to be despatched at will.

Buckingham stepped back, scarlet and furious. 'By my faith, Kit, this is not decent. What dam'd dancing master tricks are these. . .?'

'To practise on an honest English gentleman?' Kit finished, mocking him again. 'But you are not honest, George. You are my friend, and yet you used me most foully where Mistress Celia was concerned, and you tried to use her foully, too.'

Buckingham could not resist grinning at him. 'All's fair in love and war, Kit, as you should know by now.'

'Oh, indeed,' riposted Kit. 'And that being so, how many times shall I kill thee in jest before this lesson is over?' So speaking, he drove Buckingham back, back, back, to hold him against the far wall where, their foils high above their heads, they stared one another in the face until Kit, using his superior strength, twisted his wrist against Buckingham's so that George's foil flew out of his hand across the floor.

'And that,' said Kit, 'is for deceiving me yesterday, today and all the days before. Be thankful that it is buttoned foils we are using, George, or I might be tempted to kill you,' and he turned away from his erstwhile friend.

Buckingham, overcome by a rage which he had never felt before, humiliated by the other's display of skill, suddenly aware that he—and others—had never stood a chance against Kit had he ever chosen to show them that skill, bent down, picked up his foil and, tearing the button off the point, bore down on Kit from behind to plunge it in his back.

Some instinct warned Kit at the last moment. He swung around to see Buckingham almost upon him, fell intent on his face, sidestepped and began to defend himself against a man fully armed while he himself was fencing with a blunted weapon.

For a moment Buckingham, sensing his advantage, fought with renewed authority, until again he was driven back, the foil was twisted from his hand, to fall on the floor before Kit, who had stood back after disarming him.

Kit picked up Buckingham's foil, tucked it under his arm, wrenched the button from his own and threw it at Buckingham with a cry of, 'Defend thyself, George. The game is even now.'

It was not, and Buckingham knew it. It could not have been more uneven. He retreated backwards before Kit, and Kit, almost contemptuously, attacked with the lunge which he had used before. With his hand he wrenched Buckingham's foil from him again, to fall on the floor, the point of his own weapon coming to rest on Buckingham's breast.

They stood eye to eye, Buckingham breathing stertorously and Kit hardly at all. For one moment he was of a mind to lean forward and finish Buckingham's troubled life for him. He thought of the lies and treachery which his so-called friend had used towards him and others, but he thought, too, of what Celia had said to him over twelve months ago when he had offered to kill Buckingham for her. 'If you could defeat him so easily, then it would be murder.'

Murder—and for what? To die, or to fly England? How would that benefit himself, or Celia, or Adam? He thought of the years of friendship in exile, of the bitter, lost youth of the man before him, of his own bitter, lost youth; and lowered his point to touch the floor, then lifted the foil before his face to signify that the bout was at an end.

Buckingham gave a great sigh and the colour returned to his face. Oh, he did not lack courage. He had not flinched, although death had stared him in the face.

'By God, Kit, I had not known that thou were such a master. I thought my last hour had come and, knowing all, I could not have complained had you finished what you had begun. I shall have Foubert put me through a course of lessons so that I may not be so shamed again. Yet I shall never match thee.'

Kit threw the foil across the room, and said, his voice thick with some emotion which he could not identify, 'Rest easy, George. I shall never fence again.'

'That were a pity, Kit. Thy swordplay is pure poetry of the deadliest kind.'

It was typical of him that after such a testing bout he should act as though no insults had been offered him, as though he had not been ready to drive his sword through Kit's undefended back. Doubtless, if it so pleased him, he would resume his treachery towards him and Celia again, even if he risked death at the end of it.

Kit sighed. He had brought a silk towel with him, as had Buckingham, and they began to mop their faces—fencing being sweaty work and dangerous, Buckingham announced. He seemed elated, although Kit felt sad, but he knew that men who had faced death frequently felt such an elation, since he had experienced it himself, and he could guess how Buckingham meant to feed his, before the night was out.

'One thing,' said Buckingham as he unlocked the door and they prepared to part. 'I played thee many scurvy tricks, Kit, you and your doxy both. It was I who wrote the song which told of thy conquest of the astrologer's daughter, but I did not tell the fair Celia of our bet, I would not have done that. It was poor Lowther and the Castlemaine who gossiped of it in the bath-house where Mistress Celia might overhear them. I don't mind being cursed for what I have done, but I would not have thee bear a grudge against me for what I did not do.'

Kit nodded. The tale rang true. He did not feel happy, but he felt purged. He could face Celia again without blood on his hands. There was one last thing to be said.

'Latter.' His voice was low. 'I would not hold it against thy will, George. If, after this, you wish it back—then it is yours again.'

Buckingham thought for a moment. He gave a great laugh and clapped Kit on the back. 'It is thine, Kit. Fairly won. Take Celia and the babe and live there. I'll not cheat thee again. I would give you my word, but you know it is worthless. Remember me when you leave the court, for I do not think you are happy here, and you will be happy at Latter. Mistress Celia hath the art of spreading peace about her.'

That was true enough, thought Kit, finding his own room again. He would never be truly happy at Latter unless he had Celia and Adam with him. Kit Carlyon was back in the land of the living. He would never write or sing a light-minded and cynical song again, however beautiful the tune or words, for now he felt and bled not only for himself, but for others.

He wondered what Celia was doing and longed to see her. She would give him an answer soon, she had said, and for the moment he would respect her and stay away. But if her answer was long in coming he knew that sooner rather than later he would find his way to Tower Street again, and this time he would not leave without her.

August died in the week Celia had promised Kit before she answered him, and September was on them. Willem and his wife returned, but still Celia sent no answer to Kit. She was in a kind of limbo and, like Kit, wondered at herself. She cast an election—and cast Adam's horoscope again. The election told her that she had reached a crisis in her life—which she already knew; Adam's horoscope said that his life would be long, prosperous and successful—but not the fashion in which it would be.

Did that mean she would accept Kit's offer to go to Latter and that Kit would accept Adam as his legitimate heir once they were married? If so, then her deliberations were useless since Fate had already decided that she would say yes. In that case her mind, for once coldly questioning, told her that there were two major problems which faced her.

The first was that there was no such thing as human free will if the stars had already decided what should happen to her and Adam, for then her fate was determined. She had raised this once with her father, puzzling over what that did to mortal men's fancy that they made decisions based on emotion or upon reason.

'For if all is foredoomed then we are but creatures of Fate—pawns upon a giant chessboard, moved by powers outside of ourselves.'

Adam looked at her kindly. 'Why, daughter, I have often thought on this, and have concluded that we are not meant to ask such questions. We live as we will live and the stars determine our yea and our nay, yet we feel that what we do comes from inside ourselves, not from outside. And, that being so, we do well to stay with our feelings. We are all kings and queens in our own game.'

'And is the future fixed, then, or may we change it?' Celia had thought, because of her premonitions and because the reality which had followed had seen the premonitions confounded, that the future was not fixed, but Adam juggled with ideas again.

'Oh, we can only know what has happened and what is, not entirely what will be. I think that there is no future until we reach it. Some things will happen, such as the sun rising, or plague coming, but what happens to individual humans inside the future may not be exactly known.'

That had been that. She thought that she knew now what her father had meant, and she was suddenly at peace. The future would happen; she would decide to marry Kit, or not, but one way or another her doom would be upon her—and, as God occasionally chose to perform a miracle for his humble subjects on earth, then He might choose to perform a small one for Celia Archer, late Antiquis, and answer her question for her.

CHAPTER THIRTEEN

AFTERWARDS there was always argument as to where the Great Fire of London had really started, and how. The old saying had it that it began at Pudding Lane and ended at Pie Corner, but that was not entirely true. The Dutch had started it, some said, out of spite—or the French, or the Papists, or the Jews, or vague assassins, or it was an accident born out of the age of the City which had changed little since medieval times and was largely still built of wood.

Even the old wall survived—nearly two miles of it, thirty-five feet high in places—and inside the houses of rich and poor were crammed on top of one another. As Willem and Bethia and, after their return, Nan, a nursemaid for Adam, lived in Celia's house, so each house in London was filled not only with the family who owned it but servants, journeymen and apprentices—all crowded hugger-mugger in a city which had grown and was still growing.

William Lilly, Adam Antiquis's old friend and rival, whose fame was beyond Adam's had, like Adam, foretold both plague and fire. More, he had also foretold that September the third, 1666, was to be a lucky day, so a group of old Republicans had plotted to overthrow the King and restore the Commonwealth. The signal for the overthrow was to be the burning down of London on Monday,

September the third, Lilly's lucky day. The Horse Guards were to be seized and the Tower surprised.

In the event, the only people who were to be surprised were the plotters. They were caught in April, tried and executed—but Lilly's third of September proved to be a momentous day after all, one of four which changed the face of London forever, although not in the way which the plotters, or he, expected. . .

It was Celia, early on the morning of Sunday, the second of September, who was the first in Swain's Yard to see the fire. For once Adam had been restless and his cries had awakened her. Rising in the night, she found her bedroom full of light from a fire in the City, a little to the west and, Adam in her arms, she awoke Willem, who went out to reconnoitre. He returned with the news that it was the King's baker, Farynor's in Pudding Lane, which was on fire, and that the fire was moving away from Tower Street, so no reason to worry.

On the way back he had met some of the servants from Mr Pepys's house in Seething Lane nearby, also drawn by the flames and sent to satisfy Mr Pepys's insatiable curiosity about all that happened.

'No need for fear,' Willem told his anxious mistress, who sat in the parlour, a satisfied and well-fed Adam replete on her knee. 'The fire is spreading, but away from us, taken by the wind towards the west.'

There had been fires in the City before, but they had always been contained and, although this seemed a little larger than some, there was no reason to believe other than that its flames would soon be extinguished.

Reassured, Celia went to her bed. She kept Adam with her, sleeping propped up on pillows, the babe in her arms happy to be held against his mother's soft warm body. She thought worriedly of Kit for a moment, but then chided herself. He was at Whitehall, far from danger, further than she was and, thinking of him—he was seldom out of her thoughts—she slept again.

Noise from the street outside awoke the house as dawn broke. There was a great press of people all walking in the direction of the fire, which was still burning, in order to gain a better view of it. It was the one topic of conversation, but to Celia's surprise no one seemed very worried about it—rather, it was providing an excellent Sunday amusement.

Nan, who had risen early, came in full of exclamations, and excitement. 'Oh, Mistress Archer, they say that nigh on three hundred houses have gone in the night and that Fish Street, by London Bridge, is all aflame. And that poor maidservant at Farynor's was left behind when the family escaped, and is burned to cinders, they say! The family fled over the roofs, but she was afeared, would not go, and the fire took her.'

Celia shivered, and clutched Adam to her harder. Ever since his birth she had realised how true it was, as Francis Bacon had said, that children were 'hostages to fortune'. Alone and free she had felt in command of herself and the world, but having small, helpless Adam had changed all that. She feared the fire more for him than for herself, and she feared it for Kit. To love was also to give a hostage to fortune, and she remembered that her father had once said something of the sort to her, when they had been casting horoscopes for a rich merchant, his wife and family.

The smell of fire and burning was in the air. The wind changed a little in the morning, then veered round again, but during the change soot and ashes fell on Tower Street and, it being Monday, the new Mistress Hood raged at the smuts on her washing, spread on the currant bushes in Celia's garden. Willem was more worried that the changing wind might bring the fire towards Swain's Yard than about spoiled washing, but he said nothing.

'I'm off to find out what I may,' he said abruptly, and then did not return for some time. When he did the news he brought was dismal.

'Master Pepys's man told me that his master went to the Tower and climbed to the top of it with the Lieutenant-Governor and there saw all Fish Street burning, London Bridge, too, and the fire moving on. St Magnus's church hath gone, he said, and St Margaret's Fish Street Hill is going, they say, which is a great pity, but a greater pity still if the fire be not put out. Lord knows, there is not enough fire-fighting equipment to quench such a furnace! And the river is alive with the boats of those near the fire ferrying their belongings away.'

He read Celia's expression correctly. 'Come, mistress, it will not reach Whitehall, and the Lord Mayor and the Aldermen are overseeing the fighting of it and will soon have it under control.'

'Of course.' Celia picked up Adam and tried not to think of his father, but she could not help wondering what he was doing.

* * *

Kit had been awoken early that morning by the noise of men running outside and, throwing a robe over his night rail, he went to his window to look out, open the window and call down to a group of servants who were chattering loudly. 'What is it which occupies thee and keeps a man from sleep?'

'Sir Christopher.' It was one of Buckingham's men, a scrivener, his clothes thrown on pell-mell. 'They say there is a great fire in London, and that St. Magnus's church hath gone in the night, and that little is being done to contain it.'

'Doth the King know?' Kit called to them.

'Aye, and he is up and about, and the Duke of York, too.'

Kit closed the window and dressed himself hastily. The fire had not been visible from his room. but going downstairs and walking through the Privy Garden, he could see it quite plainly.

He found Charles, together with his brother, the Duke of York; Buckingham; Lord Arlington, the Secretary of State and other senior members of the court standing in Whitehall's Great Gallery. The King was speaking to the Colonel of his Life Guards—the Trained Bands of the City, Kit later found, had already been alerted—telling him to go into the City and put himself at the service of the Lord Mayor, who, Charles understood, was personally directing operations.

He saw Kit and called him over. 'Sir Christopher, the very man. I give you my orders to accompany the Guards and give my message to the Lord Mayor that he may have as many of them and my brother's Guards as he may require to help him contain the flames and be at his general bidding, for, by my life,

I have no wish to be a King of a burned capital. And you, Sir Christopher, will at all times attend my Lord Mayor and do his bidding, too.'

'I am yours to command,' answered Kit, and went at the run, calling for Caleb, his groom and his horse, to join the Life Guards and their Colonel, who were ready to march into London.

Riding along, he saw that the fire was already being driven towards him and there, in the midst of it, he found the Lord Mayor, Sir Thomas Bludworth, on horseback, his cohorts around him. Bludworth greeted Kit—not with gratitude at the King's offered help, but with distraction. He seemed, Kit thought, to be hardly aware of what needed to be done, was riding about shouting frantic orders at passers-by to stay and help, cries which they ignored.

The Lord Mayor at length dismounted among the smuts and ash and the smouldering ruins of what had once been fine town-houses, the fire roaring unhindered behind him. He said frantically to Kit, 'And of what use to me are Life Guards, sir, tell me that? And shall I pull houses down to stop the fire? And if I do, what then will follow? All is chaos, sir, chaos.' He swung an arm at the people who surrounded them—carrying goods, pushing carts, men shouting, women with children clutching at their skirts—none, as Kit plainly saw, doing anything to prevent the fire from spreading further.

An agitated man came running and fell on his knees before Bludworth, clutching at Bludworth's knees as if to find there some hope, some sustenance. 'The Merchant Taylor's Grammar School hath

been destroyed and the fire burns on. All London
will be gone.'

Bludworth began to wring his hands, turned blind
eyes on Kit. 'The Lord bless us. And what shall
follow now?'

Kit, in an effort to provide him with some stiffen-
ing, said, 'Nothing but that you pull houses down as
fire-breaks, my Lord Mayor. I am sure that the King
would wish it.'

'Aye, and, if I do, who will support me if their
fine houses go and the fire stops without them, so
that I did it all for nought? By law, having destroyed
their homes, I must then pay the cost of rebuilding
them. What then, sir? What then?'

'Send me to the King that I may advise him,
give thee further authority,' began Kit, to have
Bludworth wave a pettish hand at him.

'Nay, nay, man. I will do as you ask and pull
down houses, no need for the King. Do but stay
with me, and note what I have done.'

He seemed, Kit thought, almost more anxious to
justify himself than to stop the fire from spreading.
'Then, Sir,' Kit said, as gently as he might, for anger
and exasperation at such inneffectuality had begun
to rule him, 'we must be ahorse again, before the
crowd overwhelms us quite.' The stream of frightened people was increasing, and to the noise of the
fire—for it had a voice of its own—was added the
cries of the fearful, many of whom were making for
the river and safety, all else forgotten.

Once more on horseback, Kit followed
Bludworth, listening as news of the fire's progress
was brought in, watching Bludworth order the odd
house to be pulled down, which did nothing at all,

and merely added to Bludworth's lamentations. He had begun to fear for Celia, but it was plain that the fire had moved away from where she lived and that she was not in danger, and pray God, he thought, that she never will be.

After noon had struck, almost lost among the pealing of the bells—for some had gone to the bell-towers of London's many churches to ring the traditional warning that fire was approaching, as though such a warning were necessary, thought Kit, wryly—it was apparent that what small control Bludworth had exercised had long gone.

Riding over smouldering timbers, he suddenly turned on Kit, shouting, 'I am done, sir, done. I have been up all night and, God knows, I can do no more. I am for my bed.'

Kit rode to the distraught man's side; they were in Cannon Street, blocked with goods and carts. Furniture, virginals, the odd musical instrument, pots and pans had been thrown into the narrow street regardless of the stinking channel down its middle—all that there was in the way of drainage and sewerage.

'Then, let me ride to the King, sir, for further instructions. This cannot go on.'

'Nay, man. I order you to remain here. Oh, God, what am I to do?'

He was plainly gone beyond reason and sense. He dismounted again, leaned against the wall of a still-unburned house. Kit followed him, to see Mr Secretary Pepys approaching them, busy determination written on his face.

'My Lord Mayor, I am come from the King, having told him of the despair in which the City lives, that the fire rages and will not be stayed. He saith that he gives you orders to pull down as many houses as are needed to prevent the fire from spreading, to spare nothing, and the Duke of York hath said that he will send as many soldiers as you may require to support you in whatever is needed to be done.'

If Kit and Mr Pepys had thought that such a message would move Bludworth to action, they were mistaken. The Lord Mayor almost wailed in anguish, and continued to lament his own sad condition until Mr Pepys, shaking his head, left them, and Kit, angry at such cowardice and inanity, said abruptly, 'I will go to the King, my Lord Mayor, and tell him that the situation here is so serious that more must be done.'

'Oh, if only it were not a Sunday,' were the last words of Bludworth which followed him as he left, 'then more might be possible. But it is the Lord's Day and none are about!'

Kit found at Whitehall that the King and his ministers were more concerned than Bludworth, but still had little notion of how great the fire was—and still growing. Talking to Kit, and to others who came with further news of London's unhindered destruction, persuaded the King that he must visit the fire himself.

That afternoon the King, the Duke of York, Mr Pepys, Lord Craven and Kit, among others, went down to Queenhithe to direct operations personally, to see that large numbers of houses were pulled down to try and stay the fire but, although this answered for a little, the wind changing took the fire away, and all was to do again.

The Thames was full of craft. Lighters, wherries and barges loaded with people and goods took the refugees away into the country.

Kit took horse after a lull in the operations and rode through the as yet untouched part of the City to Swain's Yard, to see that Celia was safe. She had not sent for him, but she would surely forgive him if he called on her to assure himself that she was not in danger.

Like many other Londoners, Celia, although frightened a little by the fire, was not aware of its magnitude or that it was going to be much greater than any of the conflagrations which occasionally attacked the City.

Afterwards the authorities realised that the unnaturally dry and hot summer, following on that of the previous year, had rendered the timbers of the largely wooden houses so dry that they caught fire on the instant. The gales which swept through London that week also played their part, but that first morning the fear which overwhelmed the City when it became plain that the fire was out of control was confined to those immediately affected by it.

The first news which Celia had that matters might be serious came when Willem brought one of Mr Pepys's servants in to see her. He had news from his master, he said. Mistress Archer should be prepared to pack her goods and chattels, to bury anything of value in her garden, in case the fire changed course and began to sweep towards the Tower. He was sending word to all his friends, of whom he counted Mistress Archer one because of the service which she had rendered to himself and his wife.

'So,' said Willem, face grim. 'We must start at once, mistress. Better safe than sorry, I always say.'

They all took part in the packing of the more valuable of their possessions which they stacked in the garden at the back. Willem rolled out the handcart which he used in his gardening work and filled that—Celia's viol being carefully positioned on top of clothing wrapped around ornaments and Adam Antiquis's precious clock which Thomas Tompion had made for him.

After that Celia sat down by the empty hearth in the parlour to feed Adam while Mistress Hood prepared a meal for them. Adam's lunch was almost over when there came a loud rapping on the front door, after which Mistress Hood came in to say Sir Christopher Carlyon was here and that he must see Mistress Archer at once!

Celia did not have time to detach Adam from her breast or tidy herself before Kit entered. He was not at all his usual well-ordered self. His face was grimy, and patches of soot were on his clothing and his hands. He had taken off his broad-brimmed hat and brought into the room with him the smell of fire and burning.

They stared at one another. Kit thought that Celia had never looked more serene as she sat by the hearth, Adam at her breast. When he said, 'Forgive me for coming before you sent for me,' Adam turned his head at the sound of his voice and rewarded him with a milky smile, the green eyes sparkling at him. Celia herself was as grave as one of the painted Madonnas he had seen in Italy. He remembered what Buckingham had said of her.

'Mistress Celia hath the art of spreading peace about her,' and that was true.

Kit had an insane desire to be Adam so that he might feed from her perfect breast. He had to hold on to his duty, finish his sentence. 'But I had to check that all was well with you. I have spent the morning on the King's service with My Lord Mayor, and this afternoon came hither with the King and his brother to see what might be done to stay the fire. We seem to have blown up half London's houses to little avail, and shortly before I came to see you the water supply was dwindling to a stop.'

He had not meant to be so impersonal, but he feared that if he were not he would be unmanned, would fall before her and demand to take her and the child out of danger, out of London, forgetting his duty to his king who trusted him.

'This is indeed kind.' Celia was almost as stiff as he was. She could see the hunger in his gaze on her as she went on, 'Mr Pepys hath sent his servant to advise me to pack as many of our goods as possible in preparation for flight, and we had just finished before you came—but the fire is not heading this way yet?'

Kit shook his head, moved forward a step and said hoarsely, 'No, the wind is taking it in quite the opposite direction. The trouble is that sometimes, and how it doth this we do not know, the fire skips streets and houses to take it clear beyond all normal expectations.' Then words burst from him impetuously as he fell on his knees before her and the babe stretched out a hand to touch his cheek—a strange man being more interesting than milk now that he was almost satiated.

Kit kissed the small hand, and said rapidly, 'Oh, my dear, tell me that if the fire comes nigh you will leave at once. I cannot bear to think that you might be in danger. Promise me that you will leave. I will have a word with Willem before I go. You cannot think how dreadful the fire is until you have seen it at its pitiless worst. I have watched houses destroyed in an instant, aye, and churches, too, and people swallowed up in it without warning.'

Celia stroked his head. She could tell that he had been labouring. His curls were damp and the scent of the fire was so strong that the room seemed full of it. His face when he looked up at her was white and strained. 'And I may not stay with thee long. I have my duty to do, I will speak to Mr Pepys, ask him to keep his busy eye on you. Oh, my love, if only I could stay with you.'

His arms were around them both, and if Celia had feared that it was only for the child that he valued her, his voice and manner told her that she was wrong. For a moment they stayed like that, locked together. To Kit it was as though he had reached an oasis in the desert—he remembered visiting one on his last ill-fated journey to North Africa. He did not want to leave her, he had come home at last, and he thought that if she gave him an answer now it would be the one he wanted so desperately.

She said into his hair, 'I have cast Adam's horoscope and it promised him a long and prosperous life and, Kit, I cast an election for us both, and it said that we should come together after a fashion difficult to understand—and that was true, was it not? It did not say that we should be parted.'

Kit looked up at her. 'And now we have truly

found one another, we must be parted, I fear. I must return to Whitehall soon. The King is calling a Council this evening to decide on what to do if the fire doth not burn itself out. He has asked me to be present, and I must not fail him. It is my duty.' And he took her hand and kissed it.

No word of love had yet been spoken between them, but there was no need. Neither, apart from Celia's words of her prophecies, did they speak of the future. As her father had once said, and now Celia knew how true his words were, 'The present and the memory of the past is all we ever have.' This moment when they were together was more precious to her than a thousand hours which they might possibly share in the future.

She stroked his head again and said, her voice low, 'My love, one thing which the fire hath done is tell me how much I truly love you. . .' He lifted his head to look up into her eyes, began to speak, but she put a finger on his lips, saying, 'No, let me finish. I told a grievous lie, and grievously have we paid for it, losing a year which we might have spent together. I should have trusted thee that, knowing me, and knowing that I had begun to love thee, you had changed enough to regret the bet. My hateful pride drove me to do what I did. I loved thee then, and now I love thee more than ever. I would be thy wife when this is over, and that is the answer I promised thee. I prayed that the fire would spare thee so that thou might come to know thy son.' And she put Adam into his father's arms, adding, 'I can see by your face that you have neither eaten nor rested since the dawn. Even the King would allow you a moment's respite. Stay but a while, hold thy son, and Mistress Hood and I will prepare a meal for you.'

It was a moment out of time. Kit sat down in what had been Adam Antiquis's great chair, Adam Antiquis's grandson on his knee. His son laughed up at him and Kit stroked his chestnut curls, so like his own. He could hear Celia and her housekeeper bustling around and he had a dream of Latter with them all present, aye, and Willem, too. The dream held him, so that presently Celia, coming in with a bowl of broth and some good bread to go with it, found him dozing, his sleeping son in his arms.

She awoke him with a kiss, then fetched another bowl and they sat and ate together, the babe in his basket sleeping sweetly.

Reluctantly, his meal over, Kit at last stood up—Celia with him, Adam now in her arms. Kit took him from her, kissed the small face and walked to the window with him, to look towards London and the smoke in the sky which was shutting out the sun.

'When this is over,' he said, handing Adam back to his mother, 'I shall take thee both home to Latter with me, and I promise you that when I do I shall tell you of Adam's half-brother and his mother, for I must lay their poor ghosts to rest at last.'

It was plain that he did not wish to leave them. Mistress Hood put her head into the room and, seeing them so earnest together, withdrew. Celia said, painfully, for she could not bear to think of him going into danger, but she must not keep him from his duty, 'You must not stay, Kit. You have your duty to do as I have mine. Mine is to Willem and his wife and poor Nan. Yours is to the King. I promise that I will be careful and will flee the fire should it come near.'

Kit nodded. 'Yes, I must be a good soldier for one last time, but I promise thee if the fire makes its way to Tower Street then, God willing, I shall come for you at once.'

He could not leave her without giving her something to show how much he longed and wished for her to be his true wife, now that she had agreed to marry him.

He put his arms around Celia and his son, saying, 'My dearest love, you have told me how much you love me. Will you believe that my love for you is as deep, so much so that I could not bear a future without you?' For a long moment they clung together before he turned, and with one last glance at her and the babe he was gone.

Afterwards the four days during which the fire raged and burned down most of the old medieval city were a blur to Kit. It was difficult to remember on which day any particular event had happened. The King used him ruthlessly as a messenger and as one to send orders who would see that they were obeyed. Fire stations were set up and it was his duty to see that they remained manned. He had told Celia that he would be a good soldier and he was.

At first the King's efforts were directed to seeing that all steps were taken to prevent the fire from spreading and then, when that proved ineffectual, however many houses were blown up or pulled down to stop its advance, he resorted to other measures. Both he and his brother, the Duke of York, did what they could by their individual example to spur

London's citizens on to try to stop the fire, rather than simply fly from it as quickly as they could, leaving the City to burn down.

Night turned into day. Part of Kit's jumbled memories came from simple lack of sleep. Red-eyed, he rose, laboured and exhorted from dawn to dusk, and then at night he was called from his bed, to find that the fire was so strong that its yellow flames blotted out the moon. Men laboured and fled downriver from it as though it were day, and he was needed in London's streets to see that the fire posts were not deserted.

Once he came upon men looting a house and, enraged, he drew his rapier and cut one of them down, the rest fleeing. He said afterwards to Celia that danger brought out both the best and worst in men. By Tuesday, the fourth day of September, the fourth day of the fire, he was spent—his body aching, his voice hoarse. But when that morning the King decided to visit the fire and personally take charge of the fighting of it, Kit was one of the group of gentlemen on horseback who accompanied him.

During the day the fire destroyed Cheapside, where the goldsmiths had their shops and homes, and reached St Paul's—to destroy that, too. The fire seemed to have become a living thing, with a mind of its own. As fast as My Lord Craven, who was in overall charge of the fire-fighting, drew up plans to prevent its further spread, it twisted and turned and made its way to where it could rage unchecked.

Early that morning, Robert Renwick, who had seen his servants, apprentices and his old father leave, returned to his shop on Cheapside to recover from it the bags of gold which he had hidden in the cellars before the fire—which was now advancing rapidly towards it—could reach it. He had trusted no one to know of the size of the treasure which he had accumulated.

He was pushing a small handcart and had decided that when he had filled it with the bags, placed under blankets which he had prudently brought with him to disguise the nature of its load, he would make his way to Mistress Archer's and demand that she escape by boat with him into the country. He had decided to make her Mistress Renwick, after all.

The fire was on him sooner than he expected. Worse, as he hauled his last bag of gold from the cellar, he found that he had a companion. Leaning against the wall of what had been his workroom, but was now stripped, was One-Eye.

Robert stared at him. 'In God's name, what brings you here?' he rasped.

One-Eye leered at him. 'Not God, Master Renwick—say, rather, the devil.'

Robert registered that One-Eye had called him by his true name and said curtly, 'I think you mistake.'

'Nay.' One-Eye advanced on him and Robert saw that there was a knife in his hand, fell intent in his eye. 'It is you who mistake, Master Jude Scrivener. Didst think that I would not know who thou truly were? I thought to gouge money from thee by threatening to tell the authorities that the master fence for whom they were looking was respectable Master Robert Renwick, but the fire hath given me a better chance. Hand me thy gold, master, or worse will befall thee.'

Robert Renwick did not lack courage, whatever his other sins. Perhaps this encounter was a boon. If he disposed of One-Eye then there would be none left to tell the tale of his double life. He fumbled for the rapier which he always wore, although it was a decoration rather than a weapon.

One-Eye watched him with a grin. 'Do not think to stick me with thy little pin, master. I know a trick worth two of that.'

Robert tried to grin back. His rapier was out now and he advanced clumsily on his tormentor, who—as Kit had done—sidestepped, feinted and, seizing Robert's wrist to turn aside his sword, which left Robert's breast exposed before him, plunged his dagger into his heart.

Robert fell without a groan, One-Eye laughing down at him. What whore-son good luck! The fire would destroy Master Renwick's body and hide the evidence of his murder. Everyone would think he had been caught by it while recovering his treasure.

The fire was almost upon him. One-Eye seized the handles of the cart and trundled it into the street, running to stay ahead of the flames—a fortune in his grasp. He was almost out of the street when wicked luck had it that the house at the end, which appeared untouched but had actually been destroyed from within, fell upon him, a beam from it breaking his back—and the fire consumed him as well as his victim.

Kit knew nothing of this small drama, one among many. He only knew that Cheapside had gone, and the churches of St Mary-le-Bow and St Peter Chepe with it, and that now St Paul's was threatened. He and his King were sharing the manual labour of fighting the fire. Charles stood beside Kit and Buckingham and their fellow courtiers as they took spades and buckets and assisted in demolishing those houses which stood in the very path of the fire.

Later Kit stood between the King and the Duke of York as they and others formed a human chain to pass buckets of water to those ahead of them who fought the fire directly. Mud-spattered, grimy, soot-covered, his fine clothes torn and wet with sweat— for the combined heat of the sun and the fire made the temperature of the City almost tropical—Charles was a far cry from the man who dallied idly with his mistresses. He was, thought Kit, a monarch to be proud of.

He was rewarded by Charles gasping at him, 'You were with me under fire at Worcester Field, Kit, and now we are together in the lee of another kind of fire. Art a good fellow. When this is over, you may ask me for what you wish.'

Well, thought Kit wryly, the water slopping over and ruining his good boots, Charles had made him many promises, few of which had been kept—mostly through no fault of his own—but this one he would see was kept.

He would ask to be relieved of his post before his time was up so that he might retire with Celia to Latter. All that long and dismal day this one thought was in his mind, and to think of Celia's face was like thinking of cool water in the desert.

Kit paused in his work to mop his brow, seating himself on the remains of a wall. He was exhausted, his hair was plastered to his skull and his clothes were sticking to his back. His boots and breeches were covered with mud. The King, who was in little better case, was distributing guineas from a leather pouch slung from his shoulder, rewarding those who had laboured with him, when a wild-eyed man ran up shouting that the fire's direction had changed again and after destroying St Paul's it was making for Tower Street, and would shortly be at the Tower itself.

Kit sprang up, his tiredness forgotten. He turned to Charles, who was now shaking the hand of an honest citizen who was overwhelmed by this close contact with his monarch.

'Sire,' he exclaimed. 'You may grant me your boon immediately. Relieve me of my present post, I beg of you. Mistress Celia Antiquis now has her home in Swain's Yard, Tower Street and I beg leave to go there at once and assure myself of her safety.'

The King put a hand on Kit's shoulder. 'You have no need to ask me for permission. I know how it is between you and your lady. Buckingham told me all the other night. Go at once and take my blessing with you for all you have done for myself and England since Worcester Field.'

Oh, yes, he was indeed a king to be proud of, thought Kit, as he called for his horse and for Caleb who had been working selflessly alongside him, and he made off for Swain's Yard and Celia, praying that all was well with her. But the fire seemed to have gained a stronger hold than ever, for all their efforts.

He was not to know that this was the last flare-up before it came to a halt. All he knew was that the flames were everywhere and that Celia was in danger.

CHAPTER FOURTEEN

RIDING towards Swain's Yard was no easy thing. Kit and Caleb had to make their way through a press of people. The fire had caught most of them unawares. They had thought themselves safe but, sweeping down from St Paul's, which was all ablaze, Master Inigo Jones's façade disappearing beneath the flames, the fire had taken a new turn and a new toll.

Hysteria gripped the refugees. Struggling through them, Kit marvelled at what people thought worth saving. One man pushed a cart on which stood his virginals; another was carrying a parrot in a cage; a third a painting, blackened and scorched. A woman on a street corner had sunk down screaming: she was giving birth. Kit never knew what became of her. She had friends and neighbours around her to care for her, and he—why, he was making for Celia.

As he neared Swain's Yard his fear grew. The fire had reached that end of Tower Street. The noise of it filled his ears, smoke filled his eyes—thick, asphyxiating, choking smoke, adding to the fear of those caught by the fire.

And there before him, as he dismounted, leaving his horse with Caleb, was the row of houses in Swain's Yard and all of them, including Celia's, were aflame. A woman stood at the upstairs window of one of them screaming—she had doubtless run upstairs to rescue something and the fire had reached the stairs before she could gain safety again. A man stood shouting up at her, held back by his neighbours from entering his house to save her. His face was livid in the flames, for although the clock said that it was day, it was dark, the flames and smoke obscuring the sun and sky.

Great flakes of soot, of burning paper, of scraps of cloth, even pieces of wood, fell on Kit as he struggled forward crying Celia's name. He saw through the window in the room where Celia had received him that the fire was in the house. He touched the shoulder of one of the men holding the shouting man and shouted himself, 'Mistress Archer — what of her? Is she safe?'

The man turned blind eyes on him as the woman fell back from the window and was seen no more, her face replaced by the fire's pitiless glare. The woman's husband answered Kit. 'Nay,' he sobbed, 'that was my wife in there. Oh, cursed be the day, cursed be the day,' and he fell on his knees in the street, his head in his hands, distraught, lost to the world.

Kit turned to another standing by, questioned him, to receive a shake of the head. The man knew not Celia or Willem; he had come to see the fire, and, bewitched by it, was in danger of being consumed by it. There were many such, Kit later heard, men whom fire fascinated, who found release in it.

Kit found himself running towards Celia's house. A man sought to detain him but he ran on, to wrench open the door and be stopped by a wall of flame, its hot breath on his face.

He staggered back, heard himself shouting Celia's name. Outside again, he shattered the parlour window to look inside—to find that here, too, the fire was master, and that nothing could live there. Celia's house was a furnace.

Someone was behind him, pulling him away as he started to climb through the window, for surely, if she were there, God would let him find her. It was Caleb, shouting at him, 'Master, master, even if she be there you cannot save her. We are too late.'

Too late! The words were a knell which he had heard before. Too late, he had cried among the burned ruins of his and Anna's home. Too late, too late by a week—and now he was too late by a few minutes! He shook his fist at Caleb and at the sky, cursing God, the stars, he knew not what, and made to run at the house again.

Caleb and the man who had lost his wife held him back. He was on his knees cursing them both. Caleb said, 'You do not even know that she is there, master.'

The man beside him, his face still distorted with grief, turned ravaged eyes on Kit and asked, 'Is it Mistress Archer whom you seek?'

'Aye,' replied Kit, and was suddenly full of hope. Perhaps the man knew something. 'Had she fled before the fire came?'

'Nay, sir. I know not. I was too busy saving me and mine, and then my Mary ran back for something—I know not what—and the fire destroyed the stairs before she could return. . .' And he was sobbing again, lost to everything until Caleb, taking pity on him, led him away.

Kit stood and watched Celia's house burn. The first terror had disappeared and, like the man sobbing behind him, he was stunned. He had laboured for four days with little sleep, and only snatched food to sustain him. Exhaustion rode on his shoulders. Caleb was pulling at him.

'Come away, master, there is nothing you can do.'

Kit shook his head. 'Perchance she and the babe left before the fire. Perchance they are still in danger—the fire may have followed them.'

He had a dim memory, as of another time, that Mr Secretary Pepys lived not far from here, in Seething Lane. Perchance he knew something or, perchance, he too, had fled the fire.

His tired brain revolved possibilities. The exhaustion which he had felt back with the King, and had forgotten on his way to Tower Street, was claiming him. He must not let it.

'What now, master?' asked Caleb, seeing Sir Kit turn away from him and begin to walk to the north.

'Seething Lane,' said Kit, almost absently. 'Mr Secretary Pepys lives there. He knows many things, mayhap he knows where Mistress Celia has gone.'

Caleb thought that his master's wits were wandering through grief, but decided to humour him. Together they walked up Watermark Lane, the fire running level with them until, almost at the end of the lane, a woman ran out of a house which the fire had begun to ravage and clutched at Kit's arm. 'My boy!' she cried. 'My boy, Jem. I lost him in there. Oh, sir, I beg of you, save my boy.'

Kit took one look at her, thought of Adam and of Cecco, who might both be lost to him, and before Caleb could stop him, he ran into the house, the woman behind him crying the boy's name. 'Jem, oh, Jem.'

She stopped at the door, affrighted by the noise

of the fire and the billowing smoke, but Kit ran on, shouting, 'Jem, where are you? Answer me, Jem.'

The house was filling with smoke though the flames had not yet begun to eat it. There was a flight of stairs. He called up it. 'Jem, are you there? Jem? Answer me.' It suddenly seemed imperative that this one child should be saved if all else in London, Celia and Adam included, had perished.

A faint voice came down the stairs to him. 'Aye, I'm here, at the front. Oh, Mam, is it you?'

Kit took the stairs at a run, still calling Jem, the voice still answering. He heard it strongly as he reached a small landing, threw open a door to find flames roaring and a boy, about six or seven years old, standing against the wall on the other side of the flames, his arms spread wide, face fearful.

He saw Kit and wailed, 'Oh, good master, save me!'

Kit swung round. There was a curtain before the window on the landing. He pulled it down, wrapped it round his head and shoulders and, head down, ran through the flames—praying to God that the floor would still support his weight—to snatch at the boy, the flames licking at the curtain as he tucked him under his arm.

He made the short journey through the fire back to the landing, his eyes running from the acrid smoke which was beginning to fill it, he and the boy coughing. Somehow he found the stairs again and, pursued by the fire, ran down them as fast as he could. The boy lay limp under his arm, whether made unconscious by the smoke or through fright, Kit did not know.

Once in the open again he pulled off the flaming

curtain and threw himself and the now screaming boy down on the cinder path before the house to roll over and over to put out any remaining flames, as he had seen others do who had run out of the fire.

Someone, Caleb, perhaps, threw a bucket of water over them as he came to a stop, and then another and another. His hair was singed and the smell of burned and wet cloth was strong in his nostrils. The woman was on her knees beside him, crying and wailing over the boy who was sobbing against her, but was safe, as Kit was.

And Adam, his mind screamed, and Celia, are *they* safe?

Caleb was shouting at him, reproaching him. 'Art mad, master? Art tired of life? To run into the fire after an imp you do not know.'

Kit struggled to his feet, and knew at once that he had gone beyond exhaustion. He felt as he had done after Worcester Field, after every battle he had ever been in—that he was no longer Kit Carlyon. Kit Carlyon had gone. He was a mindless, suffering entity who endured and lived without conscious thought, able only to continue to struggle because feeling had, for the moment, left him.

He said through cracked lips, 'At least the fire did not get him.'

'It got thy eyelashes and touched thy eyebrows, though,' said Caleb grimly, leading him away. The woman and the boy had disappeared. 'And she never gave thee thanks, neither.'

'I did not want them,' sighed Kit tiredly. Simply to save the boy had been something to be done, and now that it was done the urge to find Mr Pepys was strong in him. They were almost at Seething Lane, and Caleb was having to guide him. He noted, as though he were looking at another's body, that his sleeve was burned and that the water which had been thrown over him was making him cold, adding to his exhaustion.

'You need tending,' Caleb was scolding. 'Art wet through. Should go back to Whitehall, master.'

Staggering together, for Caleb was now taking most of Kit's weight, they turned into Seething Lane and saw that outside Mr Pepys's house there was a milling crowd. Mr Pepys and his wife stood beside a horse and cart. Boxes and goods ready to be loaded on it were piled high in his garden.

A man with a handcart stood to one side. It was Willem.

Kit stared at him, then shouted, his voice as cracked as his lips, 'Mistress Celia? Adam?'

It was all that he could manage to say. The small press of people standing by Mr Pepys turned to look at him and, desperate, he shouted again, 'Mistress Celia? Adam? Oh, God, are you there? Tell me that you are safe.' He was suddenly beside himself. . .

Celia, who had been holding Adam in her arms, had heard Kit shout her name. She thrust the baby at Nan, who stood beside her, and ran towards Kit. As she did so the premonition she had experienced over a year ago took her by the throat. She had seen all this before. She recognised the dark sky, which she had wrongly thought was night, recognised the flames riding high in it and Kit's distorted face as he shouted.

Only, in the present, she knew that it was her name and Adam's that he was shouting and she ran towards him. She could hardly recognise him. His hair was singed, his face was covered in mud and smut, and what she could see of it was scarlet. Only his green eyes stared out at her, questioning, in-domitable—but it was also plain that he was near collapse.

She reached him to look into his face, to say, 'Oh, Kit. I am here, I am safe, and Adam, too. See, Nan hath him in her arms. Mr Pepys was going to take us all into the country.'

Kit could only hold her and bend his head to say, feebly now, his remaining strength fast leeching from him, 'I thought that the fire had thee. That I had lost wife and child for the second time—before I even had them. If you had perished, I think I would have done so, too. Oh, Celia. . .my love. . .my love. . .'

Celia felt him sag against her, felt Caleb lift him away from her to ease him on to the ground, growling almost angrily, 'I *told* him not to go into the fire to rescue the boy. He hath not slept properly for three nights and has been fighting the fire since dawn.'

Mr Pepys came up to them and said quietly, 'I have been watching the fire. It hath stopped, or rather, turned away again, but it is not as fierce as it was. It will not reach here now. Come, let us take Sir Christopher into my house. He is spent. Wife,' he added, turning to her as she stood, still super-vising the loading of the cart, 'leave that. Pray God we may not need to fly London, after all. Sir Christopher is exhausted and must rest a little.'

'I will look after him,' said Celia eagerly.

Caleb and Willem helped Kit walk in, for after a

moment he had stirred and tried to rise. Mr Pepys said, 'Better let him have his way if he wishes to walk,' and led them into his parlour. Celia, a little behind them, turned for one last look at the fire, which was now moving away from them, but feebler, she thought. It was, although she did not know it, the fire's swan-song. It would reach Pie Corner, almost where it had started, and then slowly die down, its end nearly as mysterious as its beginning.

Mr Pepys fussed Sir Christopher into his great chair by the hearth and fetched wine for them all, not excluding Willem and his wife, Nan and his own servants. In his busy way, he was extremely kind, Celia thought. A great burden had been lifted from her shoulders now that she knew that Kit was safe, something which had worried her grievously ever since she and Willem had decided that the fire was coming too near their home and that they must leave it, and go to Mr Pepys in Seething Lane.

She remembered as she sat and watched him wash his face and hands—Mr Pepys's serving-maid had brought a cloth and a bowl of warm water—that he had told her that he would come to her if the fire reached Tower Street, and he had kept his promise.

He was shivering, she saw, and so did Mr Pepys for he took Sir Christopher upstairs—he was most punctilious in his naming of him—to find at least a clean shirt for him. 'For,' said Mr Pepys whimsically, 'although you—like his blessed Majesty—being so tall and I being so short we may not easily exchange clothes, but a small dry shirt will do better than a large wet one!'

And so it was, thought Kit gratefully, coming downstairs in his new shirt, his hair washed and dried, to find that there was hot tea and a fruited loaf waiting—and Celia had begun to feed Adam, a sight of which he felt that he could never tire.

Except that he was still so tired that he could hardly speak. Mr Pepys watched them for a moment as they sat quiet, so full of one another that words were not needed, and presently excused himself for a time so that they might be alone.

Adam fed, Celia went over to sit on the floor at Kit's feet, Adam in her arms, Kit's hand stroking her hair. She, like Kit, was touched by the effects of the fire and felt that only a bath and new linen would make her feel fresh again, but that did not matter. Not only was he safe, but he had come for her—at great risk—as he had said that he would, and she could no longer doubt that he loved her as well as the babe, and all would surely be well.

Mr Pepys returned after a little space, and spoke to Kit. 'Sir Christopher, I have taken a great liberty. I have spoken to my friend and patron Lord Brouncker and he will put his coach at your disposal to take Mistress Celia and yourself, and your servants, back to Whitehall where there will be ample room for you all. It is not that I wish you away, you understand, but I think that you would rather be together, and I have little further room for any guests here.'

He did not tell them that out of the goodness of his heart he had already taken in several friends, and Kit and Celia were grateful for his kind consideration.

'He will send his coach for you within the hour. I trust that this arrangement is to your liking.'

'It is to mine, and you have my thanks,' said Kit

softly. 'As to Mistress Celia. . .' And he looked at her.

'Why,' answered Celia as composedly as she could, 'I, too, am grateful to Mr Pepys, but I would not trespass on Sir Christopher's kindness. . .'

'Oh, you could never do that,' interjected Kit softly. He felt drowsy but content. The wine, the tea and the food which Mr Pepys had pressed on him, and the comfort of the chair, together with the presence of Adam and Celia, had wrought on him to make him feel that after the discomforts and hard labour of the last few days he had arrived in some sort of heaven. Best of all would be simply to stay here, his hand on her head, her head against his knee, the sleeping child in her lap. He had never known such peace and contentment.

But he also wanted her to be with him where they might be alone, where he could tell her that he loved her, and where she could say the same to him. They could be alone at Whitehall, in his room above the river, and after that—why, after that, Latter beckoned. . .

He bent and kissed her head and waited for My Lord Brouncker's coach and prayed that Mr Secretary Pepys was right again—that the fire was almost over, and that not quite all London had fallen before it.

Celia was seated on Kit's bed at Whitehall. She had been to the bathing-closet and had the bath for which she had longed and changed into clean night rail, loosening her newly washed blonde hair around her shoulders. Adam was lying in his basket at the bottom of the bed, whose curtains had been looped back. Nan had just left to go to the servants' quarters where Willem and his wife were already installed.

She had not actually been welcomed in state by the King, but My Lord Brouncker and Mr Pepys between them had sent word of their coming and Celia had been installed in Kit's room by a bowing major-domo, and Kit had been given another room down the corridor. 'For,' the King had said privately to Buckingham, 'Sir Christopher hath done noble work this week and must be rewarded. Now, George, he saith that he wishes to retire to the small estate which you have lost to him, and I would not prevent his going, but I would fain give him some reward before he leaves.'

Buckingham, who had watched Celia dismount from Lord Brouncker's coach a little earlier, Kit's arm around her and the babe, was once again resplendently dressed after the labours of the day. The court might sleep in peace that night—the fire had almost ended.

'A viscountcy,' he said, at last. 'For sure, he deserves something—being with you at Worcester, and never having been a charge on you thereafter during our exile.'

This was a shrewd hit, for so many had, as both Charles and Buckingham knew.

Charles nodded, 'He is a proud man, I know. And wilt marry the astrologer's daughter, you think, not merely make her his mistress?'

'She would not have him else, or perhaps she might have been mine.' Buckingham's smile was rueful.

'A viscountcy then, and some office to give him the wherewithal to sustain it,' said the King decisively. 'My Lord Viscount Carlyon of Latter. It hath a good sound.'

'Oh, aye,' said Buckingham, affecting a Yorkshire accent for a moment—all his great estates were there. 'And he hath a ready-made heir, too, if he cannot get himself another.' It was his farewell to Celia as well as Kit that he had assisted the King in rewarding his old friend and thus cancelled out the treachery which had lain between them.

So it was done, and the King ordered the Letters Patent on the morrow. But that night Kit was still simple Sir Christopher and, wearing a great brocade gown over his night rail, was on his way to his room to see his love and his son before he retired to his bed alone.

The door opened and Celia looked expectantly towards it. At least this time, this time as Kit approached her bed he was conscious and knew who she was. What would he say and do? What would she say to him?

He paused by the basket at the foot of the bed and bent to kiss the sleeping baby's cheek. There was such tenderness on his face that Celia swallowed, her throat tight.

As he sat near to her in a chair by the bed she saw that he was clean Sir Kit again, but the stigmata of weariness was on his face. He smiled at her, the green eyes shining, and she smiled back.

'My love,' he said, and kissed her hand. 'I cannot believe that we are alone together and safe, our child sleeping near by. I should not have come, I know. You are tired, but I must have speech with thee. There is much to be said, and the first words are, I love you, and have loved you since I first saw thee in thy father's parlour and regretted the devil's bet which I made with Buckingham and which nearly drove us apart. You will forgive me for that, my heart?'

Celia nodded, her throat closing. 'Yes,' she managed at last, 'for without the bet we should never have met, and I believe now, as I told you when we spoke during the fire, that you regretted it.'

'That is noble of you,' he said. 'And now I must tell thee why I was so wild and scorned everyone, men and women both—and in exchange you must tell me why you lied about the bet and said that I had won it. You would account that a fair exchange, mistress? And after that I shall ask you to be my wife, and I hope that the answer will be the one which we can celebrate.' The green eyes were so tender that Celia pressed the hand which held hers and Kit knew, without words, what her answer would be.

Nevertheless, he must tell her his story, and quickly, for there should be no secrets between them.

He moved over to the bed and looked down at her, as she sat there in the blonde glory of her hair, the grave grey eyes shining at him filled with love and trust, and said, 'May I sit by thee, my love? I should like to hold you while I speak.'

Celia nodded and he put his right arm about her, and they sat there, companionably, too tired for open passion—but the passion was there, all the same, even if not expressed.

'After Worcester,' he began, almost conversationally, 'I fled to France to join my King. I never saw my father again, nor my home for nearly ten years. I hated being a pensioner, hated seeing what being one was doing to my King. I think that he will never recover completely from it. I left to become a mercenary soldier, a hired sword. It was not what I expected from life, but it was the only living I could earn. At last it took me to Italy, and there I hired myself out to a merchant on the sea coast well to the south of Naples to guard his little fleet of ships when they crossed the Mediterranean.

'I loved Italy. I liked the sun and the music and the people, the happiness I found there. I also found the merchant's only child, his daughter Anna, and I fell in love with her, my first true love—although as is the common way of young men, I had many light loves before her. We married—it was she who gave me the ruby ring on our wedding-day. Her father approved of me. I wanted to be more than a swordhand and, thinking that there would never again be a home for me in England, when he said that he would accept me for a son-in-law if I learned to run his business, I agreed.

'I had never known true happiness before. My mother died before I knew her, and my father was old when I was born. I had no brother or sister, just a few friends made when I was with the King— George Buckingham among them, which is why I can never truly break with him. But with Anna, her father and our little son, Francesco, I came to be happy. I thought that my life was settled, that I had renounced England and that I would live and die in Italy. After Cecco was born my father-in-law's health began to fail, and it was arranged that I would take the business over and that we would hire a mercenary to protect our ships and I would stay on shore.

'Alas, the mercenary we hired failed to arrive and Anna's father and I agreed that I would make one more voyage to North Africa with a large argosy which would seal the merchant's fortune and start me on my way as his successor.

'When I lay in your house, my wits wandering, I relived my final parting with Anna and Cecco over and over again. He was so like Adam, he had his happy nature. Anna—she was passionate and beautiful, all hot temper and fire, and I—I matched her. I was only twenty-three. For some reason she did not want me to go, begged me to stay behind, but I wanted to please her father who had been good to me and, besides, I had done the thing before, and all had been well. I remember parting from her and the babe, our last walk on the seashore.'

He paused, and looked blindly away from her.

'I never saw them again. When we got back from our venture we knew as we sailed in—even from a distance—that something was wrong. We saw, soon enough, that the small port and town had gone, burned to the ground. Nothing lived or moved there. A few who had fled to the hills came down to greet us. They told us that the Barbary Corsairs had come, had stripped the town of its wealth, looted, murdered and raped, and then had rounded up all those left alive, herded them into the church and set fire to it.

'What exactly happened to Anna and Cecco, I never knew. Only that they were gone. Some of the few survivors said that the Corsairs had taken some of the younger women away with them, others said no, that all had been slaughtered. Nothing was left to me. At first, I was stunned by what had happened, and then was almost mad with grief. I retained enough sanity to sail to Naples, sell what we had brought back and divide the money between us—for all the crew and soldiers were as broken in mind and spirit as I was.

'I cursed God, I cursed everything. My life had been destroyed twice, and the second destruction was the more painful. It changed me, Celia. I had been a pleasant enough boy, if a little hard. Now, I cared for nothing—for to care for something was to lose it. I cared for neither God nor the devil.

'I went back to France, found employment there and tried to drown my memories in debauchery—which did not answer. It never does. I next tried to drown my memories in drink—but I hated what it did to me, and to others who drank. I have seen what it does to Buckingham and Rochester. It makes apes of men, and I had enough self-respect left not to want that. In the end, I gave up both drink and the worst debaucheries and lived only for the day.

'By the time I met you I was sick of myself, my life and the world. I had drowned in self-pity long enough, but in some strange way I could not rescue myself. You seemed to me to have all the virtues which I had lost or rejected in my anger at a world which had taken Anna and Cecco from me so cruelly. You were not Anna come again, you could not be more different from what she was, but I could see in you what I might want in my life. I bet on you before I knew you, tempted by Buckingham's promise of Latter if I won. I wanted to leave the court but I had nowhere to go, only a derelict house and half a dozen barren acres in Cheshire. Latter would give me a home, and I thought nothing of the vile way in which I was trying to win it.

'I often wanted to tell you of the bet and to ask your forgiveness, but I could not. I did not want you looking at me in disgust. And then, you, my symbol of truth and purity, lied and said that you had lain with me! Why? It makes no difference to me now, although it nearly broke my heart then because I had come to love you and the last thing which I wished to do was defile you. I want you for my wife, but I would dearly like to know why you lied to the court and all the world—especially since afterwards, when I was wandering in purgatory, you lay with me to heal me and loved me so sweetly that in dreams you visit me still. . .'

He was silent at last. Celia had listened to him in mingled horror and pity. She could not have imagined such a story. She was silent for so long that Kit turned and lifted her face by the chin, to find the silent tears running down it. He bent his head to kiss them away—and passion suddenly ran through them both.

They clung to one another before Celia said brokenly, 'Oh, if only I had known, I would not have treated you so vilely. But at the time I wanted to strike at you and it seemed a suitable revenge. I had come to like you, as well as to love you, and I thought that you felt the same for me. Then in the bathing-closet I heard Dorothy Lowther and Lady Castlemaine laughing and talking about the bet. I think now that they knew that I was there and that they did it out of spite and jealousy, but, oh, I have never felt so ill. I wanted to strike at you, to hurt you as I was hurt when I discovered that I meant nothing to you, that you had bet on my virginity with such a whoremonger as George Buckingham, and that you, you were no better.'

'Nor was I then,' replied Kit humbly. 'I had been vile before—only knowing you changed me.'

'So I wanted to hurt you, and George Buckingham, and I thought that if I lied you would hate that, even if it gave you Latter, for I thought that you still retained some vestige of honour. Also, if I said that I had not enjoyed you, the court would laugh at you—which it did. And I was robbing Buckingham of Latter and losing him the bet which was all that *he* deserved. Every time you thought of Latter, or lived there, you would know that you had gained it on a lie.

'It was wicked of me, I know, but you and Buckingham had taught me wickedness and I could not unlearn it, even though afterwards when I thought of your face as I told my lie I was ashamed. And later, when Willem found you unconscious and brought you to the house, the least I could do was give you what I said that you had taken so that in the end you gained Latter fairly, even if you were not to know it. I took the ring for the same reason. In your dream you gave it to me, saying it was a wedding-ring and, knowing how much you wanted Latter—and loving you before I left you—I told you to go to Latter.'

'And I did,' said Kit wonderingly. 'I remember being with you, and thinking that it was a dream—like being on the beach with Anna. I wondered what had happened to my ring. . .'

'Which I wear still, always next to my heart,' said Celia softly, slipping it from out of her nightgown and untying it. She held it out to him, as she had done when he had come to her in mingled anger and love earlier in the year.

Kit shook his head again. 'Nay, keep it, Mistress Archer—who was Mistress Antiquis—against the time we remake our vows and you may exchange it for the one I give you. All the time that I was at Latter, healing in body and mind—for when I recovered I could remember what was happy of my life with Anna and at last accept what had happened and let her go—I dreamed that one day you might be with me, mistress of my still-room, practising thy healing arts on the villagers and the servants of my house even though you cannot be the Queen's astrologer! It is a fair place, Mistress Celia. Will you marry me, and let me take Adam and thyself there? He shall be my true heir—for were we not hand-fasted in thy bed? That is a true marriage as all English common law knows. And I love thee so dearly I would not part from thee again.'

His green eyes were glowing and he took her into his arms. 'Say yes, again, Celia. Say yes, again, as you did when I came to you in the fire, I beg of you.'

Celia said unsteadily, 'You already know that I can refuse you nothing. I love you, and today you came to save me from the fire. Caleb told me that you nigh ran mad when you thought that the fire had taken me and Adam, as the pirates had taken Anna and Cecco. Yes, I will be your wife and this time, when we celebrate our vows at least the groom will know what he is doing, as well as the bride!'

'Oh, my clever wife,' sighed Kit into her neck. 'I am marrying knowledge as well as love. I had not meant to stay with thee this night, I thought that neither of us would be fit to celebrate anything, but, oh, Celia, do not deny me, for the sight of you hath roused me, which I had not thought possible after this day. Tomorrow we shall ask the King to give us a dispensation from the Archbishop to marry on the instant—tonight we celebrate our handfast marriage.'

And so they did, except that at the end, after Celia's cries had awoken Adam, Kit left her to fetch the babe into bed with them. Celia, her eyes large and luminous after their loving, fed him, with Kit's arms around them both, while he murmured into her hair. 'The first night of many. And if I have to share him with thee, then that is his right—as long as you remember the father as well as the son.'

'I will remember them both, and all the others who will come,' said Celia drowsily, for Kit's loving and the child's feeding were slowly sending her to sleep. Kit watched over them both and planned their journey to Latter—where they went, after their marriage, at a sennight's end, for them both to enjoy what Kit had once lost and had never thought to find again, and for Celia to see the election she had cast for them both come true. They would come together after a strange fashion and would never be parted again, but would live happily together at Latter, their children around them.

 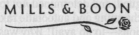

LEGACY *of* LOVE

Coming next month

CROWN HOSTAGE
Joanna Makepeace
Northampton/London, 1483

Mistress Margaret Rushton had been forced at thirteen by her father's ambition to break a childhood betrothal and in so doing had humiliated the young man. But Sir John's plans had gone awry and now, at eighteen, Margaret was still unwed.

The turmoil caused by Edward IV's death brought Sir Guy Jarvis south in the Duke of Gloucester's train, and unexpectedly Margaret and Guy met again—but *this* time Guy had the upper hand...

THE REASONS FOR MARRIAGE
Stephanie Laurens
Regency 1816

Miss Lenore Lester was perfectly content with her quiet country life, caring for her father, and had no desire for marriage.

She took steps to remain inconspicuous when managing her brothers' house parties, and so was astounded when Jason, Duke of Eversleigh, quite clearly signalled his interest. Baffled, intrigued, and determined *not* to be thrown off balance by this charming and autocratic rake, Lenore tried to deflect his attentions—to no avail! *Why* was he so persistent?

LEGACY of LOVE

Coming next month

GIFTS OF LOVE
Theresa Michaels
Washington Territory, USA, 1873

Erin Dunmore's advertisement for a husband was an act of desperation. Without help, her life in San Francisco would become intolerable.

With a secluded ranch, and two young children, widower Mace Dalton certainly needed a woman to stay long-term, but any marriage would be on his terms, and love would play no part in it. That had died with his wife...

TRUST
Muriel Jensen
Oregon, USA, 1900

Jack McCarren had worked hard to live down his upbringing, and now he had a chance to be elected mayor of Astoria. He had big plans and they didn't include newly arrived Charity Butler. Yet, somehow, whenever Charity had troubles, it was always Jack who put things right for her.

But how could Charity let their relationship deepen, when she knew her own past would ruin everything for Jack?